Hannah Emery studied English at the University of Chester and has written stories for as long as she can remember.

Her favourite things are her family, friends, books, baking on a Saturday afternoon, going out for champagne and dinner and having cosy weekends away. Hannah lives in Blackpool with her husband and their little girl.

@hannahcemery
@hannahcemery
hannahcemery@wordpress.com

Also by Hannah Emery

Secrets in the Shadows
The Secrets of Castle du Rêve

The Start of Us

Hannah Emery

OneMoreChapter

One More Chapter
a division of HarperCollins*Publishers*
The News Building
1 London Bridge Street
London SE1 9GF

www.harpercollins.co.uk

This paperback edition 2020

First published in Great Britain in ebook format by
HarperCollins*Publishers* 2020

A catalogue record for this book
is available from the British Library

Ebook ISBN: 978-0-00-838900-0
Paperback ISBN: 978-0-00-838901-7

Set in Birka by Palimpsest Book Production Ltd, Falkirk
Stirlingshire

Printed and bound in Great Britain by
CPI Group (UK) Ltd, Croydon CR0 4YY

For Hayley

Prologue

7th September 2017

I've seen another version of me.

I wonder what I'd be like, people sometimes think, *if I hadn't met that person when I did or missed that party or caught the train earlier or later or not at all. Who would I be if I'd refused that job instead of taken it, if I'd gone on the trip or if I'd stayed at home that day?*

I don't have to wonder this, because I have seen the other me. I have watched her dart between different countries whilst I stayed in the same place, ignore the job that I took, laugh on the day I thought grief would rip me into a thousand pieces.

And now, I am faced with a choice.

I stand at the kitchen window and stare out at the wilderness of our garden. The leathery green leaves twist and thrash against one another. Some of them are already edged with the gold of autumn. The wind is cold even though it's only September. It screams through the gap between the glass and the battered wooden pane and I sigh and flick on the radio beside me.

The tension is still here in the room, hanging above me like a shimmering heat. The argument, yet another, looped around and around in tiresome knots.

I close my eyes, and feel the other life calling me, promising me answers and a way out. I picture him in Luigi's, waiting for me. We haven't been in a long time, but I know where he'll sit: at the third table on the right, next to the wall with the picture of Charlie Chaplin above him. He'll face the door. He will sit fiddling with the cutlery, his jaw set with tension. If I don't arrive, he will put his head in his hands, tufts of his hair escaping through his fingers. He will sigh, and stand, nodding a goodbye to the staff, explaining nothing.

And after that I don't know what he'll do or what will happen, because I cannot imagine a life without him, a life where he hasn't met me yet and hasn't turned grey with sadness. But maybe that's the whole problem. Maybe we are together too much and our shared pain has started to weather us both like the sea has weathered our house: splintering us, cracking the beautiful strength that we started out with.

PART ONE

Chapter 1

September 2013

When Mike picks me up for the engagement party, I am distracted and wrapped up in things that seem important at the time. That's because I don't know that everything is about to change, that time is about to be sliced into one of my many Befores and Afters.

Mike drives us from my flat along the promenade and we don't talk much. We never talk much in the car because he always has his music too loud, so that the thuds of the beat wash away our words. I rest my head on the window, staring out at the soft pale blue of the sky. I'm worried that I don't know many people going to the party. I am a reluctant party-goer and leave Mike to it when I can, but he persuaded me to come to this one. That's who Mike is. He makes me socialise with his hundreds of acquaintances and stay up late when I have work the next day. He makes me eat out too much and spend my money on things I don't need instead of saving it. He makes it easy enough to be persuaded and easy enough to stand politely in his shadow. I suppose it's one of the things I like about being with him: he takes over and lets me blend into whatever crowd he's entertaining.

But tonight, Mike is still unusually quiet as we get out of the car and enter the house. When I take off my boots, shards of heart-shaped confetti stick to my feet. I glance at the huge silver heart-shaped balloons that float around like extra guests and then look at Mike with a grimace. He nods quickly, awkwardly, and I wonder for a split second if his face is tense because he's thinking of proposing to me soon, too. I laugh out loud at the thought, which is clearly ridiculous because it's *Mike*, and then I realise I've probably downed the glass of Champagne that someone gave me at the front door far too quickly.

'What's funny?' Mike asks me.

'Oh, well I ... nothing.' A tall man I don't know tops up my glass and I smile at him, say thank you, then take a sip. The man grins at me, then turns away and I look back at Mike.

'Is something wrong?' I ask Mike. He's always been the first one to do shots at parties. He's the opposite of me: a party boy who is happy to have all eyes on him. He never wants to stop drinking or dancing. On the way, I braced myself for him to hurl himself, on arrival, into amusing anecdotes and jokes at the light-hearted expense of other people. But there's none of that tonight, just quiet nods in greeting to people he knows, small smiles instead of laughter.

He shakes his head, hands thrust deep into his pockets.

'I still don't know why you brought the car,' I tell him as he shrugs. 'Are you sure you don't want a drink?'

'Mike!' Kevin, the host of the party slurs in greeting, clapping Mike on the back. 'Jaegerbombs later. Yeah?'

Mike nods, but says nothing. Kevin carries on through to the kitchen, too preoccupied to notice or care that something is obviously wrong.

'I wondered if you might be thinking of proposing,' I admit, trying to do what Mike always does and lighten the mood with a joke. And it's not just any joke; it's our very own standing joke. All of our friends are doing this all of a sudden: throwing engagement parties and planning weddings and announcing Big Things with wide smiles and helium balloons. Mike and I are avoiding all of that, and it's working for us.

Or maybe it's not.

He pales and swallows, looks away.

'Oh God, Mike? You're not actually proposing, are you?' I try to collect my panicked thoughts. I don't want to get married. He knows that. And he doesn't want to get married either. Or so I thought. I can't hurt Mike. And that would hurt him beyond repair, wouldn't it? Disregarding it as a joke? Saying no?

I touch his shoulder gently and he stands up.

'I can't talk about it now,' he says, his voice flat. 'Not in here.'

He looks at me, but his eyes don't quite reach mine. I

stand up, push my hair from my eyes, and take his hand. Is he ill? In debt? Why didn't I know about this? I lead him upstairs to a bedroom that is painted a violent purple. The house is a maze: I don't even know whose room it is, or if whomever it belongs to will mind us being in there, sitting on the matching purple duvet that hasn't been made, but left in a wrinkled heap in the middle of the mattress.

'Mike?'

And then I see that it's not what I thought at all. He hasn't hidden a solitaire in his pocket, and he wasn't anxious about proposing to me. It's not illness or debt or anything that I can support him with by being the girl who always laughs at his jokes. It's something else, and as I watch Mike's face, and see his eyes redden, it dawns on me exactly what's happening.

As I realise it, he says it, and the pain is doubled.

'I don't want to be with you anymore, Erica.'

The Champagne I had when I arrived, when things were normal and okay and I was just someone at a party, threatens to flow back up. I cover my mouth with my hand. A piece of heart confetti sticks to the edge of my palm, glistens.

'I'm sorry. I've tried. I can't.'

And that's it. Six words and it's all over.

He opens the door and noises from the party drift in. A silver balloon floats past the door.

'You can't leave me here,' I say. I see him reach in his pocket for something. His car keys.

'You knew! You knew you were going to leave the party earlier than me, and that's why you drove! Why did you even bring me?'

He shrugs. He's pale and I know that he can't want to do this to me. Yet here he is, still doing it. 'I'm sorry, Erica.'

'But we have to talk!' I say. My voice doesn't sound like mine and I'm vaguely aware that I need to reclaim it and sort out the pitch so that I don't sound like someone who has no control. 'Let's go back to mine, and talk.'

'I don't want to, Erica.'

'But I haven't!' We went on a weekend to London a few months ago. Did he know then? Does he have someone else? The dull thud of music from outside the room hurts my head and makes me feel dizzy. I lift a hand up to my temple, press it against my skin to try and numb the pain and the sensation that I might fall to the floor. 'Why now?'

He shrugs. 'I've just had enough. We've had some good times. But we're just too different.'

'But that's good!' I say. 'Opposites attract!' But even as I'm saying it, I'm wondering if it's really true.

'Nah. You're happy around here, talking about old stuff and the museum and things ... And anyway, I'm moving,' Mike says next, abruptly, his eyes still focusing on something beyond me. 'Kath, from the Cardiff branch, has offered me a position there. It's just cover for a few weeks. Then after that I'm going to go abroad for a bit,' he says, doing a ridiculous gesture with his hand to illustrate his flight, his travel, his vanishing from my life. It distracts me, and I almost don't notice the flicker in his eyes. But then I see it, and I realise why.

Kath.

Kath, the manager of the Cardiff branch of the bank where Mike works, who saved the day by doing long-term cover at the Blackpool branch last year, who always looked me up and down at Mike's work parties and threw her immaculate head back with constant, too-loud laughter.

I stare at him, at his blonde hair and the faintest acne scar on his forehead and the shadow of gold stubble on his jaw. I thought he was mine, but he's not. The thought is sharp, but I am strangely numb to it.

'So Kath doesn't talk about old stuff? She doesn't bore you like I do?' I say, trying to sound cutting, like I have my act together, but my voice is thick with hurt.

'I'm sorry,' he says. 'But you're the one who took the museum job and stopped us travelling about. And I thought I could wait, but I can't. I want to try something different right now, Erica. I'm fed up here. I'm bored.'

'Bored? But my museum job is only for three months. And then after that, I—'

'Well yeah,' he interrupts, and I recall vaguely that him interrupting me is something that has irritated me before, but that it was a small irritation, and I never really properly registered it. Now it's meaningless: a bubble floating before me and popping just as I reach out to touch it. 'But then after that there will be another reason, won't there? It's fine. But it's not for me. I want more, Erica. I literally cannot stay another second.' He lowers his eyes and shifts away from me slightly as I try to take his hand. 'Let me go.'

And then he's gone from the room, keys jangling, off to Cardiff and Kath and a world where he will talk about his ex and falling out of love and being too bored to stay for another second.

The numbness in my mind spreads to my whole body, and I don't follow him, or try to change his mind or make him stay. I sit on the bed, quite still, thinking about his words, unable to do anything with them other than hear them over and over again. And then after a few minutes, the numbness wears off. My tears are sudden and ugly, my breaths unable to keep up.

I don't know how long I've been in the room, crying in strange, gulping episodes, huddled against the purple duvet, when the door opens and someone comes in. It's the man who topped up my glass when I first arrived. I take in how he looks: perhaps early thirties, tall, dark hair, black-rimmed glasses and wide straight teeth ... He raises his eyebrows and suddenly self-aware, I put my hand up to my streaming nose.

'Sorry. I just came up to see if I can find my coat. But I can come back in a minute,' he offers.

I wipe my throbbing eyes. 'I don't mind.'

He stands by the door looking concerned. 'Do you want a drink?'

'Actually, some tissues would be really good.'

He smiles and leaves the room, closing the door softly

behind him before returning a few minutes later with a wad of toilet roll. He sits on the edge of the bed, drumming his hands on his knees.

'I had no idea,' I say. I should elaborate, but I don't have the words or the energy.

'I just saw the guy that you arrived with leave. Mike, is it? I'm guessing he's not coming back?'

I shake my head. 'Why would he bring me here and do that?'

'I'm really not sure,' the man says, even though the answer lingers between us, unspoken. Mike is a coward and if he'd broken up with me at my flat, he would have had to talk about it and I would have shouted and clung to him and not let him out of the door. I would have talked about our plans to see the world together, and asked him to just wait for me to finish my three-month job at the museum. But he didn't want me to do that.

'He's moving away,' I say. 'Cardiff and then travelling. I think he's got someone else.' I hear my own words and cringe at how open I'm being with this complete stranger. I'd never usually tell anyone something so personal. Maybe I'm a different version of myself now.

The man shakes his head. 'I'm so sorry. It was poor form, doing this at a party. So as cliched as it sounds, you're probably better off without him.'

I stare past him, trying to think, but every tangled thought leads back to Mike. I vaguely recognise a fear from my childhood snaking through my blood. Being alone and having nobody to hide behind. That's how things will be again now. 'I thought I'd always have him.' My voice shakes so much that I'm surprised he can work out what I've said. It crosses my mind that having Mike was different to wanting him and that my words might be giving away more than I even thought I knew, but the man doesn't seem to notice.

He stands up and I think for a minute he's going to leave the room, but he doesn't. He just has an apparent inability to sit still for more than a few seconds at a time. 'Well then, I suppose all you can do is find a different life to live. See what else there is, other than him.'

I close my eyes. 'We were going to travel together. Have adventures. Why couldn't he just wait so that we could stick to our plan?'

'You can still have a plan. Just not with him.'

'You seem very sure.' I sniff, then regret it because of the ugly sound it makes in front of this polite stranger. There's something convincing about his words, and I wonder if he's speaking from experience.

'I am sure. I'm an architect. It's my job to think about the bigger picture. Buildings, life, it's all the same. Each tiny detail impacts on another and that sometimes causes real problems. You start off drawing one building, but then you find something out that changes a small detail on your plan. So the building has to change into something different. You can't just carry on as though it hasn't happened.'

'Because the building will collapse,' I finish, my breathing more even now, my tears suspended.

'Well, yeah. Or it might just not be the best version of itself. You have to move with the changes and build something else.'

'It makes sense,' I say slowly. 'But it's frightening when your whole plan changes.'

He nods. 'I know. Especially when you've invested so much. You know, he's making a big mistake.'

'You don't even know me.'

'I know. I'm talking about Cardiff.'

I manage a smile, try to block non-boring Kath from my mind.

'You don't have to sit here with me,' I tell him. 'Weren't you going home? You came in here looking for your coat, didn't you?'

'I don't have to go. I'm working tomorrow so was going to head off, but I might stay for a bit. What are you going to do? This is Em's room I think, and she's passed out in the living room. I doubt she will make it to bed. So I think you can stay in here for a bit if you want.'

I nod. I can't face the party again yet, people looking at my swollen eyes and tracks of mascara and wondering what's happened to me. But then I picture my flat and feel like it belongs to somebody else who had everything worked out. I don't want to go there either. I want to press pause.

'Are you sure you don't want a drink?'

I sigh. 'It's my birthday on Friday,' I find myself saying in answer, even though I'm not entirely sure why.

'Well, that kind of answers my question,' he says. 'Tell you what, I'll stay for a bit. I'll get you a drink and if you don't want it, I'll have it.' He's gone before I can protest.

He returns to the bedroom a few minutes later with a glass of Champagne.

'Thank you. I don't even know your name. I'm Erica. I don't really know anyone here. Mike's friends with Kevin, which is why we came.'

He grins. 'Daniel.' He sips his own wine, red, and makes a face as if to say it tastes better than he thought it would. 'I used to work with Em years ago, and she's Kevin and Sophie's housemate. I barely know anyone here. I wasn't going to come, actually.'

'I didn't want to either. But I'm glad you did.' I take a sip of Champagne. 'I'm not sure I'm glad I did though. And I'm not sure I should be drinking Champagne. It hardly seems like the time for celebration.'

'It's the perfect time for a celebration. You're looking for your other life, remember. Your new building. It's the beginning.' He clinks his glass against mine and the sound rings in my ears, making me feel dizzy.

'Cheers, then,' I say. Tears threaten again, so I down the drink. Daniel takes the empty glass from me, disappearing back to the kitchen. He brings me more Champagne and then says he will come back in a bit to see how I'm doing. I sip at it and close my eyes, but dizziness pulls at me again so I sit up and then wander out into the kitchen where I help myself to some lemonade, gulping it down until my mouth is fuzzy with sugar. There is hardly anyone awake now: bodies huddled, limbs tangled, breathing heavy and even. I make my way back to the room that belongs to Em, the girl I don't even know, who has a purple duvet and doesn't make her bed, then I lie down.

That's when it happens. I have lost control. I'm not strong enough to stop it, and even if I were, it hasn't happened to me for years so it takes me by surprise. The duvet collapses from beneath me, the purple walls cave in and the world as I know it spins and shifts.

Chapter 2

I am thrown into the other world so hard that I can feel my insides slam against my skin. It's like a rollercoaster multiplied by a million. My breaths are sharp, fast, painful.

As I always used to be, once I reach where I'm going I am glued to the spot. I force my senses to catch up with the rest of me, and try to look around, take in where I am. Glossy brochures are lined up on the shelves, the air is sweet with a manufactured scent of coconut, and posters of yellow sands and palm trees and aeroplanes swooping through blue skies line the walls.

It's been years since I was thrown into another time and place. It first happened to me when I was a child: a terrifying visit to the past where I could hear people and smell their perfume but they couldn't see me. I wanted to believe it was a dream, but my mum's anger at my unexplained disappearance from our house the whole time I was in the other world told me otherwise. I know that the bedroom from the party I have just left behind will be empty, the purple bed as though I had never sat on it. The powerful dizziness that washed over me tonight should have been a warning because that's how it always used to start. But the breakup with Mike, the alcohol and the fright at the prospect of a different life without somebody all masked the feeling that I always used to recognise within seconds.

But this isn't the same as it used to be. As I finally gather breath, I know that something is different. When this happened to me as a child, I always saw things that had happened in the past. People looked different and were surrounded by strange colours and trends that I'd only ever seen in pictures. Everything seemed as though it had been seeped in low light, as though I was watching a film that wasn't quite tuned. But what I'm looking at now is bright, modern and clear. If it's the past, it's the recent past.

The woman at the desk just in front of me sighs as she taps her keyboard. Her acrylic nails clack against the keys. She glances up before checking the silver mobile phone on the desk beside her. She obviously can't see me. I try to think about who she might be, and why I'm here, watching her, but my mind is uncooperative: sticky and slow with the shock of being here, of what's just happened with Mike.

I have never been able to move or able to reach out and touch the people I can see, and I am stuck in one position now too. I turn my head slightly, the only movement I can make, to look out of the travel agent's window. I can make out cobbled streets, and I don't think it's Blackpool but that only tells me where I am not.

And then I see someone else who makes my heart stop.

She leans against the counter of what seems to be a currency change bureau and flips through a brochure, her eyes flitting over words, focusing on the shiny images of creamy sands and fluorescent blue seas.

It's me. Or somebody identical to me.

It's another Erica who has the same bone structure, the same fine dark hair and long fringe that falls into her face and green eyes and one stray freckle on her left cheek, as I do. But this Erica has a coloured braid in her hair, a sign of a recent trip abroad, an urge to change her look and shout about the fun she had. Her face is relaxed, her skin glowing. The tip of her nose is slightly pink as though she missed it with the sun cream, which I always do.

'Looking for your next trip already, Erica?' asks the woman who still clacks away at her computer as she talks. The sound of someone saying my name jolts me. I want to shout out, to say something, but nothing will come out of my mouth. I am mute, not really here.

The other Erica looks at her colleague and shrugs, a small sideways smile on her lips. Do I smile like that? Discomfort pulls at me as I watch her mannerisms that must be mine too. I can't bear to see myself from so many angles at once but can't stop looking either. How can you know yourself so well yet so little?

'Maybe,' she answers her colleague, her voice making me prickle with a self-awareness so intense I can barely stand it. It's a sound that is foreign and mine all at once.

'I'm thinking Australia. Or maybe Thailand. Just me and a backpack.'

'You've only just got back to Yorkshire,' the woman says, shaking her head and checking her phone again.

Yorkshire. The sound of the place I left so long ago quickens my pulse and I take a deep breath. There is so much that I don't understand, but Erica is talking again and I can't miss a second of it.

'So what? It's my twenty-eighth birthday next week.' Erica wrinkles her nose and I put my hand up to my own nose self-consciously. 'It'll be my present to myself. I've saved for years. And I promised myself I'd see as much of the world as I can by the time I'm thirty. So I owe it to myself.' As she speaks, she looks straight at me, as though she knows I am watching her, as though she knows I haven't done any of the travelling that seems so important to everyone else. I try to back away, panicked at the thought of our identical eyes meeting. My limbs won't move, but still I try to summon the power to try to make them. I squeeze my eyes shut to try and concentrate all my energy on stepping backwards, and as I do, overwhelming dizziness drags me down, making me fall. As I plunge through different worlds, scrambling to try and place my feet upon something solid, another scene flashes before me. A flash of road. A motorway sign.

And then I am flung back into Em's bedroom, onto the soft tangle of purple that I left behind.

I sit up and place my hand on my chest, trying to steady

my breaths. My legs are weak and nausea swirls through me. I stumble over to the window, lifting the heavy patterned curtains. It's still dark outside, but that tells me nothing really: I could have been gone hours or minutes. It felt like I was there for only seconds, but I know from when I used to disappear like this that seconds in one world can be hours in another.

As I stare out into the backyard of the house I'm in, beyond to row upon row of terraced Victorian houses and bins and gates and children's slides and cars all coated in the blue darkness of the night, I think about what I have just seen. The words I listened to whisper again and again in my mind until they take a shape and meaning of their own.

I was in Yorkshire, the place that I left when I was twelve years old and have never returned to. But the other Erica who lived there said that it was her twenty-eighth birthday next week, which means that whatever world I saw, whatever parallel universe it was, it wasn't the past or the future. It was *now*.

I adjust my focus and see my reflection in the tall sash window. I see my puffed eyes and my pale skin, the fear from Mike ending things etched, somehow, into my features. I thought my disappearances that could happen any time I was alone, the blinding headaches and dizziness followed by the terror of the ground falling from beneath me, were behind me. The last one was years ago, and before tonight they had taken on the vague, uncertain shape of very first memories, the kind with no start or end or evidence for. I wonder, hot panic snaking its way through my body why they have returned here, and now. And I wonder when the other Erica's life ended, and this one that I am living began.

Chapter 3

I'm woken the next day by the buzzer of my flat. My head is heavy, my mouth dry. My first thought is that last night my strange vision of the other me, and Mike ending things, was surely all a dream. A nightmare, I correct myself. I lurch the small distance from my bedroom to the front door. My eyes are sore with crying and the weight of anxiety and hurt slowly settles in my stomach like a rock. So, I realise, the Mike episode definitely happened.

But the disappearance can't have been real. I can't be going through this all over again. I've grown out of it. I shake off the images of the other Erica in the travel agent's that still float in my mind. I try to distract myself from seeing her tanned face, its every crease so familiar, by talking myself through what must have happened. I probably fell asleep for a few hours, because Daniel came back into Em's room as I stood at the window. It was about 3am then, and he phoned a cab to bring me home. I fell into my bed still fully clothed, peeling my boots off and throwing them across the room. I slept some more, which made the events of last night seem even more surreal. And so now, as I twist open the silver latch, it seems likely that I just drank a lot at the party and had a strange dream. Nothing more happened.

'Good night?' my friend Zoe asks as she stalks past me into my flat. She turns back and frowns at me as I stand motionless instead of following her. 'Why are you wearing yesterday's clothes?' She looks more closely at me: my crumpled black dress, yesterday's makeup smeared by tears.

'Oh, God, Erica. What's happened?'

I crumble, sobs forcing their way out of my aching body as I give an outline of the story Mike gave me. I need to let him go. He's known for a while. Kath.

Zoe's face is white. Nobody expected this to happen. I can see that everybody I tell will gasp like Zoe, their eyes wide and their faces ashen as I tell them what I tell her: that Mike's made up his mind, he's living our life without me in it, he's fallen for somebody else who won't bore him by staying in one place for too long.

'I honestly had no idea he'd do this. What a bastard,' Zoe says as she makes tea. She shakes her head. 'Well. Look at it this way. You can focus on your job now. And maybe get something similar when your contract runs out. You don't need to go away. It was Mike pushing you to do that.'

I think of the other version of me that I saw, or dreamt – surely dreamt – and what she said about travelling and try to ignore the nausea that accompanies the memory. *I promised myself I'd see as much of the world as I can by the time I'm thirty. So I owe it to myself.* Then I think of Daniel, the man at the party, making me toast my new future ... So much happened last night that a lot of it is blurred together, but his words about buildings and changing plans are bright in my mind.

'Well, maybe I will go abroad and see different places. Maybe it isn't because of Mike that I want to go away. I could do it on my own.'

Zoe looks uncertain, takes a sip of her tea. 'Do you really think it's for you? No offense, Erica, but you only just moved out of your mum's house a few years ago. You don't really strike me as the lone traveller type. You were just going along with Mike, weren't you?'

'Maybe. To be completely honest,' I say, looking down into my mug, because I feel like I'm never *completely* honest with Zoe, 'I know I've always avoided moving. I hated it so much the first time, when we first came here to Blackpool.' And I couldn't trust myself to be alone in a strange place, I add silently.

Until I met Mike, my disappearances were too frequent, too unpredictable and frightening, for me to be alone. As long as somebody could see me, I wouldn't disappear. But when they started happening less often, and then stopped altogether a few years ago, I decided that I could finally move on and rent my own flat. I swallow down my anxiety. It was a *dream*. 'But now,' I continue quickly, 'life is passing me by. I think it's time for me to be a bit braver. I owe it to myself.' I parrot the other version of me, feeling self-conscious, as though by speaking the same words she did, our two worlds will brush against one another and cause an electric surge, a jolt or a buzz of energy. But nothing happens. Zoe leans forward, oblivious, and bangs her mug down on the coffee table.

'You don't need to change just because Mike told you to. You two were really different.'

'That's what he said. I always thought that was a good thing.'

'Well, whether it was or not, you're fine as you are.'

I smile. 'Thanks. But thinking about travelling isn't for Mike. It's for me. I think on some level, I'm meant to be somewhere else.'

Zoe rolls her eyes. 'Oh no, don't go all *meaning of life* on me. If you're sure about it though ...' she thinks for a minute, then takes her phone from her bag, jabbing at the buttons before handing it to me. 'Here you go. There's Nina's number.'

'Nina?'

'Yes, Nina. You know, my cousin Jen's friend?'

I try to think, to pull a memory of Nina to the front of my heavy mind. I picture her: white-blonde hair, even whiter teeth, a smattering of piercings.

'She's going to Thailand soon. Jen was saying the other day that Nina's been trying to make Jen put off her nurse training for a year and go with her. She doesn't want to go alone. But Jen's set on staying here now. You could go with Nina instead, if you really wanted to.'

I nod and press call.

***

The conversation with Nina is short, slightly stilted at first, an awkward mix of silences and moments where we both speak at the same time so that neither of our words can be heard.

'I heard you're wanting a travelling bud—'

'How's the museu—'

'Oh sorry!'

'Sorry, go on,'

It goes on like this for a few minutes, until Nina bores of the small talk.

'Did you mention the travelling?'

'Yeah. I'm with Zoe. She said you want someone to go with?'

'Yep,' she says simply.

'Okay. Well, the thought of going alone scares me a bit too, to be honest. I've only looked into the basics before. I was going to go with, uh, Mike, my erm ... Well anyway, now I'm not with him and so I don't really know where to start.'

'You split up with Mike? God, sorry. Why?'

'Oh,' I say, waving my hand in the air pointlessly. 'Long story. But it'd be good to chat about where you're going, if you've found anywhere to work and things like that.'

'Yeah, okay. I'm working my last shift at Coffee Mansion next week. Everyone gets free coffee for friends when it's their last shift. If you want, I'll let you know when I get my rota and you can come in.'

'Okay,' I say. 'I will.'

***

It's Friday. My birthday.

'I think I'd rather stay in tonight, you know,' I say on the phone to my brother Nicholas when he calls to wish me happy birthday. Nicholas and his wife Amelia are driving up from Oxford today and we're going out for dinner later on. The past few days have shaken me and I want to snap shut, refuse to let anyone in. I can't really face the idea of going out where I might know people who will ask questions about why I'm not out with Mike on my birthday.

'Not an option,' Nicholas says. 'I've promised Amelia a pub crawl around the finest of Blackpool's bars. And Phoebe is looking forward to a night in with Mum.'

I smile, relenting. I've only seen my niece a few times since she was born last year, and the thought of her sweet, ripe skin and feathery blonde hair lifts me and makes me feel bolder somehow.

'I'm so excited to see her.'

'Oh great. It's like this everywhere we go now. All about Phoebe. I think I might pop her in a taxi to Blackpool and stay here in bed for a few days. Catch up on sleep.'

I laugh. 'No, don't do that. I need to see you too.' The image of the other Erica fills my mind, unbidden, and I ache to tell Nicholas about it. But I don't. If I tell him, he might try to persuade me that it was real, and I can't believe that right now. I can't process the possibility that this might be happening to me again, because I can't let it stop me from making the plans I should have made so long ago but was too scared to.

'Well,' he says, 'we've just got a few more billion things to pack for Phoebe and then we'll be on our way. We'll see you at Mum's, okay? She'll give you a ring when we get there.'

We say goodbye and I wander into my bedroom and make the bed, pulling the covers straight. It's ten in the morning. Nicholas won't be here until about six. I have taken the whole of next week off work and the days stretch out before me. I pick up my mobile phone. The thought that I could text Mike flits through my mind like a brittle leaf in the wind. But no. I won't do that. And I won't give up on the day either. It's my birthday. It's a day to celebrate, not wallow.

I will go for a walk along the promenade. The rush of salty air never fails to make me feel better. It's the reason I live in this tiny, boxy flat that has magnolia walls and magnolia carpets and the sound of a furious, howling baby from upstairs at regular intervals all through the day and night: I want to be near the sea. I was too angry to appreciate it when I was twelve and we first moved here. Mum and Dad had just split up, and Blackpool represented an enforced change that I didn't want to be a part of. But Mum grew up here, so when she was finding somewhere new for us to live, she felt drawn to it. Now, the sea with its constant ebbs and flows, its power and sense of freedom, has become something that I take pleasure in. I looked around so many flats, and was uninspired by every single one except this one, which looks out onto the grassy walkway and grey waves of North Shore beach.

Just as I'm pulling on my black trainers, my phone buzzes in my hand. People keep texting to ask me if Mike is spoiling me, if he's bought me anything nice. They don't know not to ask that, because I still haven't told many people that he's gone, and he obviously hasn't either. Not that he ever bought me anything nice. He was more of a joke gift kind of person.

I wait a few minutes before opening the text. When I do, I see that it's from Daniel. I vaguely remember telling him it was my birthday today. He has my number because he made me text him to say I got home okay in the early hours of the other morning, after he called me a taxi home from the party.

Happy bday. Daniel x

I'm not sure why but Daniel has had a strange presence in my mind over the past few days. His words and kindness have been a welcome distraction from the stinging memory of what happened with Mike. I've thought of getting in touch with him a couple of times but I haven't wanted to bother him after I took over his night at the party. Now, I hesitate for a moment then press the 'call' button above his message. He sounds surprised when he answers.

'Thanks for the text,' I say.

'That's okay.'

'Most people are asking what Mike bought me. It was nice to get a text that didn't ask me that.'

'Why, what did he get you?'

It's a bad joke, but I smile anyway. 'You know too well. You suffered the brunt.'

'Not really. I'm glad I was there. What are you doing today, anyway?'

I lie back on my bed, staring up at the ceiling, the cracks in the wallpaper, the ugly green lightshade that I've never changed because my path with Mike never veered near home improvement aisles.

DIY? Really? Mike would have said if I'd suggested it. He would have made me go out to the pub instead. But that was a good thing, wasn't it? As Mike fades out of my mind as soon as he entered it, I realise that Daniel is still waiting for me to answer.

'My brother's coming later with his wife. We're going out,' I tell him.

'Sounds good. Where are you going?'

'I don't know. I was meant to book somewhere.'

Everywhere seems a bit tainted now. Every restaurant that I like is now a restaurant that reminds me of Mike.

'I tried a nice new Italian last week. It's right in the town centre, opposite the Winter Gardens.'

'A new place sounds perfect.'

'I think it's called Luigi's.'

'Thanks, Daniel. I'll look it up.' I pause, listening to static, reluctant to let our conversation come to an end. 'Did you really have to work on Sunday, after the party?' I ask. 'It was late when we were talking and I was ordering you to get me drinks and tissues. And then you were still there in the early hours, phoning me a taxi. I hope you got through the next day okay.'

'Oh, I was fine. I was just finishing off some plans, so I was working from home. And I liked doing the drink and tissue runs. Although next time I see you, I hope you cry less.'

'I'll try my best.' The thought of seeing Daniel again makes something in me fizz, and then I think of Mike again, and the fizzing evaporates. 'Anyway,' I say, 'I should let you go, and stop interrupting your work.'

'No. I've got what I needed to do finished so I've got the rest of the day off. Is your brother getting there soon?'

'Oh, no. He's driving from Oxford and he has a one-year-old with him, so I think he might have to make a few stops.'

'Well, I was meant to play football over in Manchester later, but I'm awful at it. And between you and me, I don't actually really like it that much. So if you want to do something, we can. Totally up to you.'

'Are you sure?'

'Yeah. Really sure. I've never even scored a goal.'

'I meant about doing something.'

'I'm sure.'

I stand up, wander over to my window and look beyond the grassy walkways, the churning waves in the distance. The sun is bright and high, the sky marred only by a few wisps of cloud. I love September and the way it can be summer one day, autumn the next. Today is one of those days that could shape itself into anything. I'm about to say just one word. It'll take only one moment. But as I do, I feel the undercurrent of possibility – a tiny seed blooming into something bright that will change my landscape forever.

'Yes.'

Chapter 4

'Is he in love with you?' Amelia asks, eyeing me over her wine glass.

It's almost nine o'clock. We've been in Luigi's for an hour or so, eating slowly and lazily: pleasantly oily garlic bread, silky pasta and crisp salad. I've had two glasses of red wine and feel strangely detached from the last few days, as though they happened to someone I was watching.

It happened again tonight. As I waited for Nicholas to pick me up, spritzing myself with my favourite perfume, the bottle dropped from my hand onto my carpet, my head feeling as though it would burst with pressure and pain. I saw a stretch of road, debris scattered along it. And then I was back, the sweet fragrance that clouded around me suddenly too much to bear, burning my eyes and making me heave. I was gone for only a few seconds, but I missed long enough of the song that was playing on the radio to make it clear that I couldn't dismiss what had happened at the party as a dream for much longer. It was one thing when this had happened to me as a child, and it hadn't been easy then. It affected my friendships and made me scared to become too close to anyone in case they found out my secret. But fear of what this might mean for me now, for living on my own and my job and the rest of my life, has been pulling at me all evening.

'Who, Mike?' I tear apart a piece of garlic bread and dip it into my pasta sauce. 'Well, he sent one of his friends round to my flat today to pick up an Oasis CD, a toastie machine, and some socks. And I haven't actually spoken to him since we split up. So it doesn't seem as though he's in love with me, does it?'

'No, not Mike. Forget about Mike. I meant Daniel. He must have put a lot of effort into today.'

I put the garlic bread down, wipe the oil from my fingers and fan myself with the napkin, suddenly too warm. Amelia is right. Daniel picked me up soon after we'd spoken on the phone this morning and drove us to Lake Windermere. We talked all the way there, about the party, what we knew about Kevin and Sophie, our jobs and our friends and lives. Daniel parked the car a little way from the centre, and we bought ice creams on the walk towards the lake. The air was sharp with the late summer heat, salty and sweet with chips and freshly fried donuts. Daniel was energetic, his quick stride making me rush to keep up. In the end I laughed, breathless, and asked him to slow down, and he took my hand, told me to yank him back if he went too quickly and left me behind.

'I'm glad I've seen you again today,' I said to him as we

sat on a bench that faced out towards the glittering lake, eating our ice creams. 'Otherwise you'd have just thought of me as the strange crying girl from the party. Nobody wants to be that girl.'

Daniel wiped his mouth with the back of his hand, erasing a trace of vanilla I'd noticed a few minutes before. 'We've all been there. I've had a bad breakup in the past. It's just that I wasn't at a party, so nobody saw me at the worst bit. You were just unlucky.'

'I don't know. I definitely feel unlucky being dumped. But I can't help feeling like it was lucky, in the end, that I was at the party when it happened. You made me feel better. So I'm glad I went. I bet you didn't have someone to let you cry on them.'

Daniel shook his head and took out his chocolate flake before biting it in half. 'I didn't.'

'Well, it really helped me. I want to say that I'll repay the favour someday. But hopefully I won't need to.' I looked straight out at the water, at the boats, at the children throwing grains of food for the ducks onto the smooth pebbles, and then glanced sideways at Daniel.

'Here's hoping. I like to think I learnt from what happened with my ex and would do a better job of things next time. But you never quite know, do you?'

'You really don't. Are you over it?' I asked.

'What, the breakup? Yes. Completely. It didn't take as long as I thought it would. She ended it. Went off with some guy she'd met in the supermarket.'

'You're joking? I didn't think people actually met in supermarket aisles.'

'Nope, me neither, until then. Thought I was safe when she popped out for milk.' He laughs. 'But things were all wrong with us anyway. I just didn't realise it until after she was gone and I felt more like me than I had done when I was with her, if that makes sense.'

'It does,' I said. We sat quietly for a bit, the sun-scorched bench warm beneath us. 'What aisle was it?' I asked after a few minutes.

He laughed. 'I asked her that. She said it was the magazines.'

I shook my head. 'I'm so sorry. That's awful. If I were with someone like you, I'd never let anyone else chat me up at the magazines. Or anywhere, come to think of it.' My face was suddenly too warm, tingling with the surprise of being so upfront with Daniel, with myself.

Daniel grinned and jumped up from the bench, his hand outstretched for mine. 'You don't know that. You never know who you might meet in the knitting magazines section.'

I laughed. 'I don't buy knitting magazines!'

He laughed too, moved his hand closer to mine. 'Well then, I might be safe after all. Come on. You have an important decision to make. Boat trip or back home.'

***

'Daniel isn't in love with me at all,' I say to Amelia now in the restaurant, the memories dissipating in my mind as

I speak. 'We didn't even really know each other until today. I think he's just a nice guy. He saw how upset I was at the party and wanted to check I was okay. And he knew it was my birthday. Plus, he wanted to get out of this football thing, so it worked for him too.' My words rattle on and on, even though in my mind I'm willing myself to shut up.

'Well, I'm glad you went with him,' Nicholas cuts in as soon as I pause. 'It's only right that you were spoilt a bit today. It sounds like it was just what you needed.'

'Of course it was,' Amelia says with a grin. 'She was swept off her feet! I, on the other hand, have spent most of the day in motorway services changing nappies in filthy toilets. We must have stopped about six times. You should definitely make the most of having a day of romance.'

I shake my head, laughing in spite of myself. 'Anyway. Enough about me. What do you think Phoebe's up to?' I ask her. 'I bet Mum's spoiling her. We've all been so excited to see her.'

We chat about Phoebe for a while, and then Amelia takes her phone out of her bag to check it for messages. 'I've not heard from your mum, actually. I wonder if Phoebe is asleep yet,' she says. 'I think I'll pop outside where it's a bit quieter and ring, just to make sure all's okay.'

When she's gone I smile at Nicholas. 'It's so good to see you. Thanks for coming all this way for my birthday. It means a lot. I know how busy you are. It'll be lovely to spend a bit of time with Phoebe tomorrow.'

My brother grins back at me. 'It's great to see you too. It's just a shame it couldn't be for longer. But I was lucky I got out early today. No chance of getting in late on Monday. My timetable is awful.' He yawns and I laugh.

'If that's how you feel about your lessons, I dread to think how your students feel.'

Nicholas laughs too, rolling his eyes at my predictable humour. He has taught maths at a public school in Oxford for years now, and is head of department. I've always joked about his lessons, as we are so different that I can't imagine what he could possibly do to make maths engaging. His status at the school, his constant string of Outstandings and 100 per cent pass rates make my jokes funny because obviously, somehow he manages it.

'I think it's happening again,' I say next, my voice quietening.

Nicholas doesn't need to ask what. His laugh stops, and his blue eyes widen.

'I'm scared, Nick. I tried to tell myself that I was dreaming, and was almost managing to believe it. It was quite easy not to think about it too much because I was so preoccupied by what had happened with Mike. But then it happened again tonight, just before we came out. It wasn't for long. But I'm having to admit to myself that it's happening again.'

Nicholas puts his fork down. 'What did you see? When did you go back to?'

I shake my head. 'It wasn't the past I watched. It seems

to be a different kind of thing now. I think I saw myself, in an alternative life.'

'Wow,' Nicholas says leaning forward, the weak light of the candle in the centre of the table making his face glow. 'A parallel universe?'

'Yes. It was another version of me, and I think I saw what I'd be doing if I'd made different choices. It seemed like I was in Yorkshire. That was the other day. Tonight I just saw a glimpse of a road, and I couldn't tell if it was the past or the present. Nothing happened. There were no people there. And I was only gone for a couple of seconds.'

'I can't believe it's happening again. It's been years, hasn't it?'

I nod. 'Yes. I didn't do it at all when I was with Mike.'

'And what was the other version of you doing?'

'It was only a glimpse, really. But I got the feeling that she was more adventurous than I am. She was working in a travel agent's, and it seemed like that's what she was into. Travelling the world and seeing new things.'

'And were you with Mike in this ... alternate universe?'

I put my fork down. 'I don't know for sure, but I didn't seem to be.' *Just me and a backpack.*

Nicholas leans back again. 'So do you think you saw it to help you make choices, now that it's over with Mike?'

I think for a minute. 'I haven't managed to work out why it's started happening again yet. I've been worrying more about what will happen if I keep disappearing. When it used to happen, it was only ever school that I missed.

And because I knew it would only happen when I was alone, I just stayed with Mum or my friends as much as I could. Then before I met Mike, just before it stopped, I was at college. It hardly mattered that I missed the beginning of a few lessons. But now, it's different. I have my job, and a life. It's making me think I shouldn't have moved out of Mum's or taken a job where I am alone sometimes.' I finish the last of my wine, and push my glass away.

'Try not to panic. Maybe it's just because you've split up with Mike that it's jump-started the disappearances again. It might just happen to you now and again when you're going through something.'

We sit for a minute, watching Amelia hover in the doorway of the restaurant as she talks on the phone, an unspoken deal between us to change the subject as soon as she heads back towards us.

'Anyway, I suppose it has made me think about my decisions, in a way. I think Mike was right about me. I need to do something interesting. There shouldn't be anything stopping me now, should there? I'm going to get out in the world, and leave Blackpool behind.'

Nicholas narrows his eyes at me. 'What about your job?'

'I love my job,' I say, picking my fork up and spearing a piece of pasta. 'But my contract was only for three months. And that's only if I can last that long, if this keeps happening to me.' I lift the pasta to my lips. It's cold and gluey now and I chew, forcing it down.

'But it might not keep happening. And if it does then

you'll find a way to work around it. You don't have to travel just because Mike told you that you should. It's a bit cliched, isn't it? Going off and finding yourself when you have a perfectly nice life here?'

'There's another life for me, though. One where I'm not too scared to do anything.'

'There are thousands of lives for everyone. The only difference is that you've somehow seen one of yours. Come on Erica, you of all people should know it's not that simple. Whatever alternate universe you've seen a few minutes of, it wasn't your life. So you can't make your life now exactly the same as that one. You won't be able to work out where it started and the one you're living now ended.'

Amelia comes back as Nicholas and I stare at each other, our teenage selves strangely brought to life by discussing what we always used to discuss when we were younger.

'Phoebe's fine,' she announces breathlessly. 'She isn't asleep. But she isn't screaming the house down either. So that's good. What did I miss?'

'Erica was just telling me that she might be going travelling,' Nicholas tells her as she sits back down with us.

Amelia smiles at me. 'Really? Where are you heading?'

'I'm not sure. There's a friend of a friend who's going to Thailand. I might go with her if I can get things in place quickly enough.'

'Wow. But what about your new man?' she says with a wink.

I shake my head. 'My new man probably has a wife or

a criminal record he hasn't told me about. The nice ones normally do. Come on, let's go and get a drink somewhere.' I reach in my bag for my purse, and pull out something wrapped in soft blue tissue paper.

'Is this from you two?' I ask Nicholas and Amelia. 'It's not mine. I didn't know it was in here.'

They frown, shake their heads, as confused as I am, until I unwrap the paper to reveal a magnet in the shape of a boat.

I burst out laughing. 'It's from Daniel. He must have bought it for me and put it in my bag without me seeing. We looked at these in the gift shop today in the Lakes and he joked that he was going to buy me one for my birthday so that I'd remember our boat trip.' Like I'd forget it, I find myself thinking. The balmy heat of the afternoon, the lazy gliding of the boat, the way Daniel bought our tickets and batted away my offer of money, the stark differences between him and Mike, who would have rolled his eyes at the whole day: the prices of a boat trip, the predictable ice cream on a bench, the lack of beer and friends and music.

'That's cute. And totally what a man who's in love with you would do,' says Amelia with a raised eyebrow. 'But what the hell. There'll be men who fall in love with you in Thailand too.'

'Cheers to that,' I say as we clink together our glasses.

Chapter 5

'So, Erica Silver, there's something I want to know about you. It's an important question, so I want you to think very seriously about your answer,' Daniel says. It's the second time I've spoken to him since our day out. 'Are you into amusement arcades?'

He called me just as I was arriving back at my flat after meeting Zoe. I think for a moment as I take my keys from my bag and wander from the warm afternoon air into my tiny hallway. 'Well, I haven't been to one since I was about eight. But yeah, I think I could give it a go.'

'Excellent.'

I laugh. 'Are you going to tell me why this is excellent?'

'Oh, it's excellent because I have ten pounds worth of vouchers for the finest arcade on the prom. I had a meeting with the council this morning and they gave me some freebies.'

'Aw. You saw slot-machine vouchers and thought of me,' I say, smiling. 'I'm not sure how to take that.'

'Oh, it's a definite compliment. I've never said it to

anyone else. I can do my work around whenever is good for you.'

I have wanted to see Daniel again since my birthday, and even thought of suggesting it when I called him to thank him for the gesture with the magnet in my bag. But a quiet fear of what he might think, of seeming too full-on, especially so soon after breaking up with Mike, stopped me. Daniel, I think with a smile, has no such fear. I walk into the kitchen and take the magnet from my fridge. I hold it up to my face, press the cheap edges to my lips, before hastily putting it back just in case someone, somewhere, is watching.

'Any day,' I tell him. 'Any day at all.'

***

We go on Tuesday. September has brought autumn suddenly as it sometimes does, carrying with it jagged grey skies and a sharp trace of coolness in the air. We hurry from a downpour into the arcade's brassy smell of pennies and damp carpet and chips, and within about twenty minutes, we've spent all of the vouchers that Daniel split between us.

'It's quite worrying how easily ten pounds disappeared in there,' I say afterwards as we sit in a cafe in town with steaming coffees and slices of chocolate cake. 'I think they really should have given you more. Cheapskates.'

Daniel reaches into his pocket and drops some more vouchers onto the table. 'They gave us a few other ones, too. Some were only valid for a day though. And some are clearly just for people with kids.'

'Look at this one!' I say, pulling a Blackpool Tower voucher from the crumpled pile.

'Oh, I think that one's run out,' Daniel says, waving his hand.

'No, it hasn't! It's valid till tomorrow! We can do it all! Ballroom, top of the Tower, everything. This is amazing!' I grin at him. 'I'm free for the rest of the day,' I add, brave for a moment.

Daniel cranes his neck, looks out of the cafe's steamed window into the bleak street beyond. 'It's still throwing it down. We won't be able to see much from the top in this.'

'I don't mind. I love the Tower,' I tell him, feeling nervous that he doesn't seem too keen. 'I've been to the ballroom, but not all the way to the top for years. You know, when I first moved here, it was really hard. I'd left all my friends behind. I knew nobody and I was only twelve. But then I realised I could see Blackpool Tower from my bedroom window. And somehow, it made things better. I ...' I stop, laughing and putting my head in my hands.

'Go on. You can't stop there!' Daniel says.

I shake my head. 'I have to. It's too embarrassing. I've never told anybody this.'

'If you tell me, we can go to the top of the Tower right now,' he says.

I squirm. 'Fine,' I say, pushing my hair from my face. 'I used to talk to it.'

'To the Tower?' he says, markedly hiding a broad smile.

'Yes. To the Tower. I told you, I had no friends, and it was like a friend to me. I used to sit on my windowsill and chat to it. I told it about school, and how much I missed home, and the about the boys I liked. And so now, when I look at it, I feel like it knows me. I kind of feel like we're still old friends.'

Daniel smiles at me, and grabs my hand from across the table so that the vouchers dance across the wood like butterflies. 'You're completely crazy.'

'You're just jealous that the Tower knows all my secrets.'

'Then maybe I'll speak to it too. Maybe it'll tell me them. I'd love to know your crushes.'

'I can't believe I told you that,' I say, shaking my head. 'I've never told anyone.'

'Really?' Daniel asks as he begins to pile up our saucers and plates. 'Not even Mike?'

'No way. I never would have told him anything like that! I think I pretended to be normal with him.'

'No wonder it didn't last.'

I laugh, and swat him as we get up and leave our table, the neatly stacked plates and cake crumbs whisked away instantly by a waiter, as though we were never there.

***

'I love it here so much' I say as we wander through the Tower a few minutes later. 'It reminds me of an old lady. One of those people you can tell used to be so beautiful.'

'It is pretty special,' he says. 'I loved the aquarium in here when I was little.'

'Me too!' I say. 'I used to come every summer with my brother.'

'I came every summer holiday too. We might have been here together before, you know. Do you ever think about things like that?'

I nod. 'Always.' I don't say anything else, and try to push thoughts of my other life from my mind.

'I think it's the history of places like this that make you think all sorts of things about who's been here before, and what paths have crossed. You can almost feel the past. It's pretty cool.'

I glance across at Daniel. 'I've never met anyone who thinks like that before.' I try to say it nonchalantly, and I don't want to keep bringing Mike up, so I don't add that Mike would never have come to Blackpool Tower with me, even though I was always trying to persuade him. I even came on my own once. He met his friends in a pub on the prom while I was here. I remember the explosion of laughter from them when I returned to him and said I'd had a wonderful time wandering around alone and drinking coffee in the ballroom. Mike had looked pained, as though he'd wanted to tell them to be quiet but didn't quite dare.

'Do you reckon it's haunted in here?' Daniel asks as we enter the ballroom.

I turn to him, excited to tell him what I learnt recently when researching the Tower ghosts for a display at Blackpool Museum, where I work. 'Yes! I've just done some reading about that. Apparently this is the most haunted part of the Tower. The man whose idea it all was, and who started the project up to build it, apparently couldn't bear to leave. So many people have seen him here. And there are other ghosts, too.'

Daniel smiles. 'Well, it figures. This ballroom wouldn't be a terrible place to spend eternity. Especially if you knew it wouldn't have existed without you.'

I look up to the intricate gold ceiling and stalls, the glittering chandeliers above us. 'I know. It's the most amazing room I've ever been in.'

'It puts all my projects to shame,' Daniel says. 'Although it's kind of inspiring. Maybe I will put lots of extravagant gilding on my next plan.'

'What is it?'

'It's an office block in Preston.'

I laugh. 'Then you definitely should. Offices need more gold. Got to keep the workers happy.'

We sit for a while, watching the dancers glide across the gleaming floor.

'I bet you know loads about Blackpool because of your job at the museum,' Daniel says. 'Give me another fact about the ballroom.'

I think for a minute, then my eyes wander to the stage. 'See up there, the inscription below the carvings?'

Daniel looks up, and narrows his eyes. 'Yeah. What does it say?'

'It says, "*bid me discourse, I will enchant thine ear*". It's Shakespeare.'

'Okay,' says Daniel. 'I was always better at maths than English. What does it mean?'

I stare at the stage for a minute, thinking about the words. 'I take it to mean, if you give me a chance to talk, I will tell you something incredible.'

Daniel nods, and our eyes meet.

'Come on,' I say, suddenly flustered. 'Let's go up to the top.'

***

The steep iron staircases that we climb to the very top of the Tower, the whipping wind and the adrenaline of the sheer height, all contrast sharply with the ornate glamour of the ballroom. Daniel is quiet as I chatter on about everything we can see: the slopes of the rollercoasters on the Pleasure Beach; the silver sea that blurs into the sky.

'I always try and find my mum's house,' I say, leaning against the netting to squint at the thousands of rooftops. 'But it's impossible.'

Daniel nods and turns to read a sign that says we're 412 feet up. It's busy, and as I make my way round to the other side, I'm jostled by groups of people taking pictures and shouting to each other about the height, the view, the wind.

'Not much to do once you get up here, is there?' Daniel says, his hands stuffed in his pockets.

'No. But it's still brilliant. Thanks for coming with me,' I say, and before I can stop myself, I am putting my arms around him, hugging him, taking in the pleasant warmth of his body, the inky scent of his aftershave. He takes his hands from his pockets, puts his arms around me, hugging me back, and his lips press against my head.

'You're so welcome. Come on,' he says as I reluctantly draw away from him. 'Let's go and find you another ugly magnet from the shop. I won't rest until your fridge is completely covered.'

After Daniel has bought me a magnet in the shape of a Blackpool tram, we leave the Tower and step back into the bustle of the town, straight into a man who claps Daniel on the back.

'Long time no see!' he shouts, a bead of spittle flying from his lips and landing on my shoulder.

Daniel pats him on the back too, more gently. 'Erica, this is Bob. I've worked with him a few times,' he says, giving me a quick look that tells me everything I need to know about Bob and what Daniel thinks of him.

'Have you made him go in the Tower?' Bob asks me, jerking his head towards the entrance.

I nod, still burning with excitement from hugging Daniel before, and the exhilaration of being so high. 'We've just been up to the top.'

Bob frowns and gives Daniel an exaggeratedly confused look. 'You got him to go up more than a few stairs?' he asks me. 'How on earth did you manage that?'

There is a silence between us, and all we can hear is the swish of the wind, the touts of street sellers, the snippets of conversation as people walk past. Daniel is looking at Bob as though he wants him to disappear, his feelings about him not quite as skilfully subtle now.

'Had a function at the Tower with him once,' Bob says, jabbing Daniel in the side. 'We all went to the top, of course. Except, Mr Heights Phobia here turned green at the thought of it. Wouldn't entertain it. He was terrified. Almost cried like a girl when we were saying we'd carry him up there!' He leans forward, winks at me. 'He stayed in the burger bar on safe ground. Suppose if we'd looked like you, we'd have done a better job of persuading him to join us.'

I turn to look at Daniel, not understanding for a second, but then something clicks completely into place and it is as though someone has turned a light on and everything is a brighter, lighter shade of yellow.

'You know, we have a booking for dinner,' Daniel says, looking at his watch, which is an old fashioned one with a brown strap, something Mike wouldn't be seen dead in. 'We'll have to go.'

I nod mutely and wave a brief goodbye to Bob as Daniel takes my arm and guides me away. When we are at a safe distance, on the colourful commotion of the promenade, I stop and turn to him.

'A dinner booking?' I say. 'First I've heard about it.'

He reddens slightly. 'Oh, Bob would have us talking all day if we let him.'

I look at him for a moment before speaking. 'Are you really scared of heights?'

Daniel grimaces. 'Well, yeah. Pretty terrified actually.'

I reach out to him, touch his arm. 'So why did you go up there with me? Why didn't you just tell me no?'

He looks at me and grins, his face still a shade deeper than usual. 'You wanted to go up so much. You said the Tower used to be your friend. How could I possibly tell you no?'

I don't answer him, just stare at his face, which is suddenly the most perfect face I've ever seen, and savour a rush of pure happiness. It's the thrill of opening an unexpected gift, pulling off the paper and knowing, hoping you know, what's underneath: something you've longed for but never thought you'd have.

I lean forward and kiss him lightly on the lips. It's over in a second but I want it to last forever.

'Thank you.'

Chapter 6

'Do you have plans on Friday night?' Daniel asks me as we pull up outside my flat later that day. We decided that as we'd told Bob we had a dinner booking, we should really eat together too. We went to a tiny bistro and ordered huge steaming shanks of lamb and crisp roast potatoes. We talked about our families, our childhood homes, wading through the past in that detached way you do when you meet someone new. It's late now we've reached my flat, the sunset casting the streets in a pale glow. I pause before answering, trying in vain to stretch out the day.

'I do. Although I feel like I'm going to want to change them,' I say.

'Damn. Someone got to you first. What are you up to?'

'I'm meeting up with someone called Nina. I don't know her that well, but she's about to go and do some travelling. I want to quiz her about it. She wants someone to go with,' I say, the idea of joining Nina suddenly at odds with the comfort and easy happiness of the day I've spent with Daniel. 'I might go with her.' *Might?* I think to myself. I was so definite that travelling was what I wanted, and after a day out with Daniel I'm changing my mind?

I study Daniel's face for a clue to tell me how he feels, wait for him to look crestfallen or perhaps beg me not to go, but his features don't change. 'Oh?' he says evenly, 'where's she thinking of going?'

'Thailand. You know, I'm building something new,' I say, referring to Daniel's pep talk when we met at the party.

'Who told you to do that? Must have been an idiot if he's the one making you go.'

I smile at him. 'Nah. He wasn't all bad. Terrible taste in magnets, though.'

'Well, then you're best moving far away from him.'

'You think?'

'Yep.'

'I can see Nina another time. What were you thinking of doing on Friday?'

'There's fireworks on the promenade. But honestly, I just thought that if you had nothing on, we could go. I don't expect you to change your plans.'

'I know you don't. But I want to. Nina won't be bothered. She said she could see me on Saturday morning so I'll just do that instead.' I glance across at him. 'It really makes no difference,' I say, more to myself than him, but I don't believe it for a second because already I can feel the chasm between myself and the other Erica, another thousand Ericas, shift minutely with my change of plan.

Daniel taps his fingers on the steering wheel. 'Excellent.

If you're sure. I'd like to do something that doesn't involve me trying to hide the fact that I have a horrible phobia.'

'Not scared of loud bangs, are you?' I joke.

He laughs. 'Nope. All my secrets are out now. Nothing else you need to know.'

We are quiet for a moment, and Daniel takes my hand. 'I did honestly mean what I said at the party,' he says. 'You really have to do what you want to. Don't stop for anyone.'

I smile. I want to do the exact opposite of what he is telling me to do: to invite him in, to be with him for longer, to never see Nina again, to stop everything except him. But I can't do that because that would obviously be some kind of cliched rebound if I changed everything for someone so soon after what's just happened with Mike. I look at Daniel's face, his even features and his black hair that's slightly curly from the rain and his high cheekbones, his pale, smooth skin.

'I'll see you on Friday then,' I say to him as I peel myself from the car and wonder if 'rebound' is even a real thing.

***

'So what got you interested in going travelling?' asks Daniel on Friday night. We're wandering along the promenade before the fireworks start. The air is chilled and I pull my black wool jacket tighter around myself even though I spent over half an hour choosing what to wear. In the end, I went for a black dress and black tights with my chunky boots.

'Well, it was Mike who started it. We looked at places like Thailand together a lot. He wanted to go more than me. I've always been a bit scared of going away.'

'So you've never travelled before?' asks Daniel.

'No. Have you?'

'I've been to Europe a few times with friends. Nothing major. It was a while ago now though. My fear of heights kind of affects how I feel about flying so I haven't been to many different places.'

'Well, you've been more adventurous than me,' I admit. 'I even did my degree locally. I've barely been out of Blackpool since I moved here.'

'You like it here though, don't you? The history of the town?'

I nod, and stare out at the black waves that glitter with the lights from the pier. 'Yeah. I do, and that's why the museum is my perfect job. I was so excited when it came up, but I got the feeling Mike didn't even want me to apply for it. I think he knew it'd make me put off travelling yet again.'

'I thought you said the job is only a three-month contract?'

'It is.'

'Oh. So Mike's pretty spoilt.' Daniel glances at me from the corner of his eye, wondering if he's gone too far.

I laugh. 'He was a bit. I suppose it's not his fault, though. He really wanted to get away, and I'm starting to see that it was fair in a way. We wanted different things. Like you said, if you really want to do something, you shouldn't stop for anyone.'

'I suppose it depends who it is.'

I turn to look at Daniel just as he looks over at me. As our eyes meet, I see a glint in his that makes me feel as though a tiny firework has just erupted in my chest.

'Well, I'm glad now that Mike didn't wait for me,' I tell Daniel, and my words are fast, falling over one another. *Take a breath*, *Erica,* I think, smiling to myself. 'That night when we first met, there's no way I would have believed I would think like this so soon. But I'm in a different place to where I was. I'm seeing things so differently to how I have done for years.'

'I know what you mean. I think I felt the same when it ended with Sarah.'

'Sarah of the magazine aisle?'

Daniel laughs. 'Yep. Her. I think when I was with her, I couldn't see anything properly. Then I had to change places I suppose, and it was horrible and difficult because moving and change always is. But now my view is better, somehow.'

'Yes!' I say. 'You make it sound so simple.'

We walk for a little longer before Daniel speaks again. 'So anyway, you were saying about the travelling. Even though it was Mike's idea to start with, has it turned out to be something you want to do after all?'

I sigh. 'I don't even really know,' I admit. 'I think I've just been feeling a bit lost since Mike ended things. Even now I can see it was probably for the best, I do still feel like I should have a new focus once the museum job is over. I've spent so long wanting to just stay here. I'm not that adventurous really, and I always had a bit of a problem with being on my own. But now ...'

Even in a crowd of people, with the beat of music thumping from speakers above us, Daniel hears me more than Mike ever did. I watch him as he thinks about my words, turns them over in his mind. 'What about now? Do you like being on your own more?'

The first firework explodes and I watch the sky burst into a hundred different shades of green and pink. I think of the danger that has flooded back to me since I started disappearing again last week at the party, the dread of being alone and falling into another time, the raw fear of clawing at the present to try and stay and having nothing to hold on. When Zoe gave me Nina's number, and I decided that I should go travelling, I was still hoping that the disappearance and seeing the other Erica was a dream. But now, it's clear that it wasn't. Terror grips me and I swallow it down and stride forward. 'Not really. But I've decided that I should do it anyway. I want to show myself that I can be adventurous and do all the big, amazing things that other people do. But I don't know about my reasons, really. I don't know if it's just a bit of a knee-jerk reaction to Mike telling me I'm boring.'

Daniel shakes his head and grimaces. 'You know, I sometimes wish we could re-live that party. I could have beaten him up when you first arrived instead of giving him a drink.'

I burst out laughing. 'That would have been quite a welcome. I kind of preferred the Champagne. I had a toast to make, remember? The start of my new life.' My words are lost in the score of a bright blue rocket above us, and I lean into Daniel as I watch. We huddle together for a few minutes and watch the fireworks, until there is a pause in the ripples of colour and sound.

'What about you?' I ask him. 'Were you like this when you broke up with Sarah? Did you suddenly want to make plans?'

He thinks for a minute. 'Not really. My plans stayed the same. Well, other than that I thought I'd end up marrying her. We were never engaged,' he adds hurriedly. 'But you just assume when you're with someone for a while, don't you?'

'Oh, I don't know. I never thought I'd marry Mike. We always said we'd avoid it,' I tell him as the show restarts and another firework blooms above us.

'Oh, a non-believer,' Daniel says, smirking.

I jab him gently in the side, feel the warmth of his body from beneath his jacket. 'It's not that I don't believe in it. I just don't really like big weddings. And I know this is a bit negative, but I just don't think marriage tends to end well.'

'Nothing ends well!' he exclaims as we start to walk again, picking our way through all the people who are still watching the sky, waiting for more. 'All endings are horrible. If you only ever thought of the end of something, you'd never start anything, would you?'

I consider this as we weave through the children waving cheap plastic wands, the friends huddled together gazing up at the splitting sky, the hamburger sellers with their sizzling carts. We're the only ones in the crowd who are walking. He's moving faster than I am again, and I reach out and pull him back until he slows down.

'So do you want to get married?'

'Tonight?' He looks at his watch. 'Bit late. We probably wouldn't be able to get it all organised in time. Nice idea though. I'm flattered.'

I roll my eyes and try to smother my laugh.

'What are you laughing at? You'd marry me.'

'Would I?'

'Course you would. If you weren't going off to see the world with Nina, then you'd fall head over heels for me, and I'd have to remind you, one day, that you weren't even going to *get* married. But you wouldn't even be listening because you'd be too busy trying on veils and big white dresses and tiaras—'

'I would *not* wear a tiara,' I say. 'I don't like the idea of people looking at me. Plus, I always wear black, never ever white. I am definitely not a bride type of girl.'

'Yes, you'd definitely wear a tiara. And a huge dress. Not necessarily white. But not black either.' We have stopped walking now, and he is grinning at me, facing me as he talks, his words in and out of focus with the squeals and bangs of the fireworks above us. 'And I'd think of this night, the one when you swore you wouldn't ever get married because of how it might end.'

The fireworks finish in a dramatic finale, and everybody is suddenly moving around us impatiently, wanting to carry on with their lives now that there is no spectacle for them, but we stand still, frozen in our own time and moment. Daniel steps towards me, and his lips press against mine until we are jostled apart. My hair whips in front of my face and Daniel pushes it away with his hand, his fingers brushing my cheek and leaving behind a pleasant flush of heat.

You could make me stay, I think.

I know, he seems to say as we stand and stare at each other, giddy with the euphoria of the night. We're on the edge of something and we can feel it – the safe soft ground behind us; the sharp, steep drop in front that would take our breath away.

***

We move from the promenade to a sticky, busy bar where we drink warm white wine from glasses with remnants of old lipstick pressed onto the rims. Daniel pulls a face and wipes them with his sleeve, critiques the temperature of the wine, its acidity. But I don't care about the wine or travelling or being boring or brave. I don't care about anything other than drinking in every single moment of tonight: the warm, subtle buzz from spending time with Daniel, the thump of the music that vibrates in my body, the kisses and the blurred taxi ride and the press of Daniel's weight against mine, the taste of him as we fall through the door to my flat, melting into one.

***

Daniel sleeps as soon as it's over, throwing himself back onto the pillows and sighing, taking my hand and lacing my fingers through his, his eyes closed and his breathing even and deep. I drift in and out of sleep. I think fleetingly of Mike, his hard abdomen that he proudly sculpted at the gym every night, the glistening blonde hairs springing up from his stomach and thighs that always looked so angelic and childlike that they unsettled me slightly. Daniel's body hair is a stark black against his pale skin. He sleeps silently, smoothly. I curve my body up against his, the warmth of his skin spreading into mine, pleasure curling inside me.

***

I get up early on Saturday to go and meet Nina, trying to ignore my pounding head and my stomach full of cheap wine and the unexpected feelings of desire for this man who I barely know that slip over and under one another like eels.

I've arranged to meet Nina in the coffee shop where she works at nine-thirty, which now seems horribly regrettable.

But I've already cancelled her once. I shouldn't do it again. Plus, I remind myself as I drag myself from Daniel's warmth, regardless of how I started to doubt my reasons for wanting to go with Nina last night, it is something I've decided that I want to do. I would almost be cancelling myself, the very concept of which reminds me of the other Erica and makes me nauseous, so I shower and get dressed quickly and with as little thought given to the day as possible.

I whisper to Daniel that I'm going, and he nods vaguely but doesn't wake. I have a hazy but definite memory of him telling me last night that he had a meeting at eleven today in town, and that we could maybe meet for lunch if I was still around when he was done. As I walk from the bus stop to the coffee shop, I take out my phone. He'll be up now, maybe back at his place. So why hasn't he messaged me? I imagine him doing all the things I haven't seen him do, and if I go travelling might never see him do, like stretching in bed before getting up, shaking a can of deodorant and wincing at the cold as he sprays it, eating toast (or cereal? Both? Nothing?), taking short sips of hot coffee, glancing every now and again at morning television as he buttons up his shirt.

Stop it, I try to tell myself. Focus on meeting Nina. Last night was just one night. Daniel seems wonderful, but I barely know him.

Still.

It's already different to what I had with Mike – sweeter and more intense, a delicious ice cream so cold that it hurts my brain and stops me from thinking straight. I have to be careful, because even if it's not a rebound, I need to be brave enough to go and have the adventures I have promised myself. I wanted to do it, and my disappearances starting again have made me feel too cautious.

Falling for Daniel, I tell Nina, even considering staying here for him, would just be giving myself an excuse not to be brave and go away.

'Would it?' Nina asks, although from the bored look on her face I can tell she doesn't really care either way.

I look down at my napkin. 'I don't know. I thought I knew everything about myself. But now I'm second guessing every decision. Which could all be completely irrelevant anyway, because he still hasn't messaged me.'

She frowns. She's having second thoughts about travelling with me because she thinks from this short burst of time with me that I'm the kind of person who vomits up all sorts of feelings every time I'm with a stranger. But I'm not that person. I wasn't, anyway. I hate people knowing too much about me. How has Daniel, with his surprisingly broad shoulders and black chest hairs and warm skin changed that so suddenly?

'He'll message you, I'm sure. Sounds like he's pretty into you. But the thing for me is, are you coming with me? To Thailand?'

Thailand.

'It suddenly seems so far away,' I admit to Nina and she rolls her eyes, snaps a sugar sachet back and forth before tearing it open and dumping it into her half-drunk coffee.

'Well, yeah. That's kind of the point. Look, either come or have your fling. You can't do both. Which would you rather do?'

The question, a simple one in principle, has only the effect of the word *fling* sending a surge of warm pleasure through me as I am reminded of last night. I'm so busy reliving his warmth and his lips on mine and his hands in my hair, so busy itching to check my phone, relenting, pulling it out from the clutter of my handbag and seeing a glorious double green flash that signals a new message, that I barely even hear my own words.

'I don't know.'

Chapter 7

On Monday, when I let myself into the front door of Blackpool Museum, it feels like a whole lifetime has passed. I gently tear the Post-it messages from my computer screen and scan through them: people to call, emails to compose, things to collect. I picture myself as I left the museum before my time off just over a week ago. I didn't even know Daniel properly then: he was just the man I met at the party. After worrying yesterday when I met Nina that he wasn't going to get in touch with me, we messaged all day and saw each other for lunch. I smile as I think of it, a warm rush of the memory of him burning through me. I switch on my computer and take my notepad and pen from my duffel bag and then hear Katie, the curator, bustling in through the door.

'Hello stranger!' She grins as she makes her way over to me. 'I missed you! Have you had a good birthday week off?'

'Well, it wasn't quite what I expected. It definitely wasn't all bad, though.' I don't know Katie that well, and didn't tell her when Mike ended things with me. I certainly don't want to launch into the depths of my feelings about Daniel.

Fortunately, Katie doesn't seem to want to know much more. 'Fabulous!' she gives a bright laugh. 'Life would be boring if it was always what you expected.'

'I think you're probably right about that.'

'You've missed all sorts of excitement here, you know. I have a proposition,' she says as she takes off her denim jacket and throws it over her chair.

'Really? About what?'

She beams an excited scarlet-lipstick smile. 'I've fought and fought. It's been going on for weeks, but I didn't dare say anything until it was for sure. The council have funded your job for another year! And they have agreed to make it an assistant curator post. You can be involved in the spring exhibition I was telling you about!' She waves her hands about above her head in celebration, still grinning. Then she stops and frowns at me. 'You do want it, don't you? Please say you do! If not, I can advertise it ...' she lets her sentence fizzle out and arches her left eyebrow expectantly.

'I would love it,' I begin, trying to ignore the clear sense of relief that is blooming inside me. If I have a renewed contract here, Daniel here, then there is no reason to leave.

Katie frowns. 'I can sense a "but". Please don't let there be a "but".'

I smile. 'But ...' It's not that simple. I have to follow through with my plans. Plus, if my disappearances are back, then they won't work with a job. They won't work with Daniel either. Staying here and working at the museum wouldn't be excuses to make things easier for myself, I realise now as Katie stares at me expectantly. It would probably be the riskiest option to take. I could vanish at any point and let people down without being able to give them an explanation why. It could start to happen as frequently as it did when I was a child. 'You've just given me a lot to think about,' I tell Katie eventually. 'I've been thinking of going away, trying something new. I met up with someone yesterday who wants me to go to Thailand with her.'

'Oh, we can cover a holiday,' Katie says, dismissing this with a bejewelled hand.

'But I was going to go for a year,' I say, seeing Katie's face fall. 'Not that this doesn't sound amazing. And I am so grateful to you. I will definitely think about it.'

'Okay,' Katie says. She squeezes me on the shoulder 'I'll be gutted if you leave, but I do understand. Take a few days to think about it. But think hard. I feel like you're definitely the right person for the job.'

***

I try to work productively during the morning. There's a press release that Katie has asked me to prepare to promote the Tower ghost exhibition, and all the emails that I've received whilst I've been off need responses. I type slowly, the decision I need to make looming in the back of my mind. At lunch time, I go for a walk along the promenade, hoping that the fresh blast of air will help to clear my head like it usually does. The day is clean and bright, the autumn crispness that I felt the other day piercing through the wind.

I love it here, I remind myself, as I take in the grand arched windows of the Tower across the road, the tangle of rollercoasters and rides ahead, the illuminations which rock dangerously in the wind. I love the job, and I can still feel the warm, sweet excitement and flattery of Katie trying so hard to get me the permanent position.

And then there is Daniel. As I force myself through the sharp, salty air, I try to remove him and the way he looks at me, the way he faced his fear of heights just for me, from the decision I have to make.

Mike wouldn't even have gone to B&Q for me if I'd wanted him to, let alone faced his fear.

But I didn't want Mike to do that for me, did I? I'd been fine being with him because we only really circled one another; we never lived together, never got bogged down with shared money or the toll of bills or children or DIY. Mike made it so easy never to want those things with him.

I stop walking and stand still on the promenade, in the same spot that Daniel kissed me only a few days ago. People weave around me and the sea rushes towards me as I stand and stare out at the grey beach.

The two disappearances I have had in the last week have brought back everything I felt when I was twelve when they first started happening. I can taste the metallic rush of overwhelming fear that stops my heart and makes my senses strangely still: fear of dropping from the world and missing out on everything I love, fear of getting back and having to answer all the questions I don't want anyone to ask.

Where have you been, Erica?

Why do you never want to go anywhere on your own, Erica?

Why did you not turn up for the sleepover, Erica?

Why are you lying to me, Erica?

Eventually, I had to get used to answering the questions, at shaking off people's strange glances when I returned somewhere after vanishing for hours with no explanation, with my hair wet with rain even though it was a clear day. I had to stay with people as much as possible at the same time as being anonymous enough that they didn't care or notice if I disappeared for hours when I went to the toilet. And then I met Mike and slotted keenly into a life where we shared little more than a bed at the weekends, where we were constantly at parties with crowds who wouldn't have known whether I was there or not. The disappearances stopped but I never changed back into someone who opened up to anyone else because the residual fear still dripped slowly into everything I did. Because it stopped happening, I never told Mike that I was different to other people. Even if it had happened whilst I'd been with him, I wouldn't have needed to tell him where I'd been because

I'm sure he would never have asked. If I was late or unreliable then it would have just reaffirmed that we were living a cool, uncomplicated lifestyle unrestricted by all the things he hated.

I think of the other Erica I've seen: carefree, sun-kissed, happy. I don't know for sure but I would bet that she doesn't have disappearances like I do. It's in the angle of her head, the volume of her voice, the way she looks straight into people's eyes, which I stopped doing years ago. If I am brave enough to go ahead with the travelling, to try and lose the old fear that has returned to me in the last few weeks, then maybe I could be more like her.

I could change.

I take my phone out to tap out a quick message to Daniel as the wind pulls my hair around my face and tugs at my jacket. Then I turn my back to the rollercoasters and swinging lights, and walk briskly, against the wind, to the museum.

Chapter 8

Later that night, I sit in Luigi's for the second time in a month. It's busy, and waiters scurry around me holding laden trays high above their heads, but for me time seems to be ticking so slowly that it makes me feel fidgety. When I stood on the promenade earlier today and messaged Daniel to ask him to meet me, he said he'd be here at eight. I got the tram to town early so it feels like I've already been waiting a while. It's almost twenty past and with every fragile tick of the clock, doubt pulls away at me more and more.

Perhaps, I think as I fiddle with the cutlery, he's not coming. And then my decision will have no impact on him anyway. I glance outside at the darkening sky that threatens a storm.

'Drink?' An impatient waiter who has already been over once looks down at me again, pad and biro poised.

I order a glass of water and thank the waiter as he brings it over and pours it over the crackling ice. I take a sip of it and check my phone. I remind myself that he was about ten minutes late to pick me up the day we went to the Tower. Maybe he's just the kind of person who is constantly running behind.

And then before I can wonder any more, in a rush of fresh air and apologies, Daniel is standing in front of me.

'I'm really sorry,' he says a little breathlessly. 'I promised myself that I would try to curb my lateness for you. But then I had a flat tyre. Had to change it. Then I got oil on my shirt. So I had to change that.' He laughs. 'What a start to the night. Anyway. How are you? Everything okay?'

Even as I look up at him, the person I was when I was with Mike, the Erica who sat back and let everyone else talk, who never gave much away, seems to fray at the edges. Electric excitement pulses through me as the words I'm about to say float around in my mind like dancers in the wings. *I'm staying here.* I have already told Nina that I won't be joining her, and felt the soft ripple of distance between myself and the other Erica. I don't know if it's the right decision. But in the end, the decision was the best kind to make: the kind that won't go away and is impossible to ignore. The kind that you just have to make, whether it's the right one or not. Still, now, as he shrugs off his jacket and tosses it over his chair, the excitement is laced with fear. I swallow it down.

'I'm great,' I tell him, standing up and kissing his cheek. 'You're cold.'

'There's going to be a storm tonight. The wind's really

picking up,' he says as he sits down. 'You liked it in here when you came with your brother then?'

'Yes. It's lovely,' I say, but my words are suddenly slurred, blurring together. Daniel frowns at me and I take a gulp of water.

Frustration climbs inside me as I realize what is happening, that this is stronger than anything I ever felt when I was a teenager. Then, being with people was enough to stop it. *Not here*, I tell myself firmly. *Not tonight.*

'Erica? Are you okay?'

I nod, smile, and ignore the hammering in my head, Daniel's face flashing before me.

'I'm glad you asked me to meet you tonight. Today's been a bit of a strange one for me, actually,' he says.

'Why?' I manage, but even one word is difficult to get out.

He sighs and opens his menu. 'The funding for that office block in Preston's been pulled. It was a big job, and we were lucky to get it. I'm sure something else will come up though. There's actually another one in the pipeline, so really we might even ...'

I try to listen as he talks, but his words tear into fragments and lose all meaning because dizziness rages through me and I have an overwhelming, animal urge to run. I can think of nothing but leaving Daniel and our little table with its red chequered tablecloth, and going somewhere by myself so that I can be lost to another place and time. I grip the table so hard my knuckles turn white.

Stay calm, I tell myself, trying to quell the frenzied flutter of panic that rises inside me. It has never happened in front of someone before, so surely it won't now. I see Daniel frown, pause, but I can't speak to him. I am fading, and I wonder fleetingly if he can tell, if my skin is turning translucent and ghost-like in front of him.

I force my eyes to focus on what's around me – the Charlie Chaplin prints above the table, the soft flicker of the candle, the basket of rustic bread that has been placed down in front of us – trying to take it all in and somehow pin myself to the present. I try and try to force myself to stay. I nod as he says something and reach out for my water, my hand like lead. As my fingers touch the tip of the cool glass, I am brought back from the brink of disappearing, my head rushing as my senses return and the ringing in my ears is replaced with Daniel's voice.

'So yeah, I'm glad that you said about meeting because I really wanted to—'

I stand up before his words begin to blur again. I know this won't go away. 'I'm so sorry. I need to pop to the ladies',' I tell him. 'I'll be back in a minute.'

But I'm not back in a minute, and when I do return to where I was sitting, Daniel has gone. The restaurant is empty and closed. It's the end of the night. I must have been gone for hours. I hear a member of staff in the kitchen and creep to the locked front door, turning the latch and slipping out silently as I think about what I saw.

Chapter 9

I was in my old house, the soft green backdrop of Yorkshire hills outside the kitchen window.

The Erica who I saw for the first time the other day sat on a wooden dining chair that I recognised from Mum's house, that I categorically *knew* had been packed up sixteen years ago onto a van and taken to Blackpool. She wore the same travel agent's uniform as she had when I had seen her last time and typed on a PC which was set up in the corner of the lounge.

That lounge. I breathed a silent, invisible sigh. I had been longing to return to that room ever since I'd been pulled away from it all those years ago. It was the lounge of my childhood: of cartoons and play fighting and dens with Nicholas, of sleeping on the sofa when I was off school with the flu; the lounge of Christmas mornings and first-day-of-school photos. It looked predictably smaller than I remembered it and fuller somehow: a glossy fire surround took up the centre of the room where a smaller gas fire used to hang from the wall, DVDs lined shelves above the television, and the walls were busy with photos in frames. I tried to pull myself towards the photographs, but my body was as dull as in sleep. I could make out two figures in most of them, blurred in orange-tinted film. Although I had only ever seen one of them in my life, as I squinted hard at the pictures, I realised that they were my parents' wedding photographs.

I was forced to tear my eyes from them when my dad appeared in the room with the other Erica and crouched next to the computer where she sat, his hair dotted with grey.

What was this life?

'More job searching?' he asked. His voice made my eyes sting – not just the sound of it which I have barely heard in so long, but the casual closeness that we – *they* – seemed to have.

Erica nodded, clicking on a link that had caught her attention. 'This one's fine, look. A bar job.'

'In Phuket?'

'Yep. I told you I was serious about going away.'

My dad took hold of the mouse and clicked off the job advert, moving the cursor to another link. 'Plenty of jobs here in the UK. Look.'

Erica laughed and snatched the mouse back, rolling her eyes and scrolling straight past the job I know so well.

Assistant curator at Blackpool Museum

'No way. No backing out now. You're the one who has always told me to make the most of my life, and see the world. God, if I had a pound for every time you told me you'd have gone travelling if you'd been free and single for longer! You can't go back on all that now I'm actually going ahead with it.'

'I know, I know. Ignore me. I just can't believe you're actually going to leave.' My dad laughed, put his hand to his heart in theatrical mourning and I smiled at his humour, something I'd forgotten. How easy it is to forget all the little things that people do when you don't see them anymore: the way they yawn or write or hold their car keys. I ached to move closer to him, to see him, this version of him who never gave up on us.

'Yes, ignore him. Whatever he's saying, ignore him.' The tone was light, and Erica glanced up and smirked as my mum walked into the room.

'Always,' Erica replied drily as she typed quickly into another search box. I stared at her, the identicality and otherness too strange to process. My side profile that I hadn't particularly liked before, was now somebody else's too: chin a little too emphasised, eyes squinting at the screen, black hair with an annoying kink hanging down her back. She glanced up, and I followed her gaze to my mum, who was talking again.

'He says he'd have gone away and had adventures. But really, would he have coped without us all?' she said, picking up a cup from the table and wandering from the room.

'Obviously *not*,' Erica said absently as her eyes returned to the screen and she clicked on another bar job.

As I stood, like a ghost watching over its loved ones, I felt the ground shifting beneath my feet. I wanted to hold on, to stay and somehow melt into this other life where there was so much that I'd spent so long grieving for when I was younger, so much I didn't understand, but I couldn't grasp anything to hold on to. I slipped away, and plunged back into the deserted toilets of Luigi's.

Chapter 10

Now I'm outside and the storm has arrived. Thunder roars above me, the rain pounding down. I take my phone from my bag, noticing as I press buttons with my shaking hands that it's almost ten.

He answers in one ring, his voice cool.

'Daniel, I'm so sorry.'

'Why ask me to meet you, and then disappear? Where did you go?'

I'm silent, biting my lip, trembling with cold as the rain washes down over me. The other version of my family is still with me, stinging me like a vivid dream. 'I can't explain it. Not now. Not here.'

Daniel is silent. I imagine him stretched out in bed, or on the sofa perhaps, and want to curl myself around his warmth, tell him, letting him listen and asking him to put his arm around me in the hope that I might feel safe somehow. But behind my longing to anchor myself to him is a terrified urge to hang up, to never share this life with anyone.

'Erica, I don't know if this is some kind of joke, or—'

'It's not!'

He gives a dry laugh. 'Well it kind of felt that way tonight when I had to get one of the waitresses to go into the toilets to look for you and then have her tell me that you'd gone, that maybe you'd climbed out of the window. If this thing is too soon after what happened with Mike, I do understand, but you can't just take off like that without telling me why.'

'Daniel, please,' I say, wiping away my soaking hair from my face. 'Can I come and see you? I promise, I didn't want to go anywhere tonight. I wanted to be with you. It's all I wanted.'

He sighs. 'Where are you?'

'I'm outside Luigi's,' I say.

'What? It's throwing it down. Why are you back there?' He sighs again. 'Wait. I'll come and get you.'

'No, don't. I'll get in a cab,' I say. 'I'll come to you.'

'Wait there,' he says firmly and hangs up.

I stand shivering in the doorway, my arms crossed over my sodden chest, willing myself not to go again. It's about twenty minutes, and I have no dizziness, no blurring. For now, it seems, I am done. Finally, I see him running towards me. 'I couldn't stop the car near here. I'm parked nearby though,' he says.

I hold my soaking hand out to him, and he takes it, frowning. 'Erica, what's going on?'

I shake my head. I am trembling so furiously that I can

barely speak, and feel like I could be sick at any moment. Now that he is here, the thought of one day telling him, calm, collected, open-minded about his response, seems alien and far-fetched. 'I can't explain it. Not now. But it's not what I wanted.'

'You're speaking in riddles!' he explodes, throwing his hands up, letting my fingers slip from his.

'I know. I'm sorry.'

He stalks off, glancing back every now and again.

'I want to make this work, Daniel. I've changed my mind!' I shout so that my words aren't lost in the howls of the wind, in the rumbles of thunder.

He stops, turns around. 'Okay. So are you telling me ...?'

'I'm not going travelling,' I interrupt him, unable to wait any longer to tell him what I meant to tell him hours ago. 'I've told Nina I'm not going with her.'

'But Erica,' Daniel says, 'I thought that before, when you disappeared ...' he trails off and looks skyward, then bounces on his heels with his hands over his face. 'I can't believe this.'

I frown. It's not the response I was expecting. He looks almost annoyed. 'I've accepted a permanent job at the museum. I want to stay here, with you,' I tell him.

'So you didn't hear me before,' Daniel says quietly, his hands still over his words, which are so quiet that for a moment I think he's talking to himself rather than to me.

'Hear you? What do you mean?' But I know what he means: that when he was talking I was halfway to somewhere else, and only the mass of skin and bone of my body remained. He means he said something important, something that I was meant to hear every word of, that he can't understand why I didn't take it in.

'I told you about it. I had to make the call tonight,' he tells me, his voice insistent.

'I don't know what call, Daniel! Just tell me!' My heart is racing and I step towards him as a fork of lightning shoots through the sky, and shadows the town in a dirty yellow light: the pavements shining with rain, the shuttered shops, the intricate patterns of the Tower above us.

He takes his hands from his face, and takes mine in his. 'I'm going, Erica. I'm moving to Berlin,' he says, and everything is dark again.

Chapter 11

7th September 1997

The first time it ever happened, I had just turned twelve years old.

Those days were foggy with upset and confusion

My bedroom, normally crammed with photos and posters and colourful mess, was bare, swept up carelessly into pale brown boxes. The thought that I'd never sleep in there after tonight made me feel so strange – hot and cold and so nervous that I'd been to the toilet about ten times that day.

'Why do we have to go?' I'd asked him so much that even I was tired of hearing the same beaten words, but I couldn't seem to stop myself.

Nicholas smiled sadly, and I loved him for not losing his patience with me. 'We just do. And we'll be fine, you know. Mum said that our new house is five minutes from the sea.'

I wrinkled my nose. My best friend Claire had been to

Blackpool for the day last summer, and she said that the sea was brown and smelt horrid. But Nicholas was trying to help me, so I stayed quiet.

'Dad will come and visit us, you know. And Mum might be happier there. She always said she loved it.'

I thought of our mum, her mouth pulled downwards, her eyes blotchy. She never used to be like that.

'I wonder why they ended up being so unhappy,' I said, picking at the corner of a label on one of the boxes.

'They fell out of love,' Nicholas said, as though it was quite simple.

I sighed, frustrated, ripping the label off and tearing it into sad little pieces in my hands. 'That makes no sense.'

'Well, you fall in love. And then you fall out of it.' Nicholas sounded like he was okay with all of it, like it was a fact of life. But I wasn't so sure. I'd always thought that falling in love sounded nice, like falling into a giant comfy duvet or perhaps a warm pool full of chocolate. But falling out made love sound like a speeding aeroplane or a broken hammock or something at a great height that you could suddenly fall from and hurt yourself.

'Remember ages ago, when Dad used to go to work and give Mum a kiss on the cheek?' Nicholas said, seeing that I wasn't satisfied.

I nodded.

'Well, he stopped doing that. Did you notice?'

'So just because he stopped kissing her goodbye, they fell out of love?'

Nicholas looked a bit confused.

'Or did he stop kissing her because they fell out of love?'

Nicholas didn't answer me because my bedroom door opened, and Dad appeared. His face, like Mum's, was grey and tired. He stood awkwardly by the door, his hand resting on the top of his head as though there was nowhere else to put it.

'All ready for tomorrow?'

I turned away. What a stupid question that was.

'Erica, don't be like this. I might not see you for a few weeks now. I want tonight to be nice. Please know that this isn't my fault.'

'So it's Mum's fault?' I was surprised to hear Nicholas ask, and I turned back to our dad to see what he had to say.

But Dad was calm, sad, still, as he had been for ages now. There hadn't been many words at all. Philip Myers in the year above me kept having fights that year and someone said it was because his parents were getting divorced. I'd imagined divorce to be all shouting, yelling, screaming – so many words that you'd have to cover your ears or listen to your Walkman the whole time you were at home. But it hadn't been like that for us. Mum had told us last week that they were having some time apart, and that we were going to be moving to Blackpool, where she grew up, to give Dad a bit of space. Dad had been fading for a while, saying less and being at home less. He reminded me of the receipt for the cinema that I left on my windowsill the summer before, which started out with bold black letters and now looked like I never went to see any film at all, as though that night had just been erased.

'It's nobody's fault. It couldn't have been avoided. There's just no other way,' Dad said. He took something from his pocket and came and sat on my bed between me and Nicholas. My mattress sagged in the middle and I pulled up my knees to give him more room.

He held out what he had in his hand. It was an old photograph. 'Here, you've probably never seen this, have you? I brought it to try and help explain things to you. Sometimes words aren't quite enough.'

I wanted to roll my eyes at him, at his English teacher spiel. He was acting like this was a lesson, bringing a prop and planning it all out as though he could make us understand everything and get straight A's. But when I glanced at Nicholas, and saw him trying to co-operate by staring at the grainy photograph of some wedding, I tried to do the same. 'No, I've never seen it.'

'It's one of our wedding photos. The fact you've never seen it speaks volumes, doesn't it?' We were silent, Nicholas nodding. 'All of our wedding photographs were forgotten about, stored away in a box in the attic. We always meant to put them in frames and hang them up downstairs, but we never got around to it. In fact, we never got around to most things we planned.'

He passed the picture to me and I stared down at the orange-tinged figures. My dad wore huge, strange glasses and had a moustache that hung down either side of his mouth. My mum looked so young I hardly recognized her. She smiled at the camera, holding tightly onto a huge bunch of roses.

'You don't even look like yourselves,' I said eventually.

'Exactly, Erica. We're different versions of us. We were so happy then. We loved being with each other. We were excited. But that changed. We changed. So there was nothing to be done. If you compare the people in that photograph to us now, you can see that. Can't you?'

I nodded this time, because I could see it, even though I didn't really want to. Where did that leave anyone who wanted to get married? Why did anyone ever bother if this could happen to them? I didn't realise I'd asked these questions out loud until my dad put his arm around my shoulders and kissed me on the side of the head.

'There's so much you don't understand yet, Erica.'

His words lodged themselves in my mind, and I heard them again and again, long after he had closed my bedroom door softly behind him for the last time and creaked down our stairs, out of our red front door forever. He was right. There was so much I didn't understand: why they'd given up on each other, on our house and my bedroom and being my parents together, on Friday nights when we always had sausage and mashed potatoes, on watching TV all squashed together on the sofa in our dressing gowns on Saturday mornings. It worked for me, and I didn't see why it couldn't work for them anymore.

But I also didn't understand how those faces in the photograph would suddenly mean so much to me that the world as I knew it would split, changing into something that had a completely different shape, a different feeling.

And I didn't understand that this wasn't the last time I would be in our house; that at some point, way in the future, I would see it again.

***

That night, anxiety prickled at my skin as I lay wondering what the next day would bring. I left my window wide open so I could smell the last of the Yorkshire air – the warm scent of bright green fields and sweet manure and haystacks ripened by the sun. Soon, I'd be starting a brand new school where everyone else already had best friends, and I knew nobody. I'd be wearing a uniform different from Claire's, and going home to a bedroom I'd never even seen yet in a town that had a brown sea covering everything in a bitter, invisible salt. I shuffled underneath my duvet and squeezed my eyes shut, trying to block it all out, but my nervous thoughts jerked to the front of my mind and my head pounded. Amongst those thoughts about my new home and new school, the photograph that Dad had showed us flitted about like a moth. I recalled my parents' faces in the picture, hopeful and happy. As I thought about them, something that felt like a dream pulled at me, making me dizzy. I tried to sit up but I was pinned to the soft mattress by something much, much stronger than sleep. I tried and tried to force my impossibly heavy limbs to move but I couldn't even open my eyes. Time seemed to suspend, to hover over me, until my eyes flew open and my body was suddenly free again. My legs and arms flailed wildly, tangling themselves around each other. My bed, my room full of pale brown boxes, everything, fell from beneath me.

And then I found myself standing on a street in winter, as though I'd never been anywhere else.

***

I didn't know the street. I'd never been there before. I licked my lips and tasted salt. I tried to ignore my shaking legs and pounding heart, so that I could take in the shops and the people, to try and work out where on earth I was and what had happened. My breaths were fast, my head hammering, but somehow, my eyes managed to work and the street around me shimmered and eventually settled into focus.

I was dreaming, that was all. I had to be dreaming. Nicholas had told me about something like this once, a boy he'd heard about who could direct his own dreams, as though they were plays. I was like that boy.

I shivered, the winter air biting my bare skin. Glancing down, I saw that I was still in my pink and white nightie. I ached with cold. Everyone else on the street was bundled up in hats and woollen coats and scarves, their breath clouding the air with little puffs as they spoke to one another. I tried to breathe out too, but my breath didn't make a swirling cloud like everyone else's. I tried again. Nothing. It was like I wasn't really there, but I could see everyone else, and hear their conversations. A woman with long ginger hair stopped just beside me, so close to me that I could smell her perfume – sweet and sharp, like the stalks of fresh flowers. She didn't seem to notice me, but headed beyond where I was standing, where she threw her arms around a man.

'How lovely to see you!' she said as she disentangled herself from him. 'Are you still coming for the fireworks party at mine tonight?'

I turned to look at the man she was talking to. He had a shaggy beard and long hair, and wore blue trousers that flared out at the bottom. He looked familiar, like one of the men I'd seen on Mum's old records.

He frowned. 'I'm not sure I can come, actually. I—'

'Oh, please do!' the woman interrupted, touching him on the arm, her long nails making a mark on his leather jacket. 'Mary's already cancelled. I can't have people dropping out. I've bought enough potatoes for an army! Thank goodness Laurie can come in her place. You know her, don't you?'

Laurie? My mum? I frowned, watching closely.

The man nodded. 'I went to school with Laurie. Okay then, Jules. I'll be there. Can't have wasted potatoes.'

'Oh, great. You know,' Jules said with a wink, 'I was excited about sitting you with Mary for dinner. I thought you'd get along very well. But she's ill, poor thing.'

The man grinned through his beard, then stopped, as though he knew that he shouldn't, and managed to look worried instead. 'Oh dear. What's the matter with her?'

'Food poisoning, apparently.' Jules gestured down the road, and I followed the man's gaze to a window with a dead pig hanging in it, and for the first time I noticed Blackpool Tower's outline above it and something burst inside me, like a small explosion.

The man I was watching was my dad, and he was about to go to a party and meet up with my mum. This was years and years ago, before I had even been born.

Panic flared inside me. How was this happening? And how was I going to get back home, to the version of my dad that I knew with less of a beard and more lines and sadness on his face?

It was okay, I reminded myself as my breaths began to speed up and my heart began to shiver again.

'It's okay, because it's a dream,' I whispered, then I covered my mouth. I didn't want Jules and my old-fashioned dad to hear me and know that I was listening to them, to have to try and begin to explain myself and why I was there in a pink and white nightie. But they didn't hear my whispers. They were in their own world, both looking down the street at the butcher's. Or maybe I was in mine.

'Mary was silly enough to buy cheap sausages from Henderson's,' Jules carried on. 'But everyone knows he lets them hang about in his window all day. It's all well and good getting a bargain, but I wouldn't buy my meat from there if it was the last shop on earth. She's been up all night, apparently. Can't keep anything down!'

'That is a shame,' said my dad. 'But it can't be helped if she's ill.'

'Are you here for long? Maybe once she's recovered I could get you and Mary together again. Set you up. You can't stay single forever, you know. You're one of the last ones not married.'

'I'm off to London again tomorrow,' my dad said. 'I only came to visit my mother. She had a fall. But she's better now, and so I need to get back in the morning. Maybe some other time.'

His words burned through everything I knew: my grandma who used to live in Blackpool but who died when I was a baby; my Dad never mentioning London; my parents never even talking about a life before they were together.

'Ah, well that is a shame,' Jules's voice cut into my flaming thoughts. 'Poor Mary. Still, at least the rest of us will see you at the bonfire party tonight. Maybe Laurie might even do for you! I'll see you at seven,' she said as she gave his arm one final pat. 'Wrap up warm!' she called as she dashed away down the street. But her words were quiet to me, as the street suddenly broke into jagged pieces and I was flung away from her, away from the street, back into the soft mound of warm sheets on my bed.

I sat up and blinked. The curtains rippled in the breeze, my window still wide open. The late summer sun had soaked my room in golden warmth, yet the hairs on my arms stood on end, my toes stiff with the cold of winter.

My stomach swirled with fright and for a second I thought I might be sick.

From downstairs, I heard Nicholas's voice, the engine of a van outside, the beep of a horn, Mum yelling.

It was moving day, and my twelfth birthday.

I wanted to believe that I was going to go downstairs to a cake and balloons and presents that were stacked precariously on top of all the boxes, that Mum and Nicholas would want to hear all about the strange dream I'd had, that we'd have time to have the birthday breakfast of fried eggs on toast that we had every single year. Mum had even left the frying pan and the toaster out of the boxes, because I'd asked her to so many times. She was going to pack them last.

But somehow, as I shuffled shakily over to the window and saw the removal van that had been booked for 1pm, and I smelt the hint of winter frost on my skin, I knew that none of this was going to happen.

***

I could tell that Mum wanted to believe me. But would you?

I disappeared to a different time.

She frowned at me, her forehead creasing, her whole face drooping as it did so often these days. She asked me why I was lying, over and over again. Nicholas stared at me like I was a magic eye poster: closely at first, then jerking his head back as if seeing me from a different angle might help him to understand me. I wished that he could understand me, that he could explain it like he always explained everything else to me. Fear had darted around inside me ever since I woke up, or came back, or whatever it was that happened. I'd been gone for hours. Mum had come into my bedroom at nine, and again at ten, and I wasn't there. I'd listened to her shout about the wasted time hunting for me, ringing my friends, going sick with worry, but the words hadn't been processed in my mind, because there was way too much other stuff, bigger stuff, for it to deal with. It raced through what I'd seen over and over and over again, trying to find some kind of sense. How had I disappeared? Had I gone back in time? My fingers trembled as I zipped the last of my things into my battered Nike rucksack, frightened that it might happen again at any minute, that I might just fall from the world somehow, to another place where nobody knew how to find me.

The delivery driver packed everything into his huge cavern of a van, and Mum cracked eggs angrily, slamming them onto the side of the pan, muttering about us needing to follow them, about having five minutes to eat our breakfast.

We ate on the floor of the dining room in silence, even though I still felt sick, as though I had been on too many fast fairground rides after too much food.

‘I know how to make you believe me,’ I said, putting my toast down and wiping the crumbs from my fingers on my shorts.

Mum chewed slowly, swallowed. ‘How on earth you expect me to believe that, Erica, I’ll never know.’

‘I saw Dad.’

‘Dad? So you sneaked out?’ She was hurt, and her mouth drew down even lower than usual.

‘No. Not Dad as he is now. It was Dad, but a long time ago.’ My breaths were dangerously short, and I felt like I might faint, but I had to get my words out. I had to make her believe me. ‘I watched him. He was going to a party. His friend who was having the party was called Jules. It was a fireworks party, and it was going to be that night. He had a moustache and was wearing blue trousers, and a leather jacket, and—’

‘How did you know about that? The fireworks party?’ Mum had put her toast down too now, and Nicholas had stopped eating. They both stared at me.

‘What fireworks party?’ Nicholas asked.

‘That’s the first night I got to know your dad properly. We knew each other because he was in the year above me at school in Blackpool. But I didn’t see him once we’d left. We got chatting at the party and that was that. We were never really apart after that. We stayed in Blackpool for a bit, then got married, moved here and had you two. That party was where it all started. Did he tell you? He must have done.’ She shook her head and muttered to herself.

'But he's awful with names. He wouldn't have remembered Jules. We haven't seen her for years.'

'Dad didn't tell me. I saw it because I was there. It was like I went to see the past. But I don't know how, and I wanted to think it was a dream, but now I know it wasn't, because you said I wasn't in my bed this morning when you went into my room. And it was freezing in this other place, and when I woke up – or got back – I was so cold, even though my room was warm. I probably wouldn't believe someone if they were saying all this either, but I promise it's true.' I wiped my eyes because I realised there were hot tears running down my face, and suddenly Mum was rushing over to where I was sitting and putting her arms around me, squeezing me.

'Erica, it's okay. I really thought you'd run away. I'm sure there's an explanation. But if you didn't mean to leave then that's the main thing.' A step closer to believing me, but still so far from understanding what I was trying to tell her, she cupped my chin in her hand and looked into my eyes. As I looked back into hers, bright blue and sad, everything I'd seen whipped through my mind. There had to be something I could do. Surely there was a reason for me seeing what I had. And if I could work out the reason, untangle it from the knot of confusion in my mind, then maybe I could undo everything that was making us all so unhappy, everything that had led up to our home standing empty around us and all of our things whizzing towards a town we didn't really want to live in.

Chapter 12

'You're going to Berlin?' I ask. We stand apart, our whole bodies tense as we wait for each other to say more, like two bad actors in a play.

'I told you. I talked about it tonight before you left me. The Preston offices were cancelled, and there was talk of an offer in Berlin. I've spoken to my boss tonight and it's going ahead. I said I'd go.' He steps towards me. 'I *told* you about it,' he says again, frowning, not understanding. 'I told you how it had always been my plan to stay with the company, that they have a habit of sending me on random projects. I told you how much I'd dread the flight, how much I hate flying. And you didn't seem bothered about any of it. You barely seemed to listen. I wondered if maybe you just didn't feel well. But then you left. And then I wondered, amongst a hundred other possible reasons, if you'd just decided it wasn't worth spending any more time together, if I was thinking of going there anyway.'

I'd heard nothing about Berlin or his plan when he was

talking in the restaurant, because I'd been fading from him, trying so hard not to let it happen in front of his eyes. I am furious with myself, and swallow down my anger to be able to speak to him evenly. 'I would never do that.' Daniel going somewhere would not make me want to disappear. It would make me want to drink in every possible second I had with him. 'When are you going?'

'In a few weeks. There's just some paperwork to sort, and an apartment. It's a year's contract, to start with.'

I fight the sob that lodges itself in my throat. 'Are you excited?'

He frowns. 'I suppose so. It's all been quite sudden. It's just designing offices again but like I said, it kind of fits into the career plan I had. I haven't thought much about it yet though because I didn't know if I was going to accept it or not.'

'But Berlin is a good opportunity. It'll be ...'

'It'll be fine. I'll be facing my fear of flying so that's positive, I suppose. But it feels different now I know you've changed your own plans. I thought you were moving away too. But you're staying here now? Since when?'

'Since you,' I say simply.

Daniel stares at me. 'You only met up with Nina on Saturday to make plans for Thailand, didn't you? For a year? You seemed so sure that you needed to do it. I wondered if you might not go and meet Nina that morning, and I kind of hoped you wouldn't. But it was your choice, so I didn't say anything.'

My stomach crunches at his words. 'I wish you had. I kept telling myself it was the right thing to do.' I look down at the pavement that's sleek with rain, thinking of the other Erica, a strangely superior version of myself who probably wouldn't ever get herself into messes like this. 'But then I got to know you. And then when I was offered the job, it just all seemed to slot into place. I realized that staying here would be more of an adventure, in a way, than going away. I was so excited to tell you tonight.'

'I would have been excited too,' Daniel says, his voice cool. 'But you didn't tell me, did you? You left me in a restaurant making me worry about you for ages when I had no idea where you'd gone, and then eventually thinking you'd played some kind of trick on me.'

'I didn't trick you.'

'So tell me what you did do!' he explodes. 'Because I'm struggling to understand what it was that made you sneak from the restaurant, and not tell me that you were leaving me there.'

'I couldn't tell you.'

'You took your bag. You had your phone. Couldn't you use it?'

'No.'

Daniel is silent. Thunder rumbles in the distance. 'I don't understand why you couldn't just have stayed in the restaurant and told me your plans. It might have changed everything, Erica.' There's a flash of an image in my mind:

Daniel on the phone in his flat, telling his boss no, his face tense as he took a risk to stay here with me. My heart sinks.

'If I'd stayed in Luigi's with you,' I ask him, 'and told you I wasn't going, would you have told your boss that you didn't want the Berlin job? Is that what you're saying?'

He shakes his head. 'I don't want to think about it, because it's too ...' He stops, sighs, starts again. 'That isn't what happened. I don't even know what did happen, because you won't tell me. Why were you going to change your plans for me when you can't even be honest with me? It doesn't make any sense.'

'I was wrong, and I didn't have a clue what I was doing. I thought I could work round it.'

'Work round what?' Daniel's face is confused, angry.

'I ...' the temptation glimmers, a pearl in a shell. *Tell him.* But then the shell slams shut and the impulse fades. Daniel is going. He has made up his mind, and things are over between us before they've even begun. He has stepped back onto the safe ground of the precipice from which I thought we were about to jump.

'Never mind. It's not something that's easy to understand.'

'Well then tell me, Erica!' he says, throwing his arms up in frustration. 'Look, maybe you're used to someone who understands you more. Maybe Mike dealt better with these *things* than I do. Maybe we wouldn't have worked together after all.'

'Mike did not deal with things better than you. This wouldn't have happened with him. He never asked questions,' I say quietly.

Daniel lets out a bitter laugh. 'Oh, so I was right. Mike was breezy if you left him for hours on end with no explanation. I'm sorry I can't be more like that.'

'No! I meant that Mike didn't try too hard to get to know me. And I thought that was what I needed, because I didn't want people to know me properly.' Daniel pulls me into a doorway. The relief of the shelter, the absence of the sharp beads of rain pounding onto my skin, is overwhelming.

'And now?'

'A few hours ago, I felt like a completely different person. I felt like I should take a risk and forget what I thought I should do or would be safest doing. I wanted to stay. But things have changed now. It's the wrong time, Daniel. You're going away for a year.'

'So you're just going to forget it? You apparently changed all your plans for me, but now you're just going to give it all up?'

'Daniel, I ...' I falter and he stares at me, waiting. I imagined tonight over and over again. I imagined him looking at me in a way that made the pit of my stomach burn, making jokes about not being able to resist staying here and marrying him after all. The way he is looking at me is different to how he has looked at me before, and I feel a new distance springing up between us as he wonders what I could possibly say to explain away tonight. I've disappointed him, I realize. He's thinking that if I can't stick around for long enough to listen to his huge news about work or to tell him my huge news about falling in love with him – even though I vowed I'd never fall in love with anyone because of how it might end – then surely I can't be being honest.

My web of thoughts is broken by Daniel's phone ringing, the hollow polyphonic ringtone louder as he pulls the phone from him pocket. He glances at the screen and looks back up at me. Half regret, half annoyance.

'I have to take this.'

I nod.

I hear a man on the other end of the line, a man who is obviously so relieved to have Daniel on board that he is still calling him about it at this time of night, a man who has plans for a one-bed apartment in the city (compact but will do the job) and bank transfers and flights.

Daniel puts his arm around me as he listens and speaks, and I press my body against his, the cool rainwater seeping through my coat and dress onto my skin.

'It's really happening,' I say when he hangs up, my voice small.

Daniel kisses my forehead and pushes the soaking hair from my skin. 'Yeah,' he sighs. 'It's happening.'

I reach up and kiss him: salty kisses of tears and autumn rain.

'Look,' he says, the mood shifted from the call, 'whatever

is going on with you, if you want to then we can still see each other,' he tells me. 'We can visit. We can email.'

'I do want to.'

'Build around it?'

'Yes.'

He doesn't ask again tonight, and I don't try to tell him. We walk, exhausted, soaked, frozen, and fall into bed at his flat, into sleep filled with strange grey dreams of endings and secrets and sadness.

Chapter 13

'You looked different,' I say.

It's the day after Luigi's. Mum sits at the pine table we've had for as long as I can remember, on the chair which I saw in our Yorkshire house only yesterday, her slim hands around her mug of tea as I talk.

'Different how?' She became used to me talking about my disappearances in the end. It happened in bursts when I was younger – I'd vanish again and again one month, and not at all the next. Eventually, as I talked her through her life with Dad – where they'd lived, the friends they'd had, the coats they'd worn – she'd had no choice but to believe me. And then it stopped happening and we all stopped talking about it. Now, it's as though we are picking up something we put down years ago, remembering its shape, how to use it.

I gulp down bitter honesty. *Better.* 'Just different. But from what I saw, things had been easier for you. We still lived in Yorkshire. And you were still with Dad.'

She nearly spits out her tea. 'What?'

'I know.'

'And what about you? What were you doing?'

'I seemed to be close to Dad. And it looked like I was pretty fearless. Not overthinking things, just doing them. You know, the exact opposite of how I actually am. I wanted to stay, and find out how you and Dad were still married, because that seemed to be the big difference. But I couldn't. And it's good that I didn't, in a way, because I was gone for hours as it was.' I look down into my mug of tea, which is going cold. I can't face drinking it. I have felt the dizzy nausea of my teenage years since I returned from the other world last night.

'I can't believe that in some other life we stayed together,' Mum says, incredulous. 'What about Shelley?'

'I presume Dad never met her. He was quite the family man with us for some reason,' I say, and roll my eyes. 'How could someone be so different when they are still themselves? How could your marriage be so different?'

'Well,' Mum says, standing up and taking the cup away from me, pouring the cold tea down the sink and turning on the tap. 'There won't be just one reason, I suppose.'

'I think there was.'

She turns from the sink, wiping her hands on her jeans. 'What?'

'The day we left Yorkshire, and the first time this ever happened to me, I told you that I saw Dad on the day you two were going to get together.'

'At the bonfire party? What's that got to do with it?'

'Everything. You must remember that I told you about Dad staying in Blackpool just for you?'

My mum's face is blank. She blandly wipes a tea towel around the cup she has just washed and puts it back in the cupboard. 'Right?'

'He'd come back to see Grandma on that day because she'd had a fall. Then his plan was to go back to London. But then that woman who wanted him at the party told him you'd be there, and so he stayed on in Blackpool because he wanted to see you, and he never went back. He changed his whole plan for you. I told you this then.'

'Did you?'

'See? You don't even remember! I should have made more of it. I shouldn't have let it go.' My voice is louder than I intended it to be. 'You fell out of love with each other but maybe it never would have happened if you'd known how much he did for you at the start. I could have made you believe it before we even arrived in Blackpool. I tried to tell you on the way, in the car, but I gave up too easily because I was frightened of what had happened to me, and I thought talking about it too much might make it happen again.'

'You were a child. You couldn't have changed a whole relationship. There are so many tiny things that could have been different. That he stayed for me is only one of them. We did so much after that party. We made thousands of decisions. And they were already made by the time we split up. If we were already on our way here when you told me about it, then I don't think anything you'd said would have made me turn around.'

'Maybe if I'd tried harder ... He never told you that he stayed just for you, but I could have kept on telling you. It could have changed the way you saw him. It could have changed everything.'

'Erica,' Mum grabs my hands from across the table, her sudden energy surprising me. 'You're not listening to me. Yes, your dad made a mistake not telling me, for all those years, that he changed his world for me. I don't know why he chose to keep it from me. He was always preoccupied with a more adventurous life. He probably thought he'd go back to London at some point. Maybe changing his plan just happened, and he didn't even think about it.'

'If he had told you, do you think you would have seen things differently?' *Do you think you would have put your wedding photographs on the wall, and done your hair more neatly, and sighed less?*

'If he had told me what he'd done for me, when we first got together, of course we might have been happier. But you telling me that over and over again, or in a different way, or at a different time, wouldn't have changed a whole marriage. You can't put that responsibility on yourself.'

'But I do feel a responsibility. I feel like all I'm doing is letting people down, when this thing I have should be making me do the opposite.'

'Ah,' Mum says, glancing at me shrewdly. 'This isn't just about Dad. It's about Daniel, too.'

'It's about all of it,' I admit, picking at a placemat. 'I have a horrible feeling that history is repeating itself. Dad didn't tell you the whole truth, and it meant that things went wrong. I didn't tell Daniel that I was staying, so now things are probably ruined with him too. I really think I missed a chance to help you and Dad work it out. So maybe that means I could be doing more to make things right with Daniel.' I shake my head, my thoughts lost in the fog of my mind. 'I just don't know how.'

Mum swipes the placemat from me, inspecting it for damage. 'You always do make things more complicated than they need to be. You always have done.'

I frown at her. 'What's your point?'

'My point is, think about telling him the truth about where you went last night, and why you never got the chance to talk to him properly. That's probably all there is to it. Just stop shutting him out.'

I pull my hands from hers and stand up, gazing into the fading light of the garden. 'I was going to tell him. When I decided to stay, part of that was knowing that I'd probably tell him. And I was tempted for a second last night. But it wasn't like I imagined it to be, and I was so shaken and exhausted that I just kind of closed off. I couldn't.'

'You don't want to, you mean. And you were so close,' she says, sighing as though I'm a child who has failed a test for the fifth time running.

I am silent. I don't want to keep disagreeing because I

have moved past doing that. But I can feel my teenage self cloying under my skin, the familiar prickles of frustration and resentment that nobody really understands how I feel, because how can they?

'I don't want to tell him because I don't want to be closer to him,' I admit eventually. 'He would be the only person who I've ever told who isn't family. It would be huge. I would feel as though he was the closest person to me I've ever had.'

'And that's a bad thing?'

'Of course it is. He's going. I would gain something and then it would be gone.' I stare at her, wondering how she can think like this when losing my dad to a new family broke her, made her grey and sad and tired. Was the pleasure in the beginning really worth all this sadness?

'Being close to someone isn't about where you live. It's about how much you trust them and how they make you feel, whether you see them once a year or every day. Berlin isn't the end of the world, and a year isn't the end of time. You have to tell somebody one day, Erica,' Mum says, 'otherwise you'll never have anything real with anyone.'

Chapter 14

The night before Daniel is leaving for Berlin, we walk along the beach. The steely light of the moon is sharp in the autumn sky; the salty air stings our faces as we crunch along the frozen sand. He's been busy the past few weeks, preparing to leave, but tonight we have the whole night together.

'So, I've decided that before I leave for my flight, we need to know everything about each other.'

I feel a rush of happiness, tinged red with panic. We have spoken about surface things since the night of the storm: his knowledge of Berlin, the contract for my job. But now, underneath his words I can sense his need to know what happened. 'Everything?'

'Yep. I'm leaving in about fourteen hours. So I don't have much time to judge. What's not to love about that? We'll start easy, don't worry,' he says, squeezing my fingers gently in his. 'First album?'

I smile. 'Okay. Let me think. I think it was *The Wizard of Oz* soundtrack on vinyl. It ended badly, though. I took it to my friend's house and her brother snapped it. I'd only had it about a day. I was mortified, and my mum went mad at me. She'd told me not to take it round there but I didn't listen.'

'He snapped your first ever record? That's harsh.'

'I know. And every time I see that film, I think of my broken record and I'm sad all over again. Anyway. Your turn. Best day of your life so far?'

'Wow, and I went with first album? That's huge. I need to sit down and think about it.' He pulls me down onto the sand and we huddle against the wind. 'There've been a few good ones. I won a grand once. That was a pretty good day.'

'How?'

'I rang in to a radio competition.'

'Ha! And I thought you were cool!'

'I am cool. I won a thousand pounds; did you not hear that part?'

'Okay, okay,' I laugh, putting my head into his chest. 'Which other days have been good then?'

'The day I finished school was good. The day I started uni was pretty exciting. They're all cliched ones, I suppose. There was another day that I went to a party, and some gorgeous girl was crying on me, mascara all over the place, tissues everywhere. That was up there with the best.'

'It does sound pretty incredible when you put it like that. I can understand why you wanted to see me again.'

'So?' Daniel says to me. I shuffle even closer to his warmth and close my eyes. 'What else can you tell me about yourself? I'm going, remember.'

'Tonight is perfect,' I murmur. 'I don't want to ruin it.'

'You won't.'

I listen the roar of the waves beside us. 'You don't know that. If I tell you everything, you'll think I'm crazy.'

'And then I'll go to Berlin, so it won't matter. And if you don't tell me, I'll think you're crazy, and I'll go to Berlin. No difference. So you might as well tell me. I want to know you properly, Erica.'

I groan, and Daniel puts both of his arms around me, and gently turns me around.

'If you can't tell me, then tell the Tower.'

I burst out laughing.

'What?' Daniel says. 'You said yourself you've told Blackpool Tower all your secrets before. Why don't you do it again? And I'll just happen to hear you.'

I take a breath, stare up at the glow of the lights, the criss-crosses of iron that I used to stare out at every night from my bedroom window.

'Okay,' I say, shaking back my shoulders and trying to ignore the terror that is rippling through me, the desire to snap myself shut and protect myself. 'Okay,' I say again. 'I'm just going to say it. I'm not like other people. I have strange episodes that are a little bit like time travelling, but I don't always see the past. In fact, lately I've been seeing other places in the present, and my own life, but a different version of it. I disappear and seem to sort of teleport to these other times and places, and I never know how long I'm going to be gone for. My mum and Nicholas both know, but they are the only people who do. I've never told any of my friends, and I never told Mike because I never really wanted to and I suppose deep down I knew he wouldn't have believed it or accepted it, and I suppose the reason that I am telling you is that deep down, I know, or I hope, you'll do both.' I finish talking and squeeze my eyes shut for a minute. When I open them, nothing is different. The Tower carries on flashing, the sand is cool and damp beneath me and the sea gently ebbs closer. And yet everything, surely, has changed.

'Okay,' Daniel says. He looks at me for a few minutes and I say nothing else. 'So that night, in Luigi's? That's what happened?' I can see him replaying the evening in his mind. 'That's how you escaped without actually escaping? You just vanished?'

'It sounds unbelievable. I know it does. But yeah.' I look away, not wanting to look him in the eye. I stare out to the endless sea, black and glittering.

'Actually,' Daniel says after a few seconds, 'I read about something like this once. In the eighties, I think.'

'Yes!' I say excitedly. 'There was another girl it happened to. She was called Helen; I remember that. I read about her in the newspaper. I've been thinking about her lately actually, wondering if it caused her the same kinds of problems with men these days. I've tried to look her up but she's impossible to find. Maybe it's stopped happening to her. Maybe I'm the only one now.'

Daniel laughs, the sound unexpected and comforting. 'You know, the other night I thought of all sorts of scenarios, but I have to admit this wasn't one of them. Damn. Can't believe I didn't guess right.'

I look down, scoop up the cool, damp sand in my fingers. 'You believe me?'

'Why would you lie about this?'

'I wouldn't. I just never thought anyone would believe me. I thought you'd get up and walk away, or tell me I was dreaming or imagining it, and I'd end up yelling and crying. All the times I imagined telling someone, I never thought it would be calm and quiet like this. I thought there would be some kind of big explosion or something. Shouting, at least. It's such a big thing for me to tell you. It seems like it should be a big moment.'

'I don't know. The big moments are sometimes the smallest ones, aren't they?'

I let the sand fall between my fingers and press it back down. 'I suppose they are.'

'So you can't control when it happens?'

'Not really. I can just about delay it. But that's all.'

'This is incredible,' Daniel says. 'You're incredible.'

I tense, turn to him. 'You can't tell anyone. I don't want people asking me questions, writing to newspapers and following me around.'

'Of course I won't tell anyone,' Daniel says. 'It's not my secret to tell.'

We're quiet for a moment, and I watch him as he thinks.

'Are you trying to make sense of it?' I ask him.

'Not really. I'm wondering about this other version of your life you've seen, and if I'm in it, sweeping you off your feet and not having terrible timing and ending up in Berlin.'

I laugh. 'You're not in it, actually. Not yet, anyway.'

'Yet?'

'I'm sure you'll appear. You have to. The other Erica seems to travel about a lot. I'm sure she'll see you somewhere. Although I hope she doesn't get to spend too much time with you. I'd be jealous.'

Daniel leans forward and kisses me. 'At least we'd be getting it right in some other world.'

I sigh and lie back on the sand even though it is cool and damp; I feel a warmth flooding my insides. I can't believe I've told someone my secret. I feel lighter than I have since I was a child.

'You know what's weird?'

'Apart from your ability to transcend time and place?'

'Yeah. Apart from that.'

'What?'

'I feel like if you were staying, there's a chance I might not have told you.'

'Really? Why?'

'I was just so scared. I think you going away pushed me to do what I wouldn't normally do. It gave me less time to worry about what I might lose.'

He holds up his hand, lacing his sandy fingers through mine. 'Well then maybe things aren't so wrong after all.'

Chapter 15

On the day that Daniel leaves, and the ones that string themselves onto that, I am relieved to be able to throw myself into work. I have made a decision to stay in Blackpool, and I feel like I owe it to myself to make the most of that decision and put all I can into my job. The illuminations and half-term holiday both inject a last colourful flurry of life into the town and museum, and the days pick up pace. Nina sends me intermittent messages from Thailand, telling me how much I'm missing out on, telling me it would be cool if I'd changed my mind, to just let her know if I want to catch a flight and meet her.

'You still could,' Zoe says as we eat a takeaway at my flat one night. 'Or would you not want to leave your job now?'

'No, I wouldn't. I'm really enjoying planning the spring exhibition. We've done loads of promotion asking people to send in their old photographs and I'm loving seeing them all. Plus, I wouldn't want to let Katie down.' My disappearances haven't been as often as I worried they might be, so there have been no issues with Katie at the museum. We're working on a collection of photographs of people in Blackpool over time, and inviting people to send in stories of their personal histories and memories that relate to the town. We've had a good response, and Katie is impressed that I thought of the idea, and have executed it almost to the point where we're ready to start designing the final displays. So far, I feel like I have made the right decision as far as work is concerned. And although I am trying to focus on things other than Daniel, he has already mentioned the prospect of a visit back in the next few months.

'And Daniel?' Zoe says, as though she's reading my mind.

'We've been speaking most days. He's planning to come back to Blackpool for Christmas. I can't wait to see him,' I admit.

Zoe smirks and pulls a grain of rice from her sweatshirt. 'Well, it seems like Nina isn't going to get you as a travel buddy any time soon.'

'Maybe not. It's not just because of Daniel though. I am glad I stayed anyway.'

'Well, if you really mean that and you're planning on staying around here for the foreseeable after all, then you'll love to know which house is about to go on the market.'

Zoe runs an estate agent's in town. I think for a minute. 'No idea.'

'You know the house you love? The one—'

'Not *the* house?'

'Yes. The owner has been in a residential home for a couple of years now, and for some reason kept hold of the house. It's been massively neglected. Anyway, he died a few weeks ago. Some distant cousin came in to ask us if they need to do the house up or if they'll get a decent amount if they sell it as a project. They were pretty greedy, actually. It's quite sad. Anyway,' she says, her voice brightening again. 'I wish you could buy it. Although I'm not sure we'd be at yours eating Chinese takeaway for quite some time. It basically needs taking apart and putting back together again.'

'I don't think my savings would be enough to take that on,' I say. 'It's such a special house, though.'

'It'll be interesting to see how quickly it sells. Everyone in Blackpool knows it. It's almost famous.'

I nod. The strangely elegant, imposing house is on the promenade, further north than the Tower, and I drive past it every day on the way to work. When I was young and first moved to Blackpool, Nicholas and I rode for miles along the promenade on our bicycles. The new house we had moved into didn't feel like ours yet, and Mum was forever distracted. Pedalling along, away from our new house and all it stood for, the salty wind whipping against our faces, was our favourite way to pass those first, too-long weekends. The first time we saw it, we stopped and gawped at it for what seemed like hours. The owners were having a party, and guests were spilling out from the open doors onto the front garden. The weekend after, there was another party. Each week, we would pedal furiously through the September warmth, then abandon our bikes and sit on the grass verge in front of the house, the balmy evening sun warming our shoulders as we listened to the tinkling of a piano from inside, the roars of collective laughter and the clinking of glasses. Eventually, as the couple became older, the parties became less frequent, then stopped altogether, and the house began to lose its grandeur.

'It's lost its magic,' Nicholas said, on the day I first noticed the pin pricks of stubble on his chin, the way damp circles of sharp-smelling sweat now bloomed on his t shirt underneath his arms. Most things had lost their magic these days. But no. I shook my head. Not the house.

'I want to live there one day,' I told Nicholas as he rolled his eyes and hopped on his bike again to go home for tea. He was constantly ravenous in those days, eating whole loaves of bread within minutes and shovelling bowl after bowl of cornflakes into his mouth. 'I want to bring back the parties and happiness to it. I want to put a piano in it again and dance in the garden,' I told him, giggling at my own dreaminess.

'You'll need a rich husband,' Nicholas told me, his voice travelling sideways in the wind as we rode back home.

I frowned. 'No, I won't. I'm not having a husband. You know that. I'll just have some friends. They will help me to make it look good again, and dance with me. You can come and live there too, if you like.' But even as I heard my words, I heard childishness in them, an innocent belief of something impossible like fairies or magic.

Nicholas nodded, unconcerned, focusing on something else entirely – food, probably.

***

'Speaking of houses and work,' says Zoe, her words breaking into my reverie of the past and forcing me back to the present as she stands up and takes her plate out to my tiny kitchen. 'I should go. Early start tomorrow. I'll let you know what the house is like if I do the valuation. I think it'll be pretty grim inside. But I know how much you love it.'

We say our goodbyes, and Zoe leaves, but a few minutes later she's back, clutching a parcel.

'This was down the corridor, and it has your name on it,' she says.

I frown, and take it from her. 'Our post is never delivered properly at these flats. I wonder what it is?'

'Open it!'

I tear into the cardboard to reveal soft white tissue paper. Inside, there is a card with a German logo on it, with a handwritten scrawl underneath that I have to squint to make out.

What are the chances? Found this in a cool vintage record store on the first day here. Thought of you. Don't let anyone break it. D xx

'Is that *The Wizard of Oz* soundtrack?' asks Zoe, scrunching her nose up. 'Why would anyone send you that?'

I say nothing, just smile and slide the record from the sleeve and back in again, the sweet, musty smell of the past puffing up into the air.

***

'How weird,' I say on the phone about half an hour later, 'that you found the record. In Germany too, of all places.'

'I know. I couldn't believe it either. I'm glad it got to you okay. Although I know you probably don't have a record player.'

'Oh, that's an insignificant problem,' I say, giggling.

'Erica,' Daniel says, his tone becoming heavier, stranger. 'I've got something to tell you. Two things, actually.'

'Okay,' I say slowly.

He clears his throat. 'Well, firstly, Christmas. My mum and dad have just phoned. They thought they were doing something nice.'

'They're coming out to you,' I guess, disappointment springing up inside me.

'Yeah. I'm really sorry. I wish they'd told me before they booked their flights. They knew I'd rather not fly more than I need to. I wanted to see you so much, but they didn't know that. And now I can't really come back and leave them alone in my apartment with only my weird neighbours for company.'

'It's fine,' I say. 'It can't be helped now. And anyway, we're already almost two months down, aren't we? It's going so quickly.'

'Erica,' Daniel says again, more urgently this time. 'The other thing I needed to tell you ...'

There's a pause and I wonder for a minute if the line has broken up, but then I hear him sigh, a crackle hundreds of miles away.

'Go on.'

'They've changed the contract. There's funding for another similar project that's a bit bigger, and the clients want us to work on it. It's gone from one year to two. And I've been asked to sign up to it.'

'Right,' I say, my heart plummeting. I feel sick. 'So what did you tell them?'

'Nothing, yet.' I hear a slight crack in his voice and am overcome by the urge to touch him, to breathe in his inky Daniel scent, and kiss the prickly line of his jaw. I have always been quite good at reigning in what I want. Mike used to blow money on trainers or CDs or tickets to concerts because he wanted them, because he had to have them now; Zoe huffs and puffs when there's a dress or a car or a holiday she can't afford; but I have always been patient. But now, the desire for Daniel, for him to come back now and be mine, to forget Berlin and anything else that would keep him away from me, stretches inside me like elastic about to snap. It's like nothing else I have ever felt before. It is a simpler longing than I've ever had, because before, everything I have wanted has been overshadowed by my secret.

I think of the night when I disappeared and left Daniel in the restaurant. Then I think of his face when I told him the truth about my disappearances: accepting, interested. I think of the translucency of the world around me every time I fall from it, the lapses in my life and chunks of time missed every time I'm gone. I think of my mum, her face washed out by constant tears when things ended with my dad. The elastic desire pulls at me, goes against everything I have felt for so long, makes my insides ache.

Maybe I've never wanted anything else this much.

'You know, you could come out here,' Daniel says. 'Live with me for a bit. I know it would be impulsive. But you could do it. The German office is really cool, and the people here are quite good fun, actually. I can imagine you getting on with the people I've met. And we could find you a job.'

It's hesitant, hidden perhaps, but I hear it: the electric buzz of excitement in Daniel's voice. He wants to stay. He's happy to have been asked. I can't pull him back here, just to desert him in restaurants for hours on end, tangle his nice straightforward life with my own strange one.

'I have to finish the exhibition,' I say. 'I've promised Katie. And I've just signed the contract for my flat for another six months. I can't afford to go anywhere until at least the summer. But you should stay there. You know that you should stay.'

'You're right. It would be crazy to make you come here. Our timing is awful, you know,' Daniel sighs, and a tiny piece of my heart breaks because he isn't refusing to stay in Berlin, isn't challenging my encouragements. But I have told him to stay there. I shake my head, push a red-hot tear from my cheek. 'I don't know what it is about us,' he continues, 'but one of us always seems to be changing things around or deciding to move away, or changing things back again. Or teleporting. I bet you wish you hadn't told me your secret now.'

I think for a second, but my answer is clear. 'I don't wish that at all.' I say. 'You're the only person I ever wanted to tell.' I laugh, even though I'm crying. 'I don't know how you do this. You make me tell you everything. You make me feel how I swore I never would. See? I shouldn't have even told you that. I can't stop!'

He laughs too. 'Sorry about that. It's good to hear though, so I won't argue.'

There is a silence, a moment where all we can hear is the buzz of distance between us.

'I am sorry, you know,' Daniel says eventually. 'I know I can't ask you to wait for two years.'

I touch the spine of the faded record cover that lies on my bed, try to gather back some of the patience I always used to have, and pull back the elastic longing that lingers in my stomach. 'I can wait.'

Chapter 16

Christmas sweeps in and out like a dazzling guest: demanding but enchanting, arriving and leaving in a rush of glitter and money. With Blackpool's bleak, wind-bitten January comes a silent, stretched-out period for the museum. Even the volunteers don't come in. Katie and I work quietly, fuelled by hot tea and digestive biscuits, on the exhibition. Our close working together most days means that I am rarely alone at work, and I see the other version of me mainly at night: I might be sitting on the sofa, raising a fork of pasta to my lips, or crawling into bed after a late night with Zoe, or about to press call to Daniel so that we can chat about our days, and then the world blurs and tips me over into another. The other Erica taps away at foreign job applications, works at the travel agent's, sees friends who I left behind when I was twelve for cheap white wine in the local pub.

And slowly, gradually, the wind thaws and spring arrives.

***

On the opening night of our exhibition, Katie, a volunteer called William and I make the finishing touches, tying clusters of gold balloons wherever they will fit, straightening the huge black and white sign that was only delivered this morning and is suspended above us:

FIND YOURSELF IN BLACKPOOL

The hundreds of photographs of people taken in the town that we have collected over the last few months cover the walls: newly Technicolor women posing on the beach; sepia children with blurred and sombre faces caught in a moment on the promenade a hundred years ago; bathing suits and swimming hats and parasols, cars and clowns and long-forgotten hotels, shops, and stalls. We've blown up all of the images in the hope that people might recognise relatives, themselves or family businesses. Blank cards line the spaces between the photographs for people to write down names, stories, memories. As I take it all in for a final time before the doors open, nervous anticipation fizzes in the pit of my stomach.

'Katie is making me introduce the exhibition,' I said to Daniel on the phone the other day. 'She said it'll be good for me.'

'Well, she would think that. She doesn't know you have a deep-rooted fear of people looking at you just in case you disappear to a parallel universe. It's not something you'd generally expect of an employee.'

I laughed. 'You put my issues so succinctly.'

'You can do it. Make the most of the night. You've worked so hard; Katie's right to give you the credit in front of everyone. I really wish I could come. But there's no budging with the client meeting I told you about. I'm really sorry.'

'Oh, don't worry,' I told him. 'It'll hopefully all be on display for a while.'

But now, as the door opens and people begin to spill in, my chest tightens and I wish Daniel were amongst them.

'Nearly time, Erica,' Katie whispers with a grin. 'I'll set up the microphone. Ready?'

I nod, determined. The question flits through my mind: what would the other Erica do? Would she be scared of addressing a crowd, of all eyes on her? I want to think she wouldn't.

'There are hundreds of photographs here,' I tell people once I've thanked them for coming, my heart hammering. 'And we have displayed them all. But we don't know much about them. We want you to tell us anything at all that you know about them. There are thousands of moments on display, and each of those moments led to another, and another, and eventually, this one. The exhibition is about bringing all of the moments, and the people who have spent time in Blackpool, together. The town has its problems. So do most towns. But for so many people, it's a special place. It's a place where people came years ago to find fresh air and health, their future husbands or wives, a business that they would build up over generations. We want to know all of these stories – or as many as possible – and display them. So help yourself to a drink, and have a look to see if there's anything or anybody that you recognise. If there is, write it down.'

***

Once my speech is over, I feel light with relief and more than happy for people to turn away from me towards the walls of photographs. I walk with them, talking to some about the collage, others about specific places and people, just as I'd hoped. There are some pictures that I can't look directly at. Any from the 1970s, with that strange orange glow that photographs of that time exude, make my skin cool and my head ache. There's one stuffed in the back of my desk drawer because when it arrived through the post a week or so ago, I looked closely at it and saw the outline of the Tower, and the blur of a butcher's called Henderson's. I was alone in the office, and the sight of it made blood rush to my head, made my desk and everything around me hazy. The butcher's and the street of that particular era has been imprinted on my mind since the first time I travelled to see another world, a world where my existence became a possibility. I let go of the picture and let it float to the floor as I gripped the desk and willed myself to stay, but I couldn't do it. I went back to the street, back to the moment and the air that smelt of frost and damp and a heavy perfume of different times. I arrived back after only a few minutes, whipped the photograph from the floor where it still lay, and stuffed it in my drawer. Now, guilt nags at me, pulling at me like a child. I shouldn't have been selfish. Whoever sent the picture in was supporting the exhibition. I can display it without looking at it.

'Erica!' My shoulders are gripped from behind and my thoughts, my guilt, are pleasantly interrupted. I turn around and he's there, just as he promised he would be.

'Nicholas!' I hug him and he squeezes me before releasing me again. 'I'm so glad you came.'

'Wouldn't have missed it. Mum's over there with Zoe. We bumped into her on the way in.' I follow his gaze, and see Mum and Zoe chatting animatedly with Katie near the entrance, and a surge of happiness rushes through me. 'You did a brilliant job of your opening speech,' Nicholas says as he wanders along the wall of photographs with me. 'And look, people are writing stuff down already. You might have a full wall of stories by tonight!'

'I know,' I say, feeling a thrill as I see people chatting about the images and scribbling down information beside some of them. 'Some people gave stories and names with the photos they sent in, just to get the ball rolling. But it's really a long-term project. We just want to get as many people as possible looking at them and talking about them.'

'It's a great idea,' Nicholas says as Zoe and Mum join us. 'Amelia wanted to come too. She's going to visit in the summer with me and Phoebe, if it's still up then?'

'It had better be,' Katie interrupts, appearing beside us

and answering for me. 'Erica's worked so hard on this. I couldn't have done it without her.' She turns and grins at me. 'I don't know what I'd have done if you hadn't taken the job.'

If, if, if.

If I hadn't taken the job, would I have been brave enough to go to Berlin with Daniel?

Nicholas interrupts my thoughts and gives me an amused look. 'She did the right thing sticking around then?'

Katie nods, her long earrings jangling against her shoulders. 'Absolutely. I'll never let her go. Not if I can help it.'

I smile because it's nice to have someone say they will never let you go, even if it isn't the person you want to hear it from the most.

***

The night passes quickly, a blur of different conversations, people, stories. After an hour or two, the conversation slows down, the guests dwindle and William leaves, taking with him a stray gold balloon for his granddaughter. I'm left with Katie, her husband, Roger, Nicholas, Zoe and Mum. Katie drags a box of Champagne out from under the reception desk and takes out two bottles.

'Last toast to a successful opening?' she suggests.

I shake my head. 'I'm fine thanks.'

'Go on. We're celebrating. Tonight completely rocked.' She doesn't wait for an answer, snatching my glass from me and filling it with froth before topping up everyone else's. We clink glasses, a strange mix of people who all mean different things to me. I think of the photograph still stuffed at the back of my drawer and excuse myself from the group, mumbling something about having left something in my desk.

Nicholas appears just as I'm pulling out items that bury the picture in the drawer. 'So this is your office?' he asks. I nod, and reach to the back of the drawer, closing my fingers around the glossy paper.

'There's another photograph here that someone sent in. But I missed it out of the display,' I tell him. 'I couldn't bring myself to look at it.' I trace the fuzzy outline of Henderson's butcher's with my fingertip. 'It's too similar to what I saw that first time ...'

'Wow. That street where you saw a younger version of Dad?' Nicholas says. He knows the butcher's and the street in winter and the woman called Jules almost as well as I do. 'Does it make you feel strange?'

'You could say that. If I look at it, then this world starts fading away and I'm drawn to that one instead, especially if I'm on my own. Which isn't always that practical.'

'No. But it's pretty cool as well, you know. Seeing that moment.'

'It was why we exist,' I agree. 'It was the start of us, as we are now.'

Nicholas nods thoughtfully. 'It's like you said in your speech. Everything is the product of a thousand moments that have gone before. Although I have to say, technically that isn't very accurate. It's more likely millions. Billions, even, if you're talking moments.'

I roll my eyes. 'Number expert,' I say and we laugh.

We leave the silent office, flicking the lights off and throwing it back into darkness before heading back to the others. I hold the photograph out to Katie and apologise, and say that I didn't enlarge it; I don't tell her I forgot but she presumes that's what I'm saying.

'It's no problem,' she tells me. 'We'll keep rotating them anyway. They won't all fit on at once. Some people dropped some off tonight, actually, so we have more to enlarge and put up. We'll do another batch next week. I'll go and grab the new ones from reception to show you. There are some really lovely ones of the Winter Gardens, years ago.' She jumps down from where she's perched on a table, and that's when the buzzer at the front door rings.

'There's always one who can't read the times on the flyer,' she says as she heads towards the door and reception area.

I am thinking the same as Katie, that someone has arrived too late to the opening, that we'll tell them to come back tomorrow. I am thinking nothing more than that, until I hear him speak, and my heart pauses for a moment, and I feel the subtle tilt of things changing track before softly chugging along again.

Chapter 17

His hair has grown slightly longer, and the outline of a goatee is visible on his jaw in the fading light. I stare and stare. It's him. But it can't be him. He had a meeting that he absolutely couldn't get out of. He can't come back to the UK for another few weeks at least. Yet here he is.

'You came to see the exhibition?' I ask, delight making me hot, unsure. 'I thought you couldn't get the time off?'

'I couldn't.' He is breathless, pale, says nothing more until I raise my eyebrows in question. 'I've pulled out of the job.'

'The meeting?'

'The whole thing. I've ended it. I'm back.'

I take his hand, the warmth of happiness turning into a pale hot shock. 'You've changed everything? Your job? Your plan? For me?'

'I know. But it turns out that you are my plan. I just took a while to realize it.'

I throw my arms around him, crushing my body against

his, breathing in his scent and his voice and his clothes and *him*. 'You're crazy to do this for me.' He has, I think, completely lost his mind. Surely this cannot all be for me, for us. But it is. *It is*. I squeeze him tighter and tighter, as fear and excitement lace around each other in my gut.

'I'm sorry I missed your opening night,' Daniel says, his voice muffled in my hair. 'I wanted to make it so badly but the timing didn't work out.' I pull back from him slowly to see that he has suitcases with him, tatty luggage tags fluttering in the balmy sea air. 'It should have worked perfectly,' he continues. 'I was meant to get back to Blackpool at seven-ish. But my flight was delayed. I didn't know if you'd still be here, or if it was too late.'

I stand, feeling my hand in his, unable to let it go. I would have messed up my speech if he'd arrived before it, is my first thought and it's so ridiculous that it makes me laugh. And if he'd come earlier than that, or never gone, I would not have known how much I wanted him here. 'It's definitely not too late,' I tell him. Your timing is perfect.' I reach up and kiss him and feel the start of a new beginning, the one that everything so far has led us to, the only beginning that matters now.

Chapter 18

'What do you think?'

The day is bright and yellow, a sharp sea breeze that does not yet have the ripe warmth of summer nipping at our skin and tangling my long hair in dark ribbons around my face. I push it out of my eyes and look at Daniel.

He's been back for a month and in that time has been renting an overpriced furnished flat in the eaves of a large Victorian house not far from where I live. All of his books and music, his boxes of old sketched designs that have never been built, his pans and plates and mugs are all still in storage because he hopes he will be moving again soon. His tiny rented flat is like a holiday home with everything already in it. 'Which is fine for feeling like you're on holiday. Kind of nice at first, actually. But I'm starting to miss my own bowls,' he said last night as we curled together on the sofa that is not his.

I burst out laughing. 'I have to say, I kind of know what you mean. I like my home comforts too.'

'I know. Sometimes I think, why on earth did I think

that moving to a different country would be the right thing for me to do?' He leaned across and kissed me. 'I'm so glad I came back.'

'I'm glad too. Although now I'm wondering about your attachment to your crockery, and if it had more to do with your return than I initially thought.'

'Oh, of course it did,' Daniel said. 'But you'll do whilst it's all still in storage.'

We chatted late into the night, drinking tea and snapping chunks of German chocolate from the huge bar that sat between us, and woke tangled together, crooked and happy, after only a few hours' sleep.

'I have something I want to show you,' I told him this morning as he boiled the kettle a few metres from the sofa where I was still curled under a knot of soft blankets. 'A house. I think you'd like it.'

***

Now, we stand on the promenade, the house opposite us.

'It's the dream house,' Daniel says as he stares across at it.

'You know it?'

'Everybody knows it. I can't believe it's up for sale. I used to love this house. In fact, it's partly what made me get into architecture,' he adds as he turns to me. 'Every time I passed it, I'd go home and draw it, but add on extensions and renovations. It always felt like it had so much potential, even when it was at its best.'

'So we both loved it all this time,' I say.

'Yep. We have good taste, obviously.'

'So?' I ask, twisting my hair up into a bun and then letting it go again, into the wind.

'So. You always wanted it. Why aren't you buying it?'

'Because it's too much of a project and a risk. I don't feel like I'm the person who does that. You are. I can't afford it anyway.'

Daniel grins at me and a flash of happiness bolts through me. 'You can be that person too. Let's both buy it.'

The words are as bright and crisp as the air around us, sharp and pleasant all at once.

'Together? Daniel, I …' I laugh and put my hands up to my face. 'You're serious, aren't you?'

'Completely.' He grabs my hand and pulls me across the road, where we climb over the fence of the house, giggling like children, catching our trousers on the sharp, torn wood. Peering through the windows, we see threadbare carpets, mould climbing the walls like ivy. The window frames are damp as I lean against them, and I can hear the rattle of the panes of glass in the breeze.

'You want to live here with me?' My words are whispered, but Daniel hears them.

'Yep. It's just an idea. We both love the house. It would probably be too ambitious to buy it alone, impossible even, for either of us. It seems like a good solution to me. Think of all the money we're putting into renting. Dead money.

This would do something with our savings and wages, at least.' He grimaces. 'Well, when I get some work. Which I will, obviously.'

I take a few steps back and stare upwards at the blackened facade, bowing windows and the mangled pit of weeds that twists around the house like an overgrown moat. I catch my reflection in the window. Seeing myself, ghost-like and shimmering, makes me feel like I am watching the other Erica. What would she do?

What a stupid question. I scold myself, roll my eyes, and see my reflection do the same. *She is me.* I take a deep breath and wander round to the back of the house, where we press our faces up against the stained glass of the kitchen window. For some reason, there is a decaying blue velvet sofa abandoned in the middle of the kitchen, a yellow bucket, a single mug. I see in a flash the sofa dragged away, a different kitchen scattered with belongings, plastered walls dotted with photographs of happy times.

'I always wanted to live here when I was young, but with my friends,' I laugh.

Daniel laughs too and shakes his head. 'Oh. Well I'll just back off, then.'

'I think I might have changed my mind.'

Daniel nods, puts his arm around me, and pulls me towards him as we look out across the back garden, its stretch of lawn a jungle of weeds. The blossom on the tree that spreads its branches above us whispers and flutters pale pink confetti over our shoulders, and I catch a piece, feel its velvety smoothness under my fingertips. 'So you said you'd imagined buying it, making changes. Did you think about actually living here, and what it would be like?' I ask him.

Daniel thinks. 'I just wanted the house. But now, I can imagine what it would be like. And the house is only a part of it.' He takes my hand and kisses it. 'It would be a big project. I know that. But it would be so exciting too.'

A wave of anticipation bursts through me: about this garden being ours, about bringing the house back to life, doing everyday things with Daniel like choosing paint, eating toast in bed and talking about the day ahead, making cups of coffee and boiling the kettle and cooking pasta and roasting chicken, running out of milk and toothpaste, waking up together every day. *Every day*. 'So exciting,' I agree. But then immediately, I think of a life here where I disappear without warning, where Daniel might have to wait up for me because he doesn't know where I am, has no way of finding me. *He knows*, I remind myself, feeling my gathering pulse calming a little. He knows, and he still wants to do this with me. He is taking the risk. Why shouldn't I?

'So what was your way-off idea of what it would be like here?' he asks.

'Oh, romantic things like making it look beautiful, giving my guests Champagne every time they came, playing the piano and dancing in the garden.'

'I think they sound like excellent plans,' Daniel smiles.

'It was when we first moved to Blackpool that I first noticed it and dreamt of those kinds of things. But I think I've changed a lot. The more I disappeared, the more I stopped wanting anything other than just getting through each day without anyone really noticing much about me. And I spent so long wanting to go back to Yorkshire, for my parents to get back together, that when it never happened it gave me a kind of iron patience, I suppose.' I shake my head. 'I think I just shut off from life in a way.' As I speak, a cat appears and jumps onto the flaking window ledge, nuzzling its warm grey head against my hand, the soft vibrations of its purr on my skin. 'You're so different from that. You just go for what you want.'

'Oh yes. If I want something, then I usually go for it.'

'I really like that about you. And you're always optimistic that it'll turn out how you want it to.'

'Some things do.' Daniel says. He holds his hand out to the cat and touches it gently under its chin. 'Look, this could be our cat. What do you say, cat? Want to live here with us? Be impatient like me? Make Erica impatient too?'

The cat jumps down and gives a sharp meow, then squints at us haughtily, his fur gleaming in the sunlight.

'I think that's a yes,' I say.

'It's a definite yes. You don't have to be as upfront as him, though. In fact, he's quite needy. You take your time.'

I look at Daniel as he grins at me, that smile that makes me feel as though I am being lit from inside. I feel the gnawing impatience in my bones that I have had since I got to know him, an ache at the end of my nerves. If I buy this house with Daniel, then travelling won't just be postponed for now: it probably won't happen at all. The other Erica will be impossible to reach, her life opposite to mine. My whole plan will shed a skin, change into something I never thought I wanted, something I promised I would never let myself consider.

I let the petal fall from my fingers and take his hand. 'Yes.'

Chapter 19

Five months later, after I have swallowed down my fear and we've crossed our fingers too many times to count, after Daniel has managed to find a job at a small firm in Manchester and we've jumped up and down in giddy excitement, after we have spent hours poring over paint brochures then reproaching ourselves for getting ahead before we know for sure that it's happening, we get the set of rusted keys.

It's my twenty-ninth birthday.

We tread along the path of golden leaves at the front of the house, and Daniel wrangles with the front lock. Eventually, it gives way, and with a sigh, the door is released, pushing against the clutter of envelopes stacked behind it. The house seems to welcome us, its loneliness pulling us in and twisting itself around us.

'It's really ours,' I whisper, because talking out loud seems too everyday, too usual.

'And look what else is ours,' he says, so that I pull away from him and look to where he is pointing. The grey cat has followed us in, and sits by our bags casually licking his paw.

'No going back now that we have a cat,' Daniel says with a grin.

The hallway is broad, its focal point the threadbare staircase in the centre. We take the first door on the left and move into the huge front sitting room. Daniel throws open the sash windows so that September air sweetens the scent of time: dust and damp and the passing of lonely days. 'Well,' he says, reaching down to the bag of essentials we've brought with us for our first night and pulling out a bottle of cheap Champagne – our only luxury in months – and two plastic flutes.

The cork explodes from the bottle and bounces from the greying ceiling, the Champagne bursting out over the top of the bottle. The cat bounds from the room in playful terror.

'Our beautiful carpet!' Daniel exclaims as it fizzes onto the floor.

We laugh as we look down at the frayed and faded floral pattern beneath us, now stained with Champagne as well as years of use.

'Maybe that will be the first thing we replace.' I say.

Daniel plants a kiss on my forehead. 'Or maybe the last. Who cares.'

We pour and clink the plastic glasses together, toasting our future. The memory of the first night I met Daniel at the party, of our first toast together, is bright in my mind.

'One year ago today,' I say happily, 'we went to the Lake District. You bought me my first magnet.' We have a small collection of ugly magnets now from the various places we've been since then. 'We need to unpack them all and put them on the fridge as soon as it's delivered. Then it'll feel like home.'

We clutch our plastic flutes and wander around the rooms, touching the curling browned wallpaper, and taking in the vast rooms and high ceilings. The house is proud as well as lonely: its grandeur seeps through its neglect. I can imagine our lives here already: throwing the doors open to let in the summer and closing the windows to keep out the winter.

***

We sleep there even though it's not ready for us; my flat already seems to belong to the past. The pipes bang and clank as water trickles through them, bringing them to life again, and eventually thawing the damp air. Daniel builds the bed from my flat and I unpack the kettle. Our parents come for cups of tea in mismatched mugs, following us around the rooms with shocked smiles and gasps. When they've gone, we order pizza and sit cross-legged on the bed when it arrives, pulling apart the stringy slices and listening to the sound of the wind murmuring outside.

'I can't believe this is our house. And I can't believe we have five bedrooms,' I say, giddy laughter erupting from me as the day, our choice to take such a risk together so quickly, suddenly washes over me. We've been living together in Daniel's tiny flat for a few months now, tripping over one another's things since the contract on my flat ended. 'This is like a palace in comparison to your flat.'

Daniel laughs too. 'It's a bit of a derelict palace. I wouldn't call them bedrooms just yet,' he says, wiping some tomato sauce from his chin with a piece of kitchen roll.

'No. But soon.'

'Yes. Soon.' He puts his pizza down in the box, springs up and disappears. I follow him as he goes from room to room, staring at the ceilings, tearing off odd pieces of wallpaper, lifting up the dusty corners of carpets to see the floorboards underneath before returning to our new bedroom. There is a tiny black fireplace, and a bowing window that takes up most of the front wall. The grey sea spits and churns beyond the glass.

'It's draughty in here,' I say, and shiver.

Daniel wanders over to the window. 'It's because of this,' he says, tapping the rotting wood. 'There's a gap. We could try and wedge it shut, somehow. We just need to find something to use.'

'What about a book?'

We trawl through the maze of boxes downstairs until we come across the one labelled 'books'. I pull off the tape, and take out a few of the thickest ones.

'Horror?' Daniel says, surprised.

'Oh, yes. It's my favourite.' I turn one of the books over in my hand. 'I bought this copy of *The Shining* when I was really young, way too young to read it. Mum told me I had to wait until I was a bit older to start it. But I hid it in my room anyway, and read it under the covers with a torch.'

'You rebel. And you weren't frightened?'

'Nope.'

He takes the book from me, flicks through the yellowing pages, and grins. 'You're fearless, Erica Silver.'

'Me? I am not.'

'Oh, but you are. You are magical and special and scared of nothing.'

I kiss him. 'Well, it's nice that you think of me in that way. But actually, I'm scared of being cold tonight for a start. Let's see if it works,' I say. We run up the stairs, and Daniel gently jams the book between the rotted window frame and the walls. 'Perfect,' he says. 'Warm as toast in here, now. But,' he says as he runs his finger along the spine, 'if it's one of your favourites, shall we use a different one?'

'No, it's fine. This makes it even more special,' I say.

Daniel laughs. 'A romantic notion until it gets covered in mould.'

I laugh, and shiver again, something icy passing through me even though it is warmer in here now.

***

There are no curtains at our bedroom window, and as we lie in bed I stare out at the vast black sky that glitters with stars, listening to the creaks and shifts and sighs of the house. New and unfamiliar tonight, they will become the sound of my life, the sound of home. Soon, I will know them as well as I know my own body.

I listen to the rhythm of the waves, of Daniel's breathing, for what seems like hours. Eventually I sit up, slip from the bed and out of the room so that I can get a drink of water from the bathroom. I hesitate on the landing, the house vast and dark before me. And that's when dizziness swoops over me and grabs me, pulling me under with no warning. I don't want to miss tonight, I think, annoyed, as I lose my grip on the bannister, as the bannister turns to nothing beneath my fingers.

***

I don't see anything new this time. I don't see the other Erica. I see myself in my own life with Daniel, a year ago today on our trip to the Lake District. I see the fleck of vanilla ice cream on Daniel's lip and watch myself glance at it when I think he's not looking. I see him slipping the magnet into my bag when he thinks I'm not looking. And then I am back. It's still before midnight, so I can't have been gone for more than a few minutes. I sigh with relief, and climb back into bed, curling up against Daniel.

'Where did you go?' he mumbles, his words barely shaped.

'Nowhere. I was with you,' I say. I'll tell him tomorrow what I saw. I've seen it before, and I know what he will say: something about it obviously being the best day of my life.

I shut my eyes and fall into the pleasant pool of sleep.

Chapter 20

At the museum, the season is still in full swing and the exhibition that we began months ago is spreading across more and more of our walls. Handwriting flows across the cards that were once blank, fat, thin, curling cursives telling more and more stories every week. Where I once felt reluctant to speak to people, now my interest in the project takes over, and I hurry to pick up the phone or reach reception when the bell rings, wanting to know people's memories of the Tower, the long-closed, former arrangement of shops, the swarming beach of the 1950s. So many people tell me of their parents or grandparents meeting for the first time on holiday here years ago that I begin a Blackpool family tree on one of the clear walls, carefully scribing in silver paint the names of the couples who first met here, for whom the town was the very beginning of their first love, marriage, children.

I'm working on the tree one morning a few days after the house move, carefully scraping my miniature paintbrush across the smooth wall, when Katie rushes in.

'Ah, you beat me here. Sorry, I got caught up,' she says when she sees that I'm already settled into my work.

'Oh, don't worry. We have someone starting the roof today, so I needed to get out of their way. Tea?' I ask her, setting down my brush. It's still only nine o'clock; the museum doesn't open to the public for another hour.

She nods, and I go to our little white kitchen behind the reception area, click on the kettle and push two teabags into our mugs.

'You know,' I say to Katie, 'I've been thinking about somehow making the exhibition more permanent. Once we replace it, we should try to record all of these memories in some way.'

'I know,' Katie replies. 'I think so too. We'll keep it up for a long time, though. I wouldn't want you to get rid of it too soon. But I do think there's something in recording it all in another way too. What about a book? You should get some ideas together.'

'What about if we both did it?' I ask tentatively. 'We could work on it when things quieten down. It's your project too.'

Katie shakes her head. 'I think it should be your thing. The exhibition was your idea. I wouldn't mind if you worked on it here though, especially if you have time on your own here when it's quiet over the winter. You can put me in your acknowledgements and mention the museum.'

I look at Katie for a moment, feeling nauseous at the thought of regularly being on my own here. 'I would love to do it. But I'm not great at being on my own. I'm not sure I'd get much done.'

'Why not?' Katie's question is straightforward. She sips her tea, waiting for an uncomplicated answer. I have rarely considered telling her, or anyone, before Daniel. But his approach to me, his full acceptance of who I am, has started to change the shape of my thoughts. I have worked with Katie for a while now, and she trusts me.

Maybe, just maybe, I could tell her.

'Well, I've never liked being on my own,' I begin.

'Really? You're pretty quiet though, aren't you? I would have thought you were quite happy to be on your own. Strange how you can make assumptions about people, isn't it?' she says cheerfully.

'I don't think I am what people assume me to be.' I am talking in riddles, which bothers me; it makes me feel hot and unsettled. It's not as easy as I thought it would be. And while I deliberate, Katie takes hold of the conversation, moving it away from my reluctance to be on my own. She thinks that's the end of my admission, that there's no more to tell.

'Well,' she says, 'whilst we're sharing, I actually have some news.' She puts her cup down and exhales before continuing. 'I'm leaving. I'm going to another job in a month.'

'You're leaving the museum? I didn't even know you were looking for another job.'

'I wasn't. I just applied for a curator job in Brighton,

out of interest really,' she says, shrugging her slim shoulders. 'I never in a million years thought I'd get it. But I did. It's a pretty big step and I'm quite terrified. I'll miss it here so much. I kind of thought I'd be here forever. But Roger's family is in Brighton, and mine are all down south too, which is why I thought I'd give it a try. He's lucky that he works from home, so he's going to go down and sort out a flat for us while I work my notice here. It'll be sad leaving Blackpool, but it seems like it's meant to be.' She smiles her bright-red-lipstick smile at me. 'The good news for you is that my job here is up for grabs. I'll put in a good word for you, if you want it. It'll have to be a quick turnaround. That's why I thought you could consider the book. It'd be great to mention that in the interview.'

'I'd love to go for the job. I'll be really sad to see you go though,' I say.

Katie touches my arm fleetingly. 'We'll stay in touch, yeah? You can come down to Brighton and see me whenever you want. I've told Rog to find me somewhere big enough for people to stay, but he's on about bedsits and London prices.' She grimaces. 'I hope I'm doing the right thing.'

'Of course you are. You're doing what you want to do. That has to be the right thing, doesn't it?' I wonder at my temptation to tell her a secret I have guarded so closely for so long. Just because Daniel took it so well, it doesn't mean I should tell everyone. If I'd told her, she'd have taken it with her to Brighton, to people I don't know and can't trust.

Katie nods and pulls some forms from her bag. 'Here's the application form. My job is being advertised this week. I thought I'd give you a head start. You'll be the front runner anyway. I'll make sure of it.'

***

My interview is the following Friday at four o'clock. As the museum closes at the same time, I've asked William, one of the volunteers, to come in for the afternoon and help me set up an interactive exhibition for the next day in the hope that he will still be there when I am waiting for my interview.

'This job is the perfect step forward,' I say to Daniel in the morning. 'I can't be alone for even a second today. If I disappear before the interview, I might miss this whole opportunity.' I clasp a bracelet around my wrist. 'Katie is at a meeting all morning and then on the panel in the afternoon, so she won't be in the exhibition space at all today. I'm going to have to stick to William like glue.'

Daniel raises his eyebrows and pulls on a black jumper. 'Lucky William,' he says as he emerges from the neckline. He comes over to me and presses soft kisses on my collarbone. 'You'll be amazing. And maybe, if it comes to it, you'll be able to control it somehow and stay. Maybe you'll know on some level how important it is.'

Thinking about the interview, the possibility that I could

mess things up, makes my nerves roar up inside me. I try to calm my galloping breaths, to slow down. 'I doubt it. I disappeared on you, didn't I? And you were important too.'

'Erica, you're the right person for this,' Daniel tells me. 'You'll stay. You'll do the interview. You'll get the job. Katie's obviously set it up that way. I'll see you tonight, okay? We'll go to Luigi's.'

'No way! We promised we wouldn't spend money on doing things like that.'

'Oh, we need a treat. It'll be a one-off.' He kisses me once more, firmly this time. 'Got to go,' he says. His commute to the office in Manchester takes him over an hour each way. 'Good luck. I'll book the restaurant for seven, shall I? I can go straight from work and meet you in there.'

***

The day is busy in the museum, and I feel my breathing become steadier, my nerves lessen, as I guide children and their parents around the special display we've put together for half term. But by three-thirty, the fizz of visitors flattens, and I look on in horror as William gathers his things together: his navy blue flask, his coat and scarf and his empty Tupperware lunch box.

'All the best for the interview, Erica,' he says.

'You're going now?' I ask, trying and clearly failing to keep the desperation from my voice. He glances at me, amused. 'Don't be nervous, Erica. It's obviously yours. The guy in there now will have nothing on you. He's just a formality.'

So I ask William what he has planned for the evening, what he has planned for tomorrow, and when he is in next. But it's not enough. He regards my inane chatter with a warm smile, but answers my questions briefly as he retreats to the main exit, and closes the door softly but firmly behind him as though I'm a crying puppy who needs to learn how to be left for the night. I watch the closed door where Katie and a man from the council sit and interview another candidate, willing it to open, willing my interview to start, willing the dizziness that is already settling over me like gas to end.

And then I am gone.

Chapter 21

I know immediately that I am in a different country. Sweat springs from my pores. I can smell salty sand and spices. I'm in some kind of bar, and opposite me is the other Erica. A sheen of sweat shimmers on her forehead as she wipes the high wooden tables with a ragged blue cloth. I catch my breath, try to see straight, try to take in the bright blue and yellow paradise beyond Erica and the colourful clutter of bottles and glasses and straws, the raw promise of a day that is going to be scorching with heat and fun and freedom.

'What time do you open?' It's hard to hear it over the radio blaring music to which Erica dances subtly, in a way that I probably wouldn't if I thought people might see me, but the voice makes me spin around, fast and unexpectedly. I have never been able to move in this other world before. For the first time ever, I am able to go where I want, to change direction. I feel the tackiness of last night's spilt beer on the soles of my shoes as I walk towards the figure who spoke.

He has a beard, and he is tanned, more muscular somehow. But it's definitely him.

Mike.

Erica glances up at him and I take a step back again. Maybe things are different now that I can move around. What if Mike sees me? What if she does? How would I explain myself to them, dropping into their world and staring at them like a freak? But it becomes clear after only a few seconds that they don't sense me at all. I am invisible as always.

I watch Erica closely, trying to see something spark in her face, something that makes a connection with Mike and a life that she almost had. There's nothing. She pushes her hair from her eyes, and smiles at him. I can tell from the smile that she thinks he's attractive. I turn to him, try to see him as she is seeing him, without his flat in Blackpool, his job at the bank, our favourite songs and food and bars, the way he ended it all with his talk of Kath and travelling. But I can't. My eyes can't unsee everything that happened with him.

The other Erica clears her throat and looks down at her cloth. 'We open officially in about half an hour.'

Mike grabs a chair and sits down. 'So unofficially ... I can sit and wait?'

Erica laughs. 'It looks like you already are.'

'You been here long?'

'Cleaning tables? Since about nine.'

'No. In the country.'

'Oh,' Erica flushes and I can see her berate herself. *It doesn't matter*, I want to tell her. *It's only Mike. He doesn't even notice when you blush*. 'A few months. You?'

'Same. I was in Oz before this. Pretty different.'

'I want to do Australia.'

'I'll go back with you. Show you the best parts.'

Erica grins again and wipes a table that she's already cleaned. What was Mike like when I first met him? I try to remember, my mind scrabbling over the past. We met when I'd just finished my history degree. It was a few days after my twenty-third birthday and I went to the bank to pay in a cheque my mum had given me. Mike was working at the bank. He wrote his phone number on my deposit slip and gave me the same self-assured smile he is giving the other Erica now.

'Where in the UK did you come from?' he is asking her, staring up at her as though she is the only person in the world.

'Yorkshire,' she tells him. He motions for her to sit next to him and she hesitates, then puts down her cloth and joins him.

'Not far from me then. I'm from Blackpool,' he says. 'But I haven't been back for a few years. Way too many other places to see, right?'

'Definitely. I've lived in Yorkshire all my life. But I've always wanted to see as much of the world as possible.'

'And how's that working out for you?'

'It's going pretty well. I go back and stay with my parents

every so often when I need to work and save up more money.'

'Bloody money,' Mike says. 'Ruins all the best plans, doesn't it?'

Erica laughs. 'Yep. Speaking of which, I should really carry on. If the owner comes in and sees me chatting I'll be swapped for someone else by tonight.'

Mike nods, but he is preoccupied by wandering over to the counter where he finds a pen with which he writes down his number on a napkin. As he hands it over to Erica, I think of the moment he handed me my deposit slip in the bank.

'Make sure you use it,' he says to her.

Which is exactly what he said to me. I smiled at him, felt the hot creep of a blush up my cheeks before turning away and leaving the bank awkwardly, then spent days deliberating whether or not to text him.

The other Erica grins at him. 'Okay. I will.'

Chapter 22

'How did it go?' Daniel asks, rushing down the stairs as soon as he hears me come in. 'You've been so long. Were you talking to them for a while? I tried to call you from Luigi's, but I couldn't get through. So I thought that—' He stops when he sees my face.

'Let's just say it's lucky I have a key for the museum,' I say flatly. 'They'd all left by the time I got back. I was locked in.' I look at my watch. 'I'm so sorry I missed our reservation. I went straight there but you must have already left. I hate this.'

He pushes his hands through his hair. 'Oh, Erica. Forget our reservation, it doesn't matter. I'm so sorry about the interview. Have you tried to get in touch with Katie?'

'To say what?' I say, hugging him, smelling on him the stale wallpaper and dust smell I'm beginning to think smells like home, trying to ignore the fragrant scents of spices and sun that cling to my senses. 'There's no point telling her the truth. She's leaving soon. And even if I did, and she believed me, what would she tell the council guy?' I shake my head. 'She left me a couple of messages because of course my phone went straight to voicemail like it always does when I'm gone. She sounded pretty angry. She thinks I bottled it, or changed my mind about the job.'

'But she knew how much you wanted it. Why would she believe that?'

'Because I wasn't there! I vanished about five minutes before they were going to call me in to the interview and got back over three hours later.' I pull away from Daniel and look into his green eyes, push Mike and the things he said to the other Erica – the same things he said to me – from my mind. 'And not everyone is as keen to believe in me as you are.'

He pulls me back to him, presses me into his chest. 'Well they should be.'

'I think I need a different job,' I say, my voice muffled. I pull away. 'The museum just isn't the right place.'

Daniel's face falls. 'But you love it there!'

'I know. But it's not going to be long term if I couldn't even get to the interview without doing a disappearing act. Maybe I need something where I'm never on my own.' I sigh and rest my head against the damp, bare wall of the hallway.

'Okay,' Daniel says, pulling me by the hand to the dining room, where we have stacked box upon box as a makeshift table. I perch on a plastic tub, and he pulls over another to sit next to me. The cat, who obstinately refuses to leave us, and whom we have called Pip, rubs his tiny velvet chin against my hand.

'Let's think about this. Are you really saying you're thinking of quitting the museum?'

I stare at the boxes with our handwriting scribbled on them, at the peeling units and the stained sink in the kitchen to the side of us, and the overgrown, velvety green garden beyond. 'Oh, I don't know. I do really love it there. Maybe not right now. It's probably a good thing that Katie's leaving soon. She's not going to have the same respect for me now. And I can't blame her, can I?'

'Erica, you'll learn to control this,' Daniel says. 'We will learn to control it.'

I sigh. 'Daniel, sometimes you're too positive. I really don't think it'll be that easy.'

'No such thing as too positive. I didn't say it'll be easy. I said we will do it. We'll deal with it together, okay? Please don't think that this thing makes you lose everything.'

'But it does make me lose everything! And for what? I don't want to see my other life! I don't even really want to know that—' I stop myself and Daniel frowns, looking at me curiously.

'Know that what? What did you see?'

'I was in Thailand,' I say, feeling guilty, even though I know that makes no sense because I didn't choose to see my other self with Mike. 'Look, I'm sorry for being miserable. Maybe I shouldn't think about this anymore today.' I look at Daniel's face and see his disappointment that I am shutting him out again, like I did in the beginning, and I wonder if he's going to push me, to ask me for answers. But he doesn't. He holds up his hands in surrender. 'Let's just forget it for tonight. I can't think about it anymore. I'm starving. I'll go and pick up something nice for dinner,' I say. 'Any requests?'

'I'll go,' Daniel offers. 'You've had a long enough day.'

'No, let me. It's my fault we missed our meal. And anyway, I want to go out. I could do with a drive.' I reach up again to kiss him on the cheek, feel his warmth, the pleasant graze of his stubble on my skin. I will buy his favourite beer, the chocolate he loves. He is trying his best to help something that he can't possibly do anything about. 'Thank you so much for not pushing this. I will talk to you about it tomorrow, I promise.'

And that's all I remember.

Chapter 23

'So you're telling me that you're never going back home? Ever?' Erica says, her eyes wide, the dizzying backdrop of a Thai beach behind her.

Mike shrugs. It's such a Mike movement that I roll my eyes. He was always shrugging.

Where shall we go for food? Shrug.

The dress or the skirt? Shrug.

Are you really leaving me and giving up on us? Shrug.

But the other version of me doesn't seem to mind his shrugging. She probably likes his casual, rather arrogant approach to life. I liked that at first too.

'Maybe for weddings, funerals. But nah. Not long term. The idea bores me. There are so many other places in the world. Why would I want to spend any more time somewhere that I know so well? I've seen every inch of Blackpool.'

Erica laughs loudly. She's drunk. 'I bet some of the inches are pretty grim.'

Mike laughs too and takes her hand across the wooden

table where glasses and empty bottles are crowded. 'Yep. Yet another reason not to bother going back.'

'I went when I was little because my grandmother lived there. But she died when I was about six, so I've not been since then. You could have showed me around.'

'I can show you better places,' Mike says, leaning in to kiss her. It's such a cheesy line that I can't believe he's used it, and I can't believe Erica has fallen for it. Mike will taste vaguely of cigarettes, and he will pull back suddenly, as though he's remembered he has somewhere else to be.

I wonder if Erica is thinking about where this is going, about how it's going to work when Mike has just told her that he has such a problem with staying in one place for too long. Surely it won't work for them when it didn't work for us?

But Erica's eyes have no questions in them. She gazes at Mike after he jerks away from their kiss, her chin resting on her hand, her elbow on the cluttered table.

'Somewhere to be?' she says.

Somewhere to be? I said after our first kiss.

Mike had laughed. We'd been in McDonalds, of all places. He had taken a French fry and dipped it in the little tub of barbeque sauce he always insisted on. *Only the rest of the world.*

He says it again now to Erica, in a voice so low, almost seductive, barely heard against the backdrop of thumping music, a hundred different conversations in a hundred different languages, and the sizzle and crackle of cooking food.

'Only the rest of the world.'

What had I said back to him in McDonalds? Something about going with him, about seeing the world together.

Erica laughs again, even though nothing is funny, even though I didn't laugh when Mike said the same thing to me all those years ago.

'Good answer. God, I just love how you refuse to be pulled into a boring kind of life. So many people are.' She pulls him up to his feet, and they dance and kiss and I feel like a part of me is kissing Mike too. The feeling is strange, as though I am putting on a shoe that doesn't fit me anymore. As I watch them, my other life, my own life, settles down on me like a fog and I feel myself pulled towards it, away from the heat and perfume of this world. My head suddenly pounds, pain seeping through my skin and bones. I try to remember what I am returning to, what I was doing before I came here, what was interrupted by it this time and why everything hurts so much. But there's nothing, only the dull ache of confusion adding to the pain. And when I do return, I have no idea where I am.

Chapter 24

The first thing that hits me when I wake is the smell of sour air and chemicals.

I try to open my eyes, but only one will cooperate. The other sticks shut stubbornly. My mouth is dry, my throat sharp as a row of pins.

'She's waking up,' I hear Daniel say quietly, and I feel his hand on mine, see his face blurring into focus.

I hear the crunch of metal on metal, and feel the rain of glass on my head, my body jolting in fear. But then the glass and the sounds are gone, and I can only hear Daniel.

'Erica? Erica? It's okay, Erica.'

I try to focus on him, through my one eye. He stares at me and strokes my forehead. His hand hurts my skin, but I can't seem to be able to speak, so I say nothing.

I remember feeling as though I was kissing Mike. Was I kissing Mike? Or was I kissing Daniel? The sting of foreign Thai heat and the scents of cooking spices and alcohol still warm my skin and I try to push away whatever it is that is covering me, suddenly far too hot.

'Keep that on, sweetheart.' This time the voice belongs to my mum, and it sounds strangled. I turn to the side, every fibre of my neck screaming out with the effort.

'Hi,' she says, her lips in the strange shape of a forced smile. 'How are you feeling?'

I try to form words, but my mind is too slow, my mouth too dry. I nod, then close my eye again, drenched in exhaustion.

***

As the days roll by, indistinguishable from one another, I learn what happened.

I left Daniel to go out in the car. I drove alone, presumably planning to go to the supermarket. And then I lost control of the car. It rammed into a metal post, which then fell onto my windscreen. I have broken my left arm and my head is covered in cuts. Nobody else was involved or hurt. The car is a write-off.

'I'll need a new one,' I say, but as soon as the words leave my sore, chapped lips, and I see Daniel's eyes flit from me to the dull green floor, I know I won't be needing a new car. The poisonous thought that I could have hurt someone fills my mind, drowning my thoughts. I always thought I was safe driving, because I thought if there was anyone to hurt, then they would see me, and I wouldn't vanish in the first place. Now, nothing seems so straightforward. I obviously ended up back in the car after disappearing, because that's where they found me.

'We're going to do some more scans,' the doctor says. I have already had scans, tests and results, but they still can't work out why I lost control of the car. I didn't have my phone with me to distract me. The radio wasn't on. I had zero trace of drugs or alcohol in my blood. My blood pressure and blood sugar levels are both consistently normal. 'Try to think again, Erica. How did you feel just before it happened?'

'I can't remember,' I answer. Mum stares at me and I wonder for a minute if she might tell him.

Oh, she does it all the time, Doctor. She will have probably lost all control of her senses and crashed the split second before she entered the alternate world where she watches another version of herself.

My lips curl into something like a smirk and the doctor frowns.

'Erica, it's important we know as much as we possibly can about how this happened.'

Mum drops her gaze from me.

'I really don't know.'

'And nothing like this has ever happened to you before?'

I shrug, which hurts, and reminds me of Mike.

The doctor sighs and scribbles something in my notes. I imagine his impatient scrawl: *difficult and secretive.*

***

I've been on the ward for a few days when a sour-faced nurse tells me I have a visitor, even though it isn't visiting hours.

'Would've turned him away if he'd listened. Said he's had a long trip.'

I'm puzzled, and my brain is slow. When I see Nicholas I grin, my whole face hurts. He leans over and gives me an awkward hug.

'How are you?'

I shuffle around in the bed. 'I'm doing okay. Thanks for coming. Mum didn't say you were going to.'

'I told her not to. It's only a flying visit, I'm afraid. You scared me a bit. I wanted to see you. Plus, I have something for you,' Nicholas tells me. He glances at the nurse, and waits for her to move from my room and further down the ward. Once she has gone, he hands me a yellowed newspaper.

'Page twelve,' he says, gesturing to the paper that is crinkled and stiff with age.

I find page twelve and a child stares out at me: square 1980s prescription glasses, pixelated hair in bunches, a small smile.

QUANTUM CHILD PRODIGY TELLS ALL

My heart reverberates in my chest then picks up speed. 'I didn't think we'd kept this! Where has it been all this time?'

'We didn't keep it. This is a copy of the paper that we read at the time. I've only just managed to get hold of it. I kept my notes from when it first started happening to you so I still had her name and the date that she was in the paper. Do you remember when I started making notes on your case? It was in my phase of wanting to be a doctor,' he says.

I remember. I remember, in a flash, everything about that short space of time when it first started to happen: the strange new terror of being on my own in case it happened again, the September sun burning through my clothes as I rode my bike along the promenade with Nicholas, trying to talk our way through what had happened to me; the neat sharpened pencil flickering about in his small blue notebook as he tried to research his way to answers.

'I did try to find out more about her a while ago; I asked Mum if she knew where that newspaper went but she couldn't find it. And there was no internet then, so I came to a bit of a brick wall. But the other day when Mum told me about your ...' he looks around, checks for staff before he continues, 'your accident, I decided to look again. I dug out the notebook and managed to get this old copy of *The Gazette*. I thought it might help.'

I scan the faded article, which outlines eleven-year-old Helen's strange vanishing act. It only ever happened to her when she was alone. She saw moments in her personal history that held no apparent meaning, and sometimes herself, living a different life.

'I am lucky enough to have a pony in my other life, so I've had to learn to ride,' she was quoted as saying with, the journalist noted, a charming smile. I frown at the paper.

'She changed her name,' Nicholas says, breaking into my thoughts. 'As an adult, she didn't want the attention. She wanted a normal job. A normal life. I don't think it went any further because I don't think many people believed her. She could never prove it other than to her family.'

'That makes sense. Daniel has tried to do some research on it a few times, and I have too. But we've never found anything. I told him about Helen, but I couldn't remember her surname.'

He motions for me to pass him the newspaper and I hand it to him. 'Look,' he says. 'This part's interesting. She talks a bit about controlling it.'

'She could control it?' My voice is louder than I mean it to be, and now I glance out of my tiny room onto the ward.

'Yeah. That's why I brought it. I wanted you to see it. Read this.'

Helen explains to us that there is a way to stop this. "Some days I don't feel like going. Sometimes I want to just play out with my friends. And if I can touch something that I really love then I probably won't leave, so I just do that." When asked what her favourite things are, the things that can stop quantum physics in its tracks, she giggles. "My cat, Bubbles. If he's there I call him. I have to touch him though. That's the rule." And if Bubbles isn't there? To show us how this works, Helen produces a tired silver mouse from her pocket. "Oh, I have to touch something of his. That is sometimes enough. It's why I carry this with me all the time. Just in case."

'This is brilliant!' I whisper. 'She just used an anchor to keep her where she wanted to be. I should have thought of that before.'

'I know. Something so simple,' Nicholas said. He handed the newspaper back to me. 'Here you go. Keep it. Use it. Buy a cat.'

I laugh and pick up my phone to send a message to Daniel. 'I already have a cat.'

Chapter 25

'So,' I say a few days later when Daniel is visiting me. I wriggle about, trying to prop myself up a bit more in the impossibly slippery hospital bed. 'Tell me what's happening with the house. I miss it. Has the electrician turned up?'

'Yes,' Daniel grins. 'I'm hoping the nurses here take pity on me and offer me a meal because there's no electricity at home until tomorrow.'

I wrinkle my nose. 'You can have my meal when it comes. I can't stand much more of the food here. They have to let me out soon, surely.' The nurses have been muttering about me being discharged for a few days now, and I keep getting my hopes up. I want the ramshackle chaos of our new home; waking up there with Daniel; clicking on our kettle and drinking hot mugs of tea in bed in the mornings surrounded by boxes and jumbles of clothes, the cool salty air drifting through the rooms. 'Do you really think I will be able to stop this happening when I'm home by touching something of yours?' I ask him.

He thinks for a minute. 'I don't see why not. I suppose we don't know for sure. But it's not happened here while you've been on your own, has it? So it might be that it's on its way out now, anyway,' he says brightly, leaning forwards and kissing me.

'Maybe. I hope so,' I say. 'I suppose if it does then I can try what Helen did, and see if it works.'

'Exactly. Let's just get you home. Have they said any more about discharging you this week?'

I shake my head. 'Nothing specific.'

Daniel checks his phone and frowns as he reads a text message.

'What's wrong?'

'The electrics. It's more complicated than the electrician originally thought. I don't think we'll have power for another few days now.'

'Oh, well then we'd definitely better get you signed up for hospital food. Or why don't you go and stay at your parents' for a few days?'

'Nah. I'll rough it. I'll be in the office during the day and here in the evenings anyway. Just don't get too close to me because I won't smell great. The shower is electric, remember?'

He is sidling up to me, and I am laughing and moaning because my body still aches, and then the doctor comes in and we silence straight away like two suspicious children.

'Erica? I have some good news. I am happy to sign your discharge papers.'

I turn to Daniel, delight flooding through me, but when I see his face, there is a fleeting moment that makes my stomach twist. He looks thrown. Almost annoyed. I smile at the doctor, thank him, listen to his wise, quiet words about rest and prescriptions and sick notes. Once he has gone, I turn to Daniel. He's smiling now, and I wonder if I imagined it, if my painkillers are making me see things that aren't there.

'What's wrong? Why aren't you happy that I'm coming home?'

'What do you mean? Of course I'm happy.' He squeezes my knee awkwardly and I study his face.

'Okay,' I say, narrowing my eyes, unable to see anything now other than Daniel looking happy and normal. 'If you're sure. Let's go home.'

'I'll just give the electrician a ring and tell him to leave it for the day. I don't want him making a load of noise and mess.'

'It's fine. I don't mind. It needs doing. We don't want to slow him down, do we?'

'Yeah, I know, but I think we should focus on getting you better for a bit.'

With no electricity? I think, confused by his insistence. A nurse comes in, clucks around, hurries me along, helps me retrieve all my things that are scattered around the room, and Daniel slips out of the room and down the corridor. When he comes back, he grins, takes my arm, and until we arrive home and every tiny little thing clicks into place, I don't give it another thought.

Chapter 26

There is nothing out of the ordinary as far as I can see when we pull up on the drive to our house. I don't notice Zoe sneaking out of the back gate in the dark as we arrive. She will smile, pleased with herself, when I tell her this. She will tell me that luckily she was free when Daniel phoned her from the hospital, and so she was able to use her spare key to go into our house, go into the cupboard in the kitchen as instructed by Daniel, light what seemed like thousands of candles in the hall and lounge, leave a small square box on the coffee table, then leave just as she saw us pull up.

I press my hands to my mouth as I walk through the glittering miniature flames to the blue velvet box that sits on the table in the centre of the living room. It's dark outside now, and the room reflects back on us in the curtainless window, as though ours is the only scene in the world.

'Erica,' Daniel says, reaching for the box. 'I know I've joked about this a lot. I know when we met you didn't believe in marriage. And you still might not believe in it. But I don't want it to be a joke anymore.'

'Daniel, I—' I try to interrupt, but he is like a steam train, marching around the room as he speaks so that affection for him, for his way of almost never being still, washes over me and makes me quiet.

'I have to do this,' he says. 'I always told myself that I wouldn't, that I would respect how you felt and never even ask you. But this accident changed everything. Even though soon all the candles will burn out and you won't even be able to see the ring I chose for you, and even though if you do say yes, you will have to wear it on your right hand because your left is in a cast, I have to do it right now. Since the minute I thought I might have lost you, I haven't been able to think of anything else. I know you don't want a big wedding where everyone looks at you, and you don't really even want a wedding at all because you're frightened you might disappear and miss bits of it, and you don't want a marriage either because you might miss bits of that and it might end badly. But a marriage to you, even if you are only there half the time, will be better than anything I ever thought I could have. And if you say yes, and tonight is the night we decide we are going to do it, then I won't go to sleep and I won't leave your side because I don't want you to disappear and miss even a second of it.'

He is finally still, and kneels down in front of me. The ring slides on perfectly, glinting blue and yellow and white.

'Tonight is the night,' I say.

***

And so this, I think, is the start, the beginning of the real us. I feel lucky for once, to be different, to be able to feel this moment more than other people would be able to. I know what it is like in a world that was so nearly mine. I am acutely aware of what else could have been, or could not have been. Being so close to the other me as she kissed Mike, the accident, the knowledge that I could so easily have missed out on Daniel, has shifted how I feel. It's frightening having so much to lose, but whether I get married to him or not, I am high enough to fall anyway. Daniel has changed me, the accident has changed me, and I am willing to face my fear.

I am wise, all-knowing.

But really, I know nothing. Not yet.

PART TWO

Chapter 27

The following summer, on a July day that is sharp with yellow sunlight, I marry Daniel.

The night before our wedding day, Zoe stays with me at the house, sending Daniel away to stay at his best man's flat for the night. I tell her not to leave me alone for a second and she nods briskly, perhaps thinking I might be worried I'll get cold feet. Even when we need the toilet, we go together, one sitting on the edge of the bath. She curls my hair into reluctant tendrils and gently fastens each button on the back on my dress. It is tight, the satin straining over the subtle bump that has appeared over the last few weeks. Zoe raises an eyebrow but says nothing. For the last seven weeks or so, I haven't disappeared once. Pregnancy has given me a different kind of dizziness and nausea: one which fixes me firmly and pleasantly to this world, and pushes the other one away. Already, I have a pleasant difficulty remembering how it feels to disappear, how it feels to watch my other self. But I am taking no chances.

The wedding party is small, the day simple and cheap. My dress is knee length, black – everything a wedding dress shouldn't be. I broke every bride's rule when I bought it and showed it to Daniel, who kissed me and told me it was perfect. I have no tiara, no huge train, no veil. But as I walk into the room at the registry office after almost a lifetime of not wanting people to turn and look at me, I realise that it would have made no difference whether there were a hundred guests or just one, or if my dress was white or black, long or short. Because the only person I notice looking at me, as though I am all he can see, is Daniel.

Phoebe wears a dusky pink flower girl's outfit and squeals with delight as she throws petals on us when we emerge from the registry office into the summer seaside wind. The petals blow onto us sideways, clinging to our faces and hair and making us all laugh. We walk briskly, hugging each other's arms, to Luigi's, which we have hired for the evening. Daniel's parents drink too much red wine and cry and tell me with berry-stained lips that they always wanted a daughter. Zoe pushes chairs aside and dances with Phoebe after our meal; the staff turn up the volume on the speakers and play our favourite songs. Nicholas and Amelia stand up and dance too, and then we all do, even the staff.

It is a day that is vivid with hope and clear, pure happiness. At the end, when the staff are singing along to Lionel Ritchie as they clear up, and our families are swaying together, tired and full and happy, I reach up to Daniel and whisper in his ear that I'm going to the toilet. Up until now, he's sneaked in with me or I have gone with my mum or Zoe, and he raises his eyebrows. 'I will stay,' I tell him. 'I know I will.'

It is a small risk, but still, I am glad when I return, having been nowhere, seen nothing, my baby nestled firmly inside me, small as a nut.

Chapter 28

I am in the back garden.

Nothing is remarkable, except the fact I am here.

For the last three days, the air has blazed with raw white heat. Our garden, normally a damp, dark green, is burned and dry. Zoe is coming round soon with her boyfriend, Ben. We're having a barbeque, and Daniel has gone to the supermarket for the requisite charcoal, buns, and burgers.

I stretch lazily, languid in the furious sun for a few minutes before I find the energy to stand up. We've spent evening after evening pulling up weeds from the borders. I bend, pull more up now, the leaves crisp against my skin.

'Hey,' a voice says behind me, the back gate creaking open. 'I thought I told you not to move?'

I grin and shake the weeds at Daniel, who is holding huge carrier bags in each hand. 'I didn't go far.'

'Look who I found skulking around at the front,' Daniel says.

'Sorry we're early,' Zoe says, all pale, shapely legs in frayed denim shorts and huge wedge heels. 'I was boiling to death in the flat. We brought beers,' she says, lifting her sunglasses from the bridge of her nose and glancing at me.

'I'll get glasses,' I say, ignoring Zoe's expectant stare that follows me into the cool, relative darkness of the kitchen. I grab four glasses from the cupboard and then the strip of glossy photo paper that lies on the old-fashioned worktop.

'I knew it!' Zoe shrieks when I place the scan photograph in one hand and a glass for her beer in the other. She prods Ben. 'Didn't I say I knew it? Wow,' she says, beaming, and I beam too. 'This is so exciting.' She bends and rummages around in the bag she's brought. 'Good job I got these non-alcohol beers, too. You know, just in case.'

'So it was that obvious at the wedding?' I ask.

'Yes. Only because you're normally so perfectly flat-stomached,' she says, rolling her eyes, and an image of the other Erica pops into my mind for the first time in weeks, her stomach concave under her bright vest top, her body so different from mine already. 'Plus, I saw you chuck your Champagne into a plant pot after one sip. Complete waste. You should have given it to me! So how far along are you? When are you due?'

'Spring,' I tell her. 'The middle of March.'

She squints and looks at my stomach. 'Boy or girl, do we think?'

'Boy,' I say.

'Boy,' Daniel says.

'Girl,' Zoe says.

We all wait for Ben, who says, 'Boy or girl,' then we laugh.

'Well, cheers. To Erica and Daniel, and your new family,' Ben says as the sun scorches down on us.

***

Once we've eaten blackened burgers and sausages and deliciously juicy slices of watermelon, we all collapse on the stretch of crisp lawn at the back of the house. The sound of the radio floats from the kitchen and competes with a distant thump of music that comes from somewhere along the promenade. We chat, our hands dangling over our faces to shield our eyes from the glare of the sun. Zoe and Ben quiz us on names we like and the nearby schools. I ask Zoe about work and she groans, telling me about how difficult the house market is.

'What about the museum? How's the job thief?'

Now it's my turn to groan. I turn over onto my stomach, but that feels strangely uncomfortable so I flip back over and cover my face again. 'He's unbearable.'

When I didn't make the interview because of the accident, Katie had no option but to offer the job to the other candidate, Carl. He is a tall, pin-striped, loudly spoken man who seems entirely at odds with the fragile elegance of the town that we've been trying so hard to highlight.

Since he started, the museum has changed its opening hours, and the other day he called me into a private room, hands steepled, his face full of false sorrow, and told me that my hours would have to be cut due to a lack of resources and funding.

'He's already taken down the exhibition display,' I say, frowning. 'I'm really upset about it. It took so long to put it together.'

'Don't be upset,' Zoe says, standing up and peeling a cold sausage from the barbeque. 'Be angry.'

I sigh. I never told Zoe why he got the job over me, just that he did. She thinks I turned up and did my best at the interview but that the museum chose Carl, and that the accident, when I went out in the car and lost control, was unrelated, just another unfortunate event. I have never told Zoe about my disappearances. We met at school, when we were part of a huge friendship group that I tried my best to hide behind. It was only when we went to college and ended up in the same English class that I got to know her a little more. By then, my disappearances happened less often, so there was no reason to open up to her.

'I think it's good they've reduced your hours,' she says as she takes a bite of the cold sausage, grimaces, then hands the rest of it to Ben. 'I don't think being with Carl every day would be good for you. Have you looked to see if there's anything else around here?'

'Yes, I have,' I tell her. 'There's nothing similar. But Katie has been in touch a bit. She told me to bring all the exhibition stuff home, so I have.'

'She's going to be an author,' Daniel says excitedly.

'Well, we'll see about that. I've written to a few agents with my idea of a book about families whose lives started as a result of a trip to Blackpool.'

'That's so cool,' Zoe says. 'Have any of them got back to you?'

'Not yet. But it was only a few weeks ago. I think they can take a while to reply.'

Zoe springs up. 'I have a good feeling about this, Erica. Cause for another beer, I reckon. Anyone else?'

There's the clink of bottles, the blaze of sun on my skin and the tickle of grass beneath me. I close my eyes as a heavy tiredness washes over me, put my hand on my stomach and listen as Ben asks Daniel if he's played football lately. I smile to myself; Daniel still hasn't told his football-crazed friends that he doesn't want to be part of their five-aside team. Because they are friends from university, they are all spread out over the country and he spends quite a lot of time travelling to different locations, because although he doesn't particularly want to play, he likes to see them and be part of their group.

'I only go for the beer after,' Daniel tells Ben now, and Ben laughs.

Zoe sighs and looks at her watch. 'Work tomorrow,' she says. 'We'd better go soon, Ben.'

But it's one of those days that nobody wants to end and

they are still here an hour later, as the orange sun dips in the sky and a gentle breeze begins to ruffle our hair. I stand up and brush strands of yellow grass from my skirt before clearing the plates.

'You want some help?' Zoe offers, but I shake my head. 'I'm fine, thanks.'

I place plates in the sink, run the tap and stare beyond to the garden. After five minutes or so, Daniel comes into the kitchen, his hands full of bottles of ketchup and mustard, his face glowing from a day outside. He puts the sauces away in the fridge, then comes over to me and puts his arms around me. 'How does it feel?' he whispers.

It's a question that would have made more sense, in a way, before. How does it feel not knowing if you will last a whole day in this life; how does it feel when your bones and muscles are slammed into a world that is not your own? How does it feel seeing yourself whole, not one angle in a mirror or a photograph, or self-aware, behind the lens of a video camera, but as a complete person?

But it's not this he wants to know.

He wants to know how it feels for me to be alone and yet to feel safe; to watch my friends outside in the softening light of the garden after a day of lounging and food and sun; to feel full and happy and complete and like I'm never going to disappear into another world again.

I lean into him. 'It feels like ... someone has closed a door that was letting in a horrible draught. It feels warmer. Safer.'

'Good?'

I close my eyes and listen to the low hum of Zoe and Ben's voices from outside, their bursts of laughter, the wails of the seagulls that circle the house and the rolling of the waves beyond. 'So good.'

Chapter 29

'Erica?' The shout wakes me and I sit up on the sofa and stretch my distorted body. The baby jerks, nestling its foot underneath my ribcage and I wriggle, nudging the little knot that juts out underneath my jumper.

'In here,' I say.

Daniel is grinning. I stumble to my feet clumsily and kiss his cheek. 'You're frozen. Come under the blanket and get warm.'

'I can't. I haven't quite finished my jobs yet.'

I squint, trying to see into his eyes for a secret that he's been guarding in the lead up to Christmas. It's Christmas Eve now and I still have no idea what he has been planning.

'Is it another cat?' I guess, even though we've played this game before and I know it isn't.

'Nope. Bigger.'

'Dog?'

'No. It's not alive,' he says, flicking on the light and pulling closed the heavy, deep red curtains that took us months to save for. The room glows yellow with the Christmas tree lights on the tiny tree in the corner.

I think hard and pat my belly softly. 'What is it, baby? What is it?' The baby dances, pummeling its miniature fists and feet under my skin.

'I've told him not to say.'

I smile. We didn't find out the sex of the baby at our scan, but Daniel is convinced it's a boy.

'Give me a clue.'

'Okay,' Daniel relents. He hasn't given me any clues at all yet and up until now, I have been quite patient. 'It's something to do with the house. Something it used to have that you loved.'

My heart lurches as Daniel pushes the sofa in the corner of the lounge along the wall to leave a space. 'Oh! You haven't? Have you?'

The doorbell chimes. 'Go upstairs,' Daniel says. 'And come back down in ten minutes.'

***

I lie on the bed, the duvet cool underneath me, listening to the huffing and puffing of delivery men, grunts of thanks and Merry Christmas, then the roar of an engine outside. I think of the present I have bought for Daniel, an espresso machine that he's looked at a few times and never bought because we're saving everything up for the house, for the baby.

***

And then, the gentle tinkling of music floats through the house. I go downstairs carefully, gripping the bannister, my heart fluttering as the music becomes louder. I stand in the doorway of the lounge and take in the beautiful piano that sits in the corner, a red bow tied around it.

'Daniel!' I say, wanting to run to him, but having to lumber. 'You bought me a piano?'

'I saw it advertised. It was only local. It'll need tuning,' he says, kissing my forehead. 'And obviously, none of us can actually play. So in the meantime,' he spins me gently around to a record player. 'I bought us this. But then I realized that the only record we have is *The Wizard of Oz*.'

We dance, laughing as Daniel struggles to get his arms around me, as we keep bumping into one another inelegantly, as the record skips and scratches its way through the colourful songs that bring back my childhood.

'And I know you wanted to dance in the garden. But I think we'd get frostbite and it might end in possible amputation. So this will have to do.' He leans forward and whispers in my ear. 'There might be more records in your stocking tomorrow. I ran out of wrapping time.'

'Your present is nothing like this,' I tell him. 'You'll like it. But it isn't your dream.'

'Well, no, because my dream is to install bi-folding doors. Unless you've bought the doors and they're hidden under the bed?'

I feel a lump in my throat and blink, feeling silly. 'I'm so happy,' I tell him.

'Good. Happy Christmas, Erica.'

Chapter 30

Joshua arrives three days after his due date with a squashed, wise face, eyes the colour of a stormy summer sky and curled, wrinkled fingers.

'I wonder,' I say to Daniel as I stare at Joshua in his hospital cot, 'if he will count as company?'

'You mean someone who can see you and stop you from disappearing? I don't think you will now, do you? It hasn't happened for so long.'

I shake my head, unable to take my eyes from Joshua: this strange, precious bundle that I am now in charge of. The mere thought of my disappearances, of leaving him for an unknown amount of time, of being in a world where he doesn't exist, terrifies me. The fear is liquid and hot inside me, a physical entity. 'I just worry that now he's here, and not inside me, I am sort of free to go again. But surely I won't go when I'm with him?' I hear desperation in my voice. I thought, before Joshua, that I knew the taste and feel of fear more than most people. But now, I realize that I didn't.

Daniel crouches down and kisses Joshua's tiny cheek. 'I

would think he counts as a person,' he says, and I feel the knot of dread in my stomach loosen slightly. 'He's still a person, after all. He's just a very small person. But he still counts, probably more than anyone has ever counted before.' He looks up. 'So there are two of us now. Two of us to keep you here.'

I nod again, reaching out my hand to touch Daniel's, my eyes never leaving Joshua.

'You can look away from him,' Daniel says, his voice amused, affectionate. 'I'm here too. You won't go anywhere.'

I peel my eyes away from Joshua, to Daniel's face and his creased shirt that he threw on during the night when I went into labour, only hours ago but already strangely timeless. He holds out his arms and I move stiffly, sorely, towards him, letting myself be enveloped my him. 'I really hope he does keep me here,' I say quietly. 'What if he doesn't, and I—'

'Stop,' Daniel says, and his voice is forceful and different and I realize that he is already different to the Daniel of a few hours ago who wasn't a father, that this Daniel is firmer because he has to be and because he wants to be, that the other Daniel has melted into the past. And I think, as I turn my head ever so slightly to steal a glance at Joshua who is still safe in his cot, I am different too. I am a mother now. That will change everything because it has to and because I want it to.

And so I push the worry away.

***

Once we are released from the hospital, the days with Joshua and Daniel pass sweetly and quickly. I feel the other Erica ebb again, bobbing gently away in the sea of my consciousness. I spend lazy showers alone in a blissful haze of vanilla bubbles, lie in bed and listen to Daniel chat and sing made-up songs to Joshua downstairs as he gives him his last milk of the evening. I am alone, and I go nowhere.

'You're going to be fine when I go back to work, aren't you?' Daniel asks the night before his return.

I nod, sit Joshua on my lap and hold his tiny chin in my hand, rubbing his soft little back in my other. 'I will be more than fine,' I say. 'I feel like a different person compared to when it used to happen. Everything has changed for the better.'

I spend my mornings walking along the endless promenade, climbing up to the grassy slopes and looking across at the sea with my Silver Cross pram bouncing gently in front of me. I tell Joshua about the snowdrops and clouds and the changing colours of the sky and he watches me curiously, his sharp blue eyes following my every move, his mouth making little o's in response to my words, bubbles escaping from his tiny pink lips. As we turn and see our house in the distance, I feel a thrill that it belongs to us.

Each night when Daniel gets home from work, we stare at Joshua in his Moses basket, stunned by the way he has changed since the day before, and the day before that. We settle on our grey sofa, flicking through the television channels lazily, eating stews and curries to warm us from the eternal cold that has settled in our house. Pip the cat curls up with us, always on my lap. The days are laced with a kind of magic that comes only with new beginnings.

An agent has been in touch to ask me to complete my book, and so I'm spending any time that Joshua sleeps working on it. There are a surprising amount of stories to include, and within those, histories of buildings, homes and family businesses. I spend evening after evening surrounded by sprawling memories of Blackpool, faded photographs and scribbled phone numbers of people who might agree to tell me their stories. There is the eighty-four-year-old woman who met her husband on a holiday to Blackpool that she wasn't meant to go on and the fifteen great-grandchildren who now exist as a result; the man whose mother, a performer with the Blackpool Tower Circus, left him wrapped in a blanket in the doorway of Blackpool Tower when he was just two days old; my own dad's visit back to Blackpool that he extended so that he could stay with my mum, the visit that turned into his life and then mine.

***

It's in the middle of this stretch of pleasantly repetitive days that I stand in the back garden, rocking Joshua gently and breathing in the sweet spring air. It's been raining all day, and we've been inside, listening to the constant tapping of water on the windowpanes. As soon as the rain stopped, I unlocked the heavy back door and pushed it open, Pip winding himself around my ankles.

The sodden garden is gnarled and wild as an old witch, bypassed completely in the fruitless and seemingly growing pursuit to try and get the house done first. I brush some sticky cobwebs from the bench that has been sheltered by the house, and sit down with Joshua nuzzled into my arm. I hear the rhythmic whooshing of the sea, in and out. The gulls cry and cry. And then, the unexpected: footsteps from the back of the house.

It's Daniel. He's grinning, waving some papers around in his hand. I stand up to kiss him.

'Why are you home so early?' Usually, he doesn't get home until at least six. It's only about four in the afternoon.

'Because,' Daniel says, pressing the papers into my free hand and scooping up Joshua from me, 'I have something important to run by you. You can say no if you want to.'

'Yes,' I tell him, and he laughs loudly so that Joshua is startled in his arms.

'You don't even know what I'm going to say!'

'It doesn't matter when you look this happy. How can I possibly say no? I think I have an idea of what you're going to say anyway,' I tell him as I look down at the papers in my hand. When Daniel came back from Berlin and we bought the house a couple of years ago, he got his job at Palms Architecture in Manchester. When he joined the company, it was only small. Daniel helped it to grow by expanding the client list and developing its reputation which is now strong, with businesses returning and encouraging others to do the same. Although the commute is long, and the work trails home with Daniel like a stray dog – into our bedroom, our kitchen table, our car – Daniel's designs are consistently well-received and John, the owner, has become a good friend. He's mentioned Daniel taking more of an active role in the business a couple of times now.

'John wants to move offices,' Daniel says, as we both sit back down on the bench. 'The one we saw a while ago is still up for rent, and it's in a much busier area of the city which would obviously mean more exposure and hopefully new clients. He says that whilst we do that, we could go for an expansion. We've been discussing me buying shares of the limited company. But it would mean using all our savings for the house, Erica. They'd be gone.'

'Daniel, I really don't mind. You need to say yes.'

'At least think about it. We've lived so carefully for so long. In a way, it feels wrong to spend our money on something other than what we planned.'

I shake my head firmly. 'It doesn't. It feels right. You've said to me so many times that sometimes plans need to change. This is a big opportunity. You love working with John. You know this is what you wanted.'

'Obviously, I'll meet with the bank and I need to see a solicitor as well. We'll probably just have to hold off on the windows.'

'And the plastering.'

'Carpets.'

'Bathroom.'

'Everything. I'm sorry, Erica. I really don't have to do it if you're not sure.'

'Oh,' I say, waving his worries away with my hand. 'You know how much I love old stuff. I'm in my element.'

Daniel looks at me, and the house and its temperamental toilets that only flush sometimes, its rusty taps and cracked floor tiles, its crooked windows that don't open or shut properly and threadbare carpets, seem like nothing – tiny dots, like boats on our smooth blue horizon. All I can feel is new beginnings. Our endings are a million worlds away.

Chapter 31

It is going to rain any minute now.

I have been walking along the promenade for an hour or so, and although the May air has been warm, the sky has been grey. Now I'm reaching home, the afternoon is darkening, the clouds black and heavy. There are steps up to our front door that I can't get the pram up, so I unstrap Joshua to take him into the house. I should hurry, I think as I feel for my keys in my bag with my free hand, because if I leave the pram outside it'll get soaked. I should not, I think, and not for the first time, have been seduced by this bargain coach-built pram just because it looked nice and had a bit of history. I should have got a light one that I could fold up at the touch of my toe, and fling into car boots and hallways. I'm thinking this, hurrying to get Joshua in and on his mat, when I abruptly trip on a snapped tile in our hallway and sail through the air, Joshua loosening in my grip. My spare arm flails and I somehow manage to keep hold of him, to stop myself from crashing down or dropping him, by grabbing hold of the bannister.

'I dread to think what could have happened,' I say to Daniel that night, shuddering. 'We really need to make a few improvements on the house, even if they're only really small.'

A day later, an odd-job man arrives in a small red van like a postman's and cringes when he enters our hallway.

'Taken on a project and a half here, haven't you? I saw this house on the market a few years ago and thought to myself, whoever buys that is either brave or stupid,' he shakes with laughter and turns pink with pride at his own joke. 'Especially with a little man to look after too,' he adds, pointing to Joshua who I'm holding with one aching arm.

'Yeah,' I clear my throat. 'It is a big project. We love it, though. We have lots of plans. But for now, I just wanted to know how much would it be to sort the floor in here?' I gesture to the tiles in the hallway and the man shakes his head like a dog. 'Big job, love. We can't just make a tile out of thin air. You'd need to get the whole thing replaced. Laminate would look nice. These tiles need ripping up. You can't have these once your little one starts crawling about. He'll be into everything.'

I adore the black and white tiles that stretch from the front door through to the kitchen. Some of them are cracked, but to me that's part of their charm: if they could talk, they'd have so many stories to tell about the different shoes that have walked on them over the last hundred years.

'It's fine,' I sigh. 'Thanks for coming anyway.'

'If you get yourself a job lot of laminate, then give me a ring and I'll lay it for you. Or if you come to your senses, and need help moving house, let me know. Got a few mates in removals.' He hands me a red leaflet which reads:

Handyman Neil.
No job too big or small.

***

'What did he say?' asks Daniel later that night as he takes off his coat and flings it over one of our mismatched dining chairs.

'He suggested taking the whole lot off and replacing it with laminate flooring.'

'Oh, Erica! It's like he swore at you!' He comes over to where I sit and kisses me lightly on the forehead. 'I'll call round some reclamation yards and ask if they have any similar tiles or any ideas. He just didn't get it. But someone will help us sort it out.'

'I've been wondering,' I say quietly, looking past Daniel to the crooked old kitchen cabinets, 'if we should just give it up. Put it on the market and move on.'

'What? Quit on the house?'

'I don't know. It's since I tripped with Joshua. It's just kept going through my mind that we could look at what else there is,' I admit. 'I didn't say anything because it felt wrong, like we'd be giving up too soon. But I just don't know if this house is too much of a project. We don't seem to be getting anywhere.' I see guilt flash across Daniel's face and immediately regret my words. 'I don't mind that – I really don't. You having shares in Palms is something we both wanted to put our money into.' I watch him, wanting him to feel okay about his choice. I would do anything for him and I know how he feels about his work. 'It was fine just for us. But now we have Joshua, things are different. We didn't really know what having a baby would involve when we bought it, did we? And we definitely didn't properly think through the costs and the time it would take.'

We stare around us. The mould that we scrubbed at only last week is sprouting from the wall again in mini black swirls. The kitchen units are hanging from the walls like crooked teeth, the wood brittle and stained. Daniel, in his suit, with all his fine features, is at odds with the chaos.

'I know,' he sighs. 'I have been trying to ignore it, but you're right. Let's think about it, then,' he says.

***

We find a house to go and view at the weekend. It's newly built, a few streets back from the promenade further towards St Anne's. Zoe is away for the weekend, and I have been in touch with a different agent. I feel disloyal when I think of her but then I remind myself that we haven't made a decision yet, that we are only seeing another house to try and help us work out the best thing to do.

'Look,' says Jack, the estate agent, as we stand awkwardly in the master bedroom. 'If you look past those houses on your right, you can just about see the sea. Perfect.'

We crane our necks until we catch the glint of waves between buildings. If you didn't know to look you wouldn't see it at all.

'We're in a house on the promenade at the moment,' Daniel tells Jack. 'We're a bit spoilt with the view.'

Jack shudders. 'All that maintenance though. Salt corrosion. Floods. Nah, this is what you need. You get the view but none of the problems. Once I'm back in the office I'll have a look at the diary and arrange to come and value yours, if you like. Once you're on the market you're in a much better position. This one will probably be snapped up if you hang around.'

We follow the estate agent around the rooms, which are all completely spotless: lush cream carpets, every surface gleaming with glossy white paint, immaculate wardrobes and en suites. Beneath is a bright, square garden with a swing set standing proudly next to the orange brick garage. Joshua stares up at the bright gold spotlights in the ceilings as Daniel carries him round. The room that would be his is painted a soft lemon. I imagine his cot in there, turn to Daniel and wonder if he is imagining the same.

'It's the complete opposite of our house,' Daniel says afterwards when we sit in a cafe in St Anne's square.

I peer into Joshua's pram and adjust his blankets, touching the tip of his tiny nose as he gives me a gummy smile. 'I know. It would be so strange to live somewhere so ...'

'Nice? Clean?' Daniel offers and we laugh.

'Well, yeah.' I stir my coffee and stare at the swirling foam. 'It would be better for Joshua, wouldn't it? So much cleaner and *finished*.'

'Better in those ways. But we need to love it too. Do you really love it? Or any other house like it that Zoe could find us?'

'I think I would, eventually.'

'So do you think we should get ours valued?'

I say nothing, taking a sip of coffee and feeling sick as it slides down my throat.

Daniel throws up his hands. 'Erica, what are we doing? Do we really want this? Do you want this? Be totally honest.'

I shake my head. 'No, I don't. I feel like I should. But that house is not our home. And what I want is to go to our home right now and stay there. Of course I want to do what we can to make it safer for Joshua. But I want to live there forever and make it beautiful, even if it takes fifty years. I want to stick at this plan.'

'Me too,' Daniel says, downing his coffee even though it must be way too hot. 'So let's.'

***

A few weeks later, we find some tiles at a reclamation yard to repair our hallway. Daniel takes a day off to do the job himself, and once he has carefully fixed them into place we ooh and ahh over the transformation, congratulating ourselves. Why, we laugh happily, did we ever consider moving? It looks as good as new. It looks better. And it will be safe for Joshua when he starts to crawl, walk, run.

And as we talk about tiles and houses and hallways and live a beautiful normality, life careers on, speeding to its next destination.

PART THREE

Chapter 32

7th September 2017

I always thought the problem would be my disappearances.

Now, it seems they are the solution.

The biggest events that crash into our lives seem so insurmountably huge: lightning and fireworks, so loud and bright we think we'll be deafened and blinded. It seems impossible that we didn't know they were on their way to us. It seems that if we'd listened harder, stayed still for a moment, we might have heard the distant rumble of the approaching storm, felt that something was off kilter somehow, that life was about to split into two.

So many Befores and Afters seemed to be important before that day. Before my parents divorced. After, when we moved to Blackpool. Before Mike ended things with me and I met Daniel, and After. Before we bought the house and got married, and After.

Now, they are all mangled, crushed into the bigger Before, the only one that seems to matter.

I stab at a slice of dry cake with a fork before lifting it to my lips, but then drop it back down with a clatter. An autumn chill snakes its way through the air and I pull my cardigan around me. I frown as I look across at the broken window.

I can't help but feel like part of the problem is the house.

They all *said* it wasn't the house. They said it was unexplained. *Unascertained.*

But what if there was something we could have done to stop it? What if there was some way of explaining it?

What if we had never bought the house? What if we had never stayed?

What if, what if, what if.

What if I don't meet him in Luigi's? What then?

Chapter 33

Joshua is six months old. It's a hot day, one of those September afternoons that refuses to let go of summer, that won't let in even a whisper of autumn. I'm going to get my hair cut and so I am leaving Joshua with Daniel, who assures me that he is more than capable of looking after our son.

I take Joshua's chubby curled hand in mine across his yellow highchair table, and I kiss his smooth cheek that is stained with impossibly bright carrot juice, and tell him that I will be back soon.

'It's the first time he's having carrot,' I tell Daniel, who is sitting at the table, and doesn't look up from his laptop, but reaches out and strokes my thigh absentmindedly as I speak. 'I don't think he'll be allergic, but if he is sick or anything and you want me to come back then I have my phone, okay? I shouldn't be too long.'

'Hmm. Yep. Got it.'

'You need to watch him,' I say to the side of Daniel's

face, trying to keep my tone light. 'You can't not watch him while he eats.'

He looks up then, finally, and I laugh at myself.

'Got it. Watch him eat the carrot.' Daniel shuts his laptop and pushes it away, moving his chair closer to Joshua, who squeezes his puree with his fat little fist.

***

I think about the carrot, and tomorrow's potato and swede that I need to take from the freezer as the hairdresser chops and chops, black strands decorating my shoulders like feathers. I don't hear a distant rumble, or the crackle of something about to catch alight and rip through my world in a furious blaze. I sit there, staring at my own face in the mirror, thinking about how it is too hot and how I am looking forward to winter: candles and blankets and long winter walks; cinnamon coffee and satsumas in stockings; Joshua's first Christmas.

Chapter 34

I hear Joshua's indignant howls before I even open the front door after returning from the hairdresser.

'He spat out the carrot,' Daniel says when I arrive in the lounge. 'Wouldn't touch it. More on his face than in his belly. He's super grumpy.' He does an amusing dance in front of Joshua, who is propped up on the sofa. Joshua's face, still tinted orange, crumples and is still for a moment before another holler erupts.

'It's too hot.' Loose strands of sharp hair prickle at my skin and I tear my black cardigan off. I touch Joshua's clammy forehead and whip off his little blue t-shirt, which makes him scream even more, and pick him up. 'He's tired out. I'm going to put him to bed.'

Daniel looks at his watch. 'It's only six.' He glances at me and smiles. 'Your hair. I love it.'

I touch the nape of my neck which is strangely exposed. 'Really? They always do it shorter than you want.'

Daniel reaches out and touches my hair, and Joshua

grabs his hand, his little face scrunched up in anger. 'It suits you.'

'Come on,' I say to Joshua. 'Let's see if a nice sleep sorts you out.'

'He'll be up at the crack of dawn if we put him to bed now,' Daniel groans.

I yawn, the very mention of sleep making me want to crawl under the duvet and close my eyes. Joshua still doesn't sleep through. I've spent so many blue dawns rocking him and shushing him that I am constantly exhausted. 'I know.'

Joshua wails again and I pat his downy head gently as we go up the stairs.

I peel the rest of his clothes off and fight his little thrashing body as I give him some liquid paracetamol. Daniel appears with a bottle of milk. Joshua calms as he drinks, his eyelids flickering, drooping. It's Sunday tomorrow, but I will, I decide as I place him in his cot, take him to the doctor on Monday if he doesn't seem any better. He's probably coming down with something. I try to open his window, but Joshua's window is one of the many in the house that doesn't open. The catch is infuriatingly stubborn, caked in years of gloss paint. Daniel tries too, and gives up.

'These windows!' I hiss, annoyed. 'It's too warm in here.'

'I'll get a fan tomorrow,' Daniel says.

We go downstairs, me clutching the baby monitor, pressing it to my ear and hearing the steady rise and fall of Joshua's soft breaths. We order a pizza and fall asleep on the sofa when we've eaten. I wake in the early hours, thirsty from the pizza and aching from sleeping at a strange angle. Remember, I think to myself, the early days, when we used to fall asleep together on the sofa because we were talking and kissing, not because we were exhausted to the bone. How things have changed. *Remember, remember.*

I force myself to stand up and go to the kitchen, then get a drink of tap water that makes me grimace because it is too warm, too metallic. I climb the creaking stairs, open Joshua's door and make my way to his cot to check on him. I place my hand on his cheek.

And that is the end of Before.

Chapter 35

Our world is smashed into pieces, unrecognizable in seconds.

I scream Daniel's name again and again, my voice someone else's, someone who lives in a horror film of nightmares and terror and life that cannot, cannot carry on.

He appears in the room, sleepy and confused. I can't say anything but hold my hands up to my face. Daniel looks down into the cot, and I recognize something like hope in his face, a hope that makes my insides feel as though they are being twisted and crushed.

Your phone, he is saying, patting his pockets in a crazed way. A phone.

He calls an ambulance somehow, tells them. Cold skin. No. Yes. No. And then he stops talking, starts to wail instead. The sound winds itself around my mind like a snake, and I will never ever stop hearing it.

The paramedics arrive even though I don't remember either of us telling them our address. This is how life will be now. Memories and thoughts won't make sense. They will be sharp fragments, pieces of broken mirror in which I cannot recognize myself.

***

It's inevitable, isn't it? As soon as the paramedic turns to me and I hear his mouth saying the red-hot, burning words that brand themselves on my mind, I want to rush from it all, to escape to a world where this isn't happening, where it never could.

I close my eyes, press my hand into Daniel's so hard that it should hurt us, yet we feel no pain other than the roaring hot one that is inside us both.

The front door opens and closes, opens and closes.

The air smells too sweet, of late summer and sickly honeysuckle. It sticks in my throat and makes me gag as we climb into the ambulance.

When we get to the hospital, I don't let go of Daniel's hand at first. I have to stay with him. Vanishing now would be too cruel.

A man says that he needs to ask us some questions. He tells us that he is an investigator but he doesn't wear a uniform. He has coffee spilt on his shirt, an ugly brown pock on the pale green fabric. That's the worst bit of his day, I think bitterly. A spilt drink. I glare at him as he asks us thousands of questions that make me feel as though I can't breathe: questions about stuffed toys and bedding and the cot and how much of his milk Joshua had before bed. I think vaguely, horrifyingly, of the heat of Joshua's room, of the window that wouldn't open. I think of us sleeping on the sofa as he took his last breath and I scream.

And then I am running.

I hear Daniel calling my name, the thumping of his fist hammering at the door of the hospital toilets. He comes in and bangs on the cubicle but I have locked it. Sadness drowns me. I try to call out to him but my voice won't leave my body.

I will not recover from this, I think again and again. I cannot live without him. Flashes of Joshua burst into my mind: his milky warmth, his utter dependence; his *things* at our house. How will I ever, ever look at his things? I vomit, acid sorrow rushing from me and I hear Daniel shout at me again, his voice cracking with the rawness of grief and shock. The desperation in his voice almost keeps me here, but it is not enough.

Nothing is enough now.

My limbs collapse and my world caves in.

***

The other Erica is laughing. A delicate gold bracelet twinkles on her wrist. Her wedding finger remains bare. Her hair is long, raven black, hanging all the way down her back. Freckles brush the bridge of her nose.

'It's my last night here,' she says to the person next to her, a tall man with bright red hair.

'Shame,' the man says. 'I like it when you're on shift. You'll be missed.'

'Ha,' Erica says, sipping wine from a murky glass. 'I'll be easily replaced. I'm an awful waitress,' she grins. 'I'm meant to be still on shift right now, and I'm drinking instead.'

I tremble as I watch, try to swallow down the lingering taste of acid. She has no idea what is happening to herself, to me, as she sips this wine and talks about moving on to Italy, about a friend with a villa.

'He's absolutely loaded,' she laughs. I search her face for a flash of anxiety, a sudden feeling of inexplicable emptiness, but there's nothing.

And then she is sitting alone. The man with the red hair has wandered off to find someone who is sticking around. As I watch her sip her wine and gaze out at the utopia beyond, I feel a longing stirring inside me, to be living her life, one where existing is so simple, so free from the agony that still burns through me, even here. I reach out to her, but as I do, her face becomes hazy, the bright colours behind her blurring into a rainbow that I don't want to leave behind.

I'm not ready, I think. I can't go back.

As I fade, I think I see it: a sense that she might have felt a glimpse of her other life. She shivers even though the heat shimmers around her. She hugs herself and glances to her side, but nobody is there.

And then I am back, slammed against the cool hard floor of the hospital.

Chapter 36

I am outside. I don't remember getting dressed, or brushing my teeth or hair. Maybe somebody did it for me. Maybe they helped me pull a brush through the tangled knot my hair has become, or pulled my heavy limbs into the black leggings and dress I am wearing. But I don't know who it was. It's like I am fading in and out of existence. At the moment, as I fade in, I can feel the unfamiliar brush of cool air against my face, the sharp and jagged colours and sounds of the outside world too bright and loud. I don't know how long I have been inside for and I don't know how long ago the day was when everything ended, or the black day of the funeral that followed. I don't know how long ago *Before* was. It isn't September any more. I know that because when we were all in the car I heard a too-jolly DJ say 'October' and grief ripped through me. I think I might even have screamed. When September began, I was Joshua's mother. He was in the world. I don't want to part with September, with all the months that went before.

We are in a park. It isn't one I ever went to with Joshua.

They aren't that stupid. They are all here: Mum, Nicholas, Amelia, Phoebe. Daniel isn't with us. I remember him telling me about today this morning, his lips moving and words flowing from his mouth. How was he doing it? How was he stringing sentences and meaning and sounds together? I couldn't process the words. I heard some of them but didn't put them together. Park. Out. Air. Nicholas. The air smelt of toast and coffee, of horribly normal things that the world should smell of in the morning but that I felt it shouldn't smell of, because my world had stopped.

Now we're at the park, I can't stop staring at Phoebe. Her tight, milky-white skin. Her mass of brown hair that is casually scraped into a ponytail on the top of her head. It isn't extraordinary hair. It's Nicholas's mousy brown, dead-straight strands. But the fact that it continues to grow, that it has moved beyond the white-blonde duckling fluff of babyhood, that her feet and hands and skin and bones continue to thrive beneath her bright pink leggings and Clarks trainers and striped top fascinates me. Suddenly, I can't believe that anyone manages to live, manages to make it out of the tangle of terrible possibilities we're all part of.

Phoebe tosses out bread to the ducks. When her bread has all gone, she holds out her hand to Amelia for more. Amelia gives another slice to her, and their fingers touch for a brief moment. It is the smallest of transactions, not even worthy of words. The passing of cheap, hardened bread from one hand to another – a mother to a daughter who are so in tune, so used to each other, that they are almost bored. But it raises something in me, a strange beast of emotion. I yell and scream. People stare. A man in a yellow coat runs over, panting, a sheen of twinkling sweat on his forehead. He helps as I am bundled into the car again, thrashing my legs and arms like something from a horror film.

***

Daniel tries to talk to me when we arrive home. I don't know where the others have gone. These days, they are here one minute then gone the next, then back again, with no clue as to when they will disappear or vanish again. It's like a nightmare that makes no sense, that shifts from one scene to another with no warning.

Someone – I don't know who or when – has attempted to clear the detritus of Joshua away from downstairs. There are no bottles in the kitchen, no boxes of formula, no rattles or muslin cloths or rogue nappies. But now and again I open a cupboard or a drawer and a missed dummy or toy appears and stings me like electricity so that my nerves sizzle and make me cry out.

I have spent so long needing company, wanting to be weighted to this world, this life, this house and these people. A dizzy rush, a wave of nausea, a blackness of my senses, has always frightened me, made me clutch onto what I'm holding so tightly that my knuckles turn white. I never wanted to go before this. I have always longed to stay. Now this longing is bleeding away, seeping from me and making things so different. A desperate urge to run from everything, to escape this strange world where nothing makes sense anymore, pulses through me every day. Every time I feel the start of light-headedness, the temptation to rush away and give in to it washes over me. But when I stand up, try to dart from the room to the isolation that I always feared so much, someone always jumps up with me, places a gentle hand on my shoulder, takes hold of my wrist, coaxes me back down again.

And then there is Daniel.

I have to stay for Daniel. I remind myself of this daily.

I try to hear him. I see his mouth moving, agony pulling at his face.

He is going through it too, he says. He is hurting too. He knows.

He pulls me to him and I find myself resisting him, guilt springing up inside me as I pull away, squeeze my eyes shut, crave space and time alone. His inky, warm scent traps me in the scent of Before, hurts me, makes things too real and too much to bear.

I do try. Of course I try. I love Daniel and I want to make things better for him. I want to stay in the place and time where I would do anything to help him. But it is like trying to help someone to see with my own eyes shut.

I watch him struggle on, like he has been placed in a world where the balance of everything is off and it is an exertion just to stay upright. His mind, always sharp and fast, has become slower, but his movements have stayed the same. He drops things all the time: knives clattering to the floor as he tries to butter toast that we won't eat; his phone sliding constantly from his hands as he fumbles with the keys. I pick things up for him, hand them to him silently. He nods thanks. But we speak less and less. Words are strange to me. I float through each day, terrifying floods of emotion gushing from me without warning every so often, like the day in the park.

I see on Daniel's newspaper that it is now November. The air is bitter with cold, the leaves that fall into our garden are the fierce orange of flames, and the sky and sea seem to be closing in on the world.

Time, it seems, is not waiting for us.

***

I don't know what day of the week it is when Daniel's parents arrive at our house. They are here because I forced myself to pick up my phone and dial their number, because I know that I am barely living, and that somebody needs to be here for Daniel more than I am.

Daniel's father is a greying, chunkier version of Daniel. He pulls me into a strange, strong hug when they arrive, and says something quietly about grief that I can't quite catch. His mum bustles straight into the lounge, putting fresh flowers into a vase that I have never seen before.

I help them unload their things from the car. They

probably don't want to sleep here. The house is more dilapidated than ever and they only live about half an hour's drive away. So I say thank you but they wave the words away.

His mum, Diane, is busy putting eggs in our fridge, wiping the surfaces that are freckled with crumbs and subtly dusting around us. His dad, Paul, sits at the table with Daniel. Daniel clicks on the coffee machine that I bought him last Christmas, less than a year ago yet so, so long ago. It makes the kitchen smell bittersweet and warm. They talk quietly, calmly, sipping their drinks, Paul standing up to fill their cups as soon as they are empty.

***

'Thank you,' Daniel whispers as we crawl into our cool bed next to each other the night of his parents' arrival. We still have no curtains in here. With the sea as our only onlooker, we've never felt the urgency. The sky is inky black, dotted with burning bright stars and an eerie full moon that illuminates our bedroom.

I turn my body to face his.

'For asking Mum and Dad to come,' Daniel continues. 'It's really good having them here.'

I listen to the clattering of pots downstairs. Diane cooked us roast beef for dinner. I even ate some, and drank some of the deep red wine she placed in front of me. Now, she is washing the dishes in a steaming sink of bubbles, and Paul is drying them, putting them away in places where they don't normally go. I can hear them talking in low voices.

'I wanted to help you,' I tell him. 'It was the only thing I could think of. I want to help you with this, but I can't do it.'

Daniel finds my hand under the covers and squeezes it in his. 'But you did. This helped me. It was good talking to Dad. I wouldn't have asked them to come. And you knew that. That's why you did it. So thank you.' I feel him moving towards me, feel his lips press against mine. I push aside my sorrow and let him.

'It's not the only reason. I wanted them here because I can't really focus on anything.'

Daniel takes my hand in his and sighs. 'I know.'

'I feel,' I begin, my chest tight, 'only sometimes, tempted to let myself go.'

He drops my hand. 'Erica, don't.'

'I'm just being honest.'

'Well, don't be. We're not strong enough for this at the moment.'

My heart stops and my blood chills. Daniel always, always believes we're strong enough. He never doubts anything.

'I dealt with it the day when we were at the hospital,' Daniel continues, sitting up. 'Almost an hour of people asking about you. They needed us both there. They needed to ask their questions, and you made us look ...' He doesn't finish.

'I couldn't help it.'

'I know. And that's why I dealt with it, on top of everything else.'

'I'm sorry,' I say, because it's all I can think of. A conversation that started with thank you has ended in apology. Guilt strangles us. It threads itself through every single one of my thoughts. I have been told time and time again that Joshua's death was not because of just one, avoidable reason, but a plethora of bad luck flowing through his tiny veins, his miniature heart. But people could tell me a million times a day and the guilt would still never fade.

'Let's forget it now anyway,' Daniel says, collapsing back down on the bed, turning from me again. 'I don't want to talk about your disappearances. They ... well, let's just forget it.' There is an edge to his voice, a bitterness that cuts through me.

'What?'

There is silence. But I know what he was going to say.

'You think they had something to do with Joshua,' I whisper, because the words terrify me.

'Erica, I'm tired. Just forget we even had this conversation.'

I lie back. Daniel has never made me feel bad for my disappearances before. He has only made me feel special, ethereal. But he is not the same Daniel now. He is not the Daniel who will assuage my guilt just by looking at me or taking my hand or brushing my hair from my face.

We are both different people, and the path we are on is

not the one we thought, not one we are in any way equipped for with its strange lurking beasts of fear and guilt and pain. We have lost our way and our compass is shattered.

***

Daniel's breathing becomes steady within minutes. Even now, he sleeps as easily as he wakes.

I think about what he said. Nothing. Everything.

Somewhere, beneath all the pain, I can recognize the shape of his hurt, his exhausting search for some kind of answer to the worst question: why?

Why? All day long. As I lie in bed and wait for the night to turn to day. In the bath, as the water cools around me. As I stand at our window, staring out at the endless grey sea. *Why, why, why.*

I clutch at possible answers, flailing, reaching for something, anything, that is solid enough to absorb some of this pain. Sometimes it is the house. The windows, the heat, the damp. And it doesn't stop there. It never stops there. Who really wanted this house? Really, really wanted it?

I wanted it. Daniel wanted us both to have it. We both decided to stay, but who wanted to stay, really?

I get nowhere. And so I move on: a weird genetic throwback of my disappearances. My fault completely. I rest momentarily at this, but then I remember, I don't know that. It's unexplained.

But *why*?

My thoughts circle like crows, cawing and cawing.

So I do understand Daniel, and what he said. I have blamed him too, in moments of strange make-believe. I should be able to tell him this, to put my arms around him, to feel his warmth spread to me and try to fit next to him as closely as I used to. But I can't. All the fibres in me have snapped, and I have no bend left, no give.

***

I sleep for short bursts. When I wake, the morning air is sharp with cold. Daniel's side of the bed is smooth and cool, as though he was never there.

'Coffee?' he asks as I shuffle into the kitchen. I shake my head and he gazes at me for longer than he needs to. 'What?'

'I blame myself too, sometimes.' The words that have been festering inside me all night, leaking into my dreams, rush out all at once. 'It might have been something to do with my disappearances. He might not have been quite normal.'

Daniel stares and stares, his bloodshot eyes boring into me. 'That is not what I meant. I meant nothing. I was exhausted. I wanted to go to sleep.'

'Maybe I should have told them. When they asked all the questions and we got to the hospital.'

'For what? To make them think you were imagining things? To make them think you hallucinated? That would only have made them ask more questions. The closest to the truth you could have told them would have been about your accident, but that's on your medical file. They'll have seen it. They will have accessed all our records, everything. And they found nothing to say it was anything to do with any part of you because Joshua didn't just vanish to another place, Erica. It wasn't the same.'

'Okay. But even if it was nothing to do with that, you'd also be right for blaming me for not knowing somehow. I, more than anyone, should have seen this coming. I should have been able to change it.'

He laughs sourly, puts down his mug but misjudges it so it bangs on the worktop. 'I wish you could have done. But it's a bit much to think of yourself as some kind of psychic.'

'I don't. I'm not giving myself credit here. I'm saying I have a stupid, weird *thing* that you'd think would help avert disaster in some way. But it didn't help. And I'm sorry about that.'

'I don't connect the two.' Daniel downs his drink, puts his empty cup neatly under the machine and presses the button until new coffee spews out. 'I meant nothing by it.'

I am silent. *I don't believe you*, I say with a look as Diane appears in the kitchen.

'Let's go out today,' she says quietly, so that at first I think she is only talking to Daniel. But then I see that she is looking at us both, that she is trying to get us to make friends: two stubborn children who have fallen out over their favourite toy breaking.

It was her fault.

No, it was his.

'Where?' Daniel asks, tossing his mug into the sink as though it is made of paper.

'I don't know,' she says. 'Anywhere but here.'

***

I dress slowly, my back to Daniel as he dresses too.

'I know you don't want to go out,' Daniel says. 'I don't either, really.'

I turn to him. 'Don't you?'

'No. I don't want to do normal things. But I'm forcing myself to. I'm hoping that it will get easier. It *will* get easier,' he tells himself. A glimmer of the hope that is so typical of Daniel and that I thought had deserted him last night, is still there.

'Nothing seems normal now,' I say.

'I know. But I'm doing them anyway. I'm getting up, and I'm drinking coffee even though I don't really want to, and I'm getting dressed and going out today because at some point, time will have passed and hopefully we'll be a step closer to getting through this.'

I sigh and sit on the bed, half-dressed. Daniel sits next to me. 'The counsellor gave me a good tip,' he says. 'I don't know if she gave it to you, too.'

I look up. We haven't talked about the counsellor before,

I realize. Or not that I can remember anyway. She is a tiny, greying woman who wears colourful brooches and smells of Elnett. I want her to help us, but such insurmountable pain surely can't be touched by such a small person.

'She said it's okay to have time off from the grief. A break. It made sense to me,' Daniel says.

I am silent.

'Does it make sense to you?' he pushes.

I think of Joshua and clamp my eyes shut. The tension that had begun to melt is suddenly there between us again, hard as ice. 'No.'

'Well, I'm trying it. I have to try something, Erica. Otherwise I'm going to go mad.' Daniel pulls a black jumper on, takes a cardigan from a pile of tangled clothes on the chair and hands it to me. 'Please. Get dressed. And if you manage to get dressed, we might manage to go out. Take one second at a time. Just try.'

I take it, and our fingers brush.

***

We pile into Daniel's parents' car and his dad drives us into town where we walk through bitterly cold streets and wander in and out of shops that blast us with false warm air. Daniel's parents are struggling too: I can see that. It's like we're all trying to stay afloat in a frozen sea. We need to hold on to each other, and get the balance just right. Too weak a grip and the others will fall under the black waves. Too strong and they might pull us down with them.

Diane herds us into a crowded coffee shop and sits us all down at a cramped table in the centre before disappearing to the counter. She returns with a tray loaded with seasonal, too-sweet concoctions involving whipped cream and cinnamon. Paul tells us he's thinking of retiring from his hardware store job that he's done since before Daniel was born. Diane tells us they have booked a trip to Scotland for the New Year, that the cottage has two bedrooms and we'd be welcome to join them for all of it or some of it, or even just one night. They all avoid mentioning the baby that gurgles in a high chair next to us. I see from the corner of my eye it is a girl. A gaudy ribbon is tacked onto the side of her blonde head. She slams a plastic toy down on the floor and her mother sighs and bends to retrieve it. The baby cackles and repeats the slamming. She's scooped up by the mother, her cackling swiftly transforming into howls as she is stuffed into a pink coat covered in prints of dancing mice. She is a few months older than Joshua was. She is about the age he should be now. The thought jars in my mind. It is too big for my head. I am still thinking it, trying to process it, when I realise that the mother's companion, her own mother probably, is staring at me. Her eyes are large and hooded, her hair arranged in a greying halo around her head. I don't know her, but she is looking at me as though she knows me.

I stare back, vaguely aware that Daniel has noticed too, that he is suddenly holding my arm protectively.

'You're the couple,' the woman says slowly, a frown deepening her features. 'I saw you in the paper. You bought the house that everyone talks about, and then your baby ... You poor, poor things.'

I continue to stare. The sweetness of cinnamon rises in my throat and I can't believe I ever liked the taste. I catch my reflection in the mirror on the wall above her head and barely recognise myself: short, crazed hair and horrified eyes. I can't remember the last time I looked in the mirror properly.

I glance at Daniel. He is tired and his heart is broken and he is a different kind of Daniel. But he is still Daniel. He is still attractive, I realise with a jolt, as though I am seeing him for the first time again. The image of when I saw him for the very first time at the party flits across my vision: younger, unfamiliar, pouring Champagne into my glass. That moment, I think, was the start of it all. I feel a pull to the other Erica, a longing to try and unravel my life from this point, to undo all the grief and pain. Press rewind.

'If it had been our Dotty,' the woman continues, like an express train hurtling towards me, 'I don't know what we would have done. I don't know that we'd be able to carry on like you. Look at you, out having coffee. I admire you.' She sniffs, wiping her nose on the cuff of her walking jacket. She motions to her daughter, who is now putting her howling baby into a polka-dot buggy. The daughter looks up and gives me a small neat smile. She doesn't acknowledge that her mother is still talking at me about what happened to Joshua as you might talk about a recent rainstorm or power cut or something else mildly disruptive.

I see Daniel looking at the younger woman and I wonder what he sees as he watches the two of us next to one another. She in freshly laundered clothes, gleaming hair and skin, contentment making her glow from within. Me, who he has to be begged even to finish dressing, who has some strange affliction that he can't help but think I might have passed on to our baby and somehow damaged him. Surely, surely Daniel cannot want me. I am failing to function. My grief is all-consuming, and I can't take a moment off from it like he wants me to. Yet I can't bear for people to see it either because it seems so personal and raw, as though people who are looking at me can see me naked.

Daniel would definitely be better, I decide in this instant, with someone who can take him forward to a new happiness. I am trapping him in the past, the wrong future.

And so I run. I run from the cafe, out into the street, where I take big gulps of dark, November air as though I am drowning. I hear Daniel's shouts, his voice fading through the slamming door of the coffee shop. I carry on running until I reach a deserted alleyway, its darkness beckoning me.

Just once, the alleyway with its shadowy recesses, its isolation, whispers to me. *Escape it all. Let Daniel escape you and your sadness. Just once. He said to have a break from the grief. This is the best way. Give him a break from you, too.*

I stop, gasping for breath, leaning back so that the rough brick of the wall behind me scrapes my head, tugs at my hair, until a delicious blackness washes over me and takes everything away.

Chapter 37

There is a cottage with smooth white walls and warm terracotta tiles; the scent of fresh bread and the tang of tomatoes; a deep blue sky dotted with cotton wool and patchwork fields for miles beyond.

Erica is there with some friends. They all wear the same carefree, pleased-with-themselves expression like a uniform.

'Your turn,' a girl with pink hair says to Erica.

Erica places her hands over her face and I try to see through her fingers to gauge her expression and what might be happening. Music thumps and candles flicker. An empty wine bottle tips over by Erica's feet and rolls away down the cobbles to the pool where it lands with a gentle splash.

'Truth or dare,' Pink Hair continues.

'She always picks truth. She has to do a dare,' a man says. The voice is familiar, from another time.

'Fine,' Erica says, peeling her hands away to reveal her blushing face. 'Dare.' She juts her chin out determinedly.

I look around, moving towards the group. I smell cigarette smoke and red wine and the salty fragrance of warm bodies. I see Mike; I hear his voice again.

'One kiss,' he says. 'For old time's sake.'

Erica drops her jaw, outraged. The group cackle like teenagers, clinking their bottles. The breeze picks up and ruffles Erica's hair as Mike steps towards her and cups his hands around her face, kissing her theatrically and ending by throwing her back in a dramatic embrace. They emerge, eyes shining, laughing, and as the group moves on with its drunken dares and demands for truths, I see Mike take Erica's hand in his.

When most of the bottles have been cleared, the candles blown out, and the terrace is dark, Mike and Erica sit alone at the table.

'I'm glad you came to join us here,' Erica says to him. 'It's gorgeous, isn't it? And we've not all been together for ages.'

'I know. It's cool being back with you all. Joel's so lucky to have this house.'

'We're lucky he's letting us stay here rent-free too.'

'So he should. Share the wealth and all that,' Mike laughs, lighting a cigarette and offering it to Erica. She shakes her head, pulling her red cardigan around her.

'Cold?' he asks.

'A bit.'

'You don't miss British weather, then?' Mike asks before taking a swig of beer.

'I do, actually. I don't mind the cold.'

He hates it, I think absently, as though I'm watching a film I've already seen. He'd rather have summer.

'Ah, I hate it,' Mike says. 'Give me summer any day.'

Erica smiles. 'I quite like candles and blankets. And I love cups of tea. I miss English tea and—'

'Don't tell me you're going to quit on this big adventure for a cup of PG Tips?' Mike interrupts and laughs, flicking a glowing ember from his cigarette onto the terrace.

'No. Not yet.'

I sigh, then place my hand over my mouth. I'll never get used to the fact that I am invisible and silent here, no matter what I do.

'So they're the things you miss the most?' Mike is asking Erica, the tip of his cigarette glowing red in the pale darkness.

She shrugs. 'I suppose so. They're home, aren't they? The little things.'

Are they? They probably were at one time. I can't remember the last time Daniel and I lit a candle in the lounge and cuddled under our favourite grey blanket. I don't drink tea these days because it makes me nauseous, like everything else.

Mike is nodding. 'Yeah, yeah, totally,' he's saying, even though I know he thinks candles are unnecessary and tea is only for old ladies.

'I do miss my family too, obviously.'

'But not as much as candles,' Mike says with a grin.

'Oh no. Nowhere near as much.' Erica takes a swig of her beer then looks at Mike. 'Actually, you're like my dad. I think he—'

Mike interrupts with a hooting laugh. 'Cheers. Just what I want the girls to tell me.'

Erica laughs too, more loudly than I ever do. 'No, I don't mean it in a bad way. You don't look like him.'

'Well, that's a relief.' Mike puffs out his chest. 'How are we the same then?'

I watch as Erica cocks her head to the side and smiles as she thinks about her dad – my dad. I haven't seen him since I was a teenager. He emails every now and again, but I know so little about him. He doesn't even know what has happened to Joshua because I haven't been able to face telling him, and Nicholas hasn't spoken to him in years either. Has not having my dad in my life, seeing his marriage to my mum fade and fall, changed me this much?

'He has the travelling bug,' Erica tells Mike. 'He really loves the idea that I'm out here seeing the world, being adventurous. At first, when I was planning to travel more and more, he seemed to kind of get cold feet for me. But now I'm here, he's so glad I've gone ahead with it. He loves getting pictures from me of all the things and places I'm seeing.'

'So he's a bit of a traveller too, then?'

Erica shakes her head. 'No. He never got the chance. He was too bogged down, I think. He never said that, obviously, because it was us who tied him down. But I get the feeling that he wants me to live out some of the stuff he never got to do. And I suppose I feel like I owe it to him. And myself. I never want to be in that position, where you're trapped somewhere you don't want to be.'

I shiver, even though I'm warmer than I've been in weeks. *Trapped.* Just how I've felt every time someone places their hand on mine, stops me from leaving a room, or keeps me from coming here and seeing this.

Mike shakes his head. 'Nah. I never want to be trapped either. Can't stand to stay in the same place too long. We're living the dream.'

They laugh, and clink their bottles together. Erica accepts Mike's cigarette, and inhales lazily, puffing out delicate rings of smoke that drift away into nothing before giving it back to him. He moves closer to her again, takes a strand of her hair and twists it in his fingers, then whispers something to her that I can't hear. It'll be something flirtatious, something Erica probably won't even remember tomorrow. I wonder what it is.

It seems impossible that once, I wasn't able to move when I saw these other worlds, that I was stuck in one position. Now, I am able to move closer to Erica and Mike, so close that I can smell the perfume I always wear – deep red roses and sweet vanilla – and Mike's smoky breath and sharp, citrus aftershave. I can see each strand of Erica's hair shimmering in the moonlight, each curved eyelash, each pore.

And that's when I do it. It's instinctive. I tried to do it

once before, on the worst day of my life, but I didn't actually touch her. Now, as I reach out, I feel her skin beneath my fingers and there is a flash, a moment of pure, blinding light.

And then there is only one version of me. I face Mike, and he leans into me, oblivious to any change. He kisses me softly on my neck.

I am myself, in my own body. I feel the same. I also feel completely different: looser and freer and lighter, without any of the weight of sorrow that has been pulling at me for so long now. I know that I lost Joshua, but I can't feel it. I close my eyes and feel the familiar touch of Mike's lips which are rougher than Daniel's.

Daniel.

I jerk backwards, and am thrust back into the wet November that I left behind.

Chapter 38

I slam into the wall of the alleyway, grazing my cheek so sharply that I cry out.

It is pitch black. There is no moon, no stars. There is just a sky that is low and purple-black with rain and darkness. When the first fat, cold drops start to fall I pull my coat around me. There's enough loose change in my pocket to catch a tram, so I walk to the tram stop, the rain stinging as it pounds against my throbbing cheek. I pass the coffee shop that I ran from and hear the metallic hammering of rain on the shutters that were pulled down hours ago. The tram is silent, with only one other passenger who sleeps and snores gently. When I get off, it's raining even harder and frozen water pounds at me, soaking through my clothes and skin into my bones.

When I finally reach home, I have to knock quietly on the front door because I have no key with me. It swings open almost immediately, and behind it is Diane. She holds out her arms to me, then helps me out of my soaking coat, gesturing for me to take off my shoes.

'Go and put something dry on,' she says. 'I'll make us a cup of tea.'

***

Daniel is in bed, and I whisper his name as I stumble through the darkness to find some pyjamas. His breathing changes so subtly I might have imagined it.

'Daniel?' I say again. My voice sounds weaker than the version of it that I have become used to in such a short space of time. It's quieter than the other Erica's, I realize, and I long to tell Daniel because the Daniel from Before would have sat up in bed, switched on the light and asked me to tell him more, fascinated by the difference.

But from this Daniel, the Daniel of After, there's nothing.

'I'm so sorry,' I tell him. 'I'm sorry for everything. I missed you. I wanted to come back. I only had to think of you,' I begin, but then I see the other side of the sentence, flashing red: *when I was kissing Mike*. I stammer, and wonder how to finish, or even start, but then Daniel shifts under the covers and sighs.

'It's late, Erica. It's too late for this.'

***

Diane hands me a steaming cup of tea that I can't face as soon as I walk into the lounge. I should go back upstairs with it, stay distant from her. She knows nothing of my disappearances, and so trying to explain where I've been for the past who knows how many hours will be impossible. Usually, it would come naturally to me to avoid her. But everything is on its head these days, grotesque and foreign. And so I press myself onto the sofa next to her, unable to stop myself from shivering. My body pulses with confusion, is hot and cold, exhausted and stimulated all at the same time.

'He's mad with me,' I say, my teeth chattering. 'And he should be.' I face her. 'I'm sorry. It was awful of me to go off like that when you've come to help out. I know you must be thinking that I should be there more for Daniel. And I think so too. I'm just finding it so—'

Diane holds up her hand in gentle interruption. It is delicately lined with age, her wedding band solid and fuss-free. 'No more. I don't want you to spend energy explaining yourself to me. You're entitled to grieve in whatever way you need to.' She cocks her head to the side, frowning as she sees my cheek, then stands up. 'Let me get something for that.'

She is back in a few minutes, pressing warm cotton wool against my skin, and I feel like a child. Tears spring to my eyes, and guilt floods me, pulling at every single nerve. 'I should have looked after him,' I say.

Diane looks down at the cotton wool, speckled with blood from my graze. 'Yes. And you did.'

'Joshua, I mean.'

'I know. And you did.'

'No. Not enough. I didn't look after him enough.'

Diane shakes her head, placing the cotton wool in her

small, neat lap. 'This is exhausting for you. But I won't tell you not to do it to yourself, because I know you can't help it. We just need to hope that one day, it will end for you and you will somehow accept it.'

I nod, unable to look at her.

'Daniel seems to think he knows where you went before. But I won't ask you because it doesn't matter. What matters is that you came back, and you're safe, and even though you are going through the worst thing that life could possibly dole out, you're going to get through it somehow.'

'Do you think I am?'

Diane laughs. It's a short, sharp burst of a sound that I'd forgotten people could make. 'Well, Erica. What choice do you have?'

I swallow, busying myself with gathering the soggy rounds of cotton wool. *Choice*. The times I have disappeared since we lost Joshua have been almost animal urges, too strong to fight and too sudden to think over. And I reached out to touch the other Erica without even thinking about it.

'I came back,' I say out loud. 'Just thinking of Daniel made me come back. I didn't want to leave him, you know.'

Diane puts her steady hand over my jittery one. 'I know,' she says.

'Do you think little things are important? Things like candles and blankets and making cups of coffee for each other?' I ask next. It's like I have taken a drug. My thoughts collide into one another, erupting from my lips before I can stop them. 'And do you think our old selves are still underneath all of this? Could doing the little things that we used to do get the old us back? Or are we gone forever?'

Diane isn't the kind of person to dwell on philosophy, on the mysteries of hypotheticals. But she will do anything to help me, so she furrows her thin brow and tries to look as though she's debating it. 'Maybe,' she says in the end.

'I hope so. It scares me that we might have changed too much.'

'Everything changes anyway,' she says. 'It's just that this change was a little too fast.' She stands up, swiping the cotton wool from my hands. 'Come on. Drink your tea, and then we can get some sleep.'

I get into bed next to Daniel a few minutes later, but there's no way I can sleep. The room spins, my senses still ringing the way they do long after you've left a nightclub.

I throw off the duvet again and step quietly across the floorboards, through the crooked corridors of our house, and down the groaning stairs to the lounge, clutching my phone.

I don't sit down, but pace from one side of the room to the other as I dial, waiting for him to answer.

'Erica?'

'It's different now,' I say. 'I suppose I probably knew on some level I could do it.'

Nicholas is silent. He doesn't bring up the fact that it's the early hours of the morning, or make us do hellos, for which I am grateful. I wonder fleetingly about Amelia, and if she'll be annoyed that I have phoned at this time, but then my bigger thoughts take over.

'You know the girl from the 1980s, Helen Boswell?' I ask breathlessly.

'What about her?'

'She said she had learnt to ride horses, didn't she?'

'Yes,' Nicholas says after another minute of silence. 'She did.'

'Did you realise? At the time? Were you waiting for me to realise too?' I know as I'm asking that he knew. I know that, ever fair, he gave me the information but didn't point me directly to it, was perhaps even hoping it would always escape me. 'You should have told me, Nick.' I am digging through the dresser in the lounge now, papers and bills and receipts and photographs fluttering out like moths onto the fraying carpet beneath. 'It's here somewhere,' I tell him, and just at that moment my fingertips touch the firm, yellowed paper. I pull it out, squinting in the weak light of the lamp.

'In the article, Helen says: "I am lucky enough to have a pony in my other life, so I've had to learn to ride". So she actually lived her other life sometimes. She somehow managed to dip in and out of her two worlds. If she'd only *watched* her other life, like I always have, then why would she have said she'd actually learnt to ride horses? It's been there, all this time. I've had a feeling that there's something more, ever since you gave me this newspaper, but with everything that's happened it's kind of been locked away in my mind. What's happened has almost made me go crazy with grief, but it's led me to this. I reached out and touched her, and then I was her. So this means that I could live a different life sometimes. I could have a break from the grief. And that would be better for Daniel, wouldn't it?'

'Okay, Erica. We have to clarify right now that you disappearing, no matter what reason you have for it, will never make things better for Daniel. You have to forget this. It's not fair on him,' Nicholas says. 'It's too much of a risk. This isn't riding ponies, Erica. It's bigger than that.'

I close my eyes. 'I know. It's too big. That's why it's so impossible.'

'Not impossible. Just difficult. There's a huge difference.'

'You're so awkward, you know.'

'I'm right though. Promise me you'll forget what happened? Don't even tell Daniel. Don't think about it. Just get through each day.'

I sigh, my pulse finally slowing. Nicholas's voice, his tone with me takes me back to being a teenager and reminds me of a time when he was my number one person, the one who would slowly and gently pull me back down when my disappearances and everything that had changed for us sent me sailing off into the heights of panic.

'By the way,' Nicholas says, a yawn stretching his words. 'Phoebe got star of the week in assembly. She wants to phone you and tell you about it.'

The thought of Phoebe with her pure, bright laugh that

is as clear as a bell, her eager questions, her luminous skin that is as yet not darkened by life, isn't as difficult as it was in those first few days. So maybe I am moving on, after all.

'Put her on,' I joke, glancing at the clock. It's just after 3am.

'I'll get her to ring you tomorrow. So don't go anywhere.'

'I won't. I promise.'

As I hang up, and the promise of sleep finally washes over me, I realize that if the teenage version of myself is still in me somewhere, brought back by talking to Nicholas, then maybe the one I think I've lost forever might still be somewhere too.

Chapter 39

'Your mum was good to me last night,' I tell Daniel the next morning. He is eating a bowl of cereal before work. There is a spot of milk on the corner of his lip and it reminds me of the scene I have lived, and watched, where we sat in the Lake District on my birthday, and he had a fleck of ice cream on his mouth. I lean forward and kiss him. It is unexpected for him, strange for both of us. Daniel wipes his mouth, brushing away the milk and my kiss. He stands up and stalks over to the sink and the dish crashes into it.

'What happened to trying? To taking a second at a time?' He still has his back to me, facing the back garden. The bare branches of the tree tap against the glass of the window, punctuating the pause before I speak.

'It was all just too much, with that woman in the coffee shop and the baby ... I wanted to escape. Surely you can understand that?' I started with so much hope, but already I can feel the day unspooling as they all do, tangling beneath my feet and threatening to trip me up.

'No. Not really. Because I can't escape like you can, Erica. I have to live this. Every second.'

'I know. But you even said yourself that you wanted to take a break from the grief.'

'No. I said I wanted *us* to take a break from it. Together.'

'I saw that other woman, with her baby, and I ...' My words fade. Was a random woman in a coffee shop being prettier, cleaner, and calmer, really a reason for me to desert him? It was so clear at the time, but now it seems so trivial, too childish to even say.

We hear the clearing of a throat and both turn. My face burns as I see Diane.

'We've had a think, and we're going to leave you to it,' she says. 'Being here with you both when you have so much to work through ... well, we just think you need a bit of time on your own. Some space.'

Daniel puts his jacket on and winds a blue scarf around his neck. 'Thanks for coming, Mum.'

I should feel relieved. Daniel's parents being here wouldn't help us to get back to the way we were, to return to what I now know I've been missing almost as much as Joshua. I know logically that I want to keep to my promise not only to Nicholas and Phoebe, but to myself and to Daniel. I know I have a concrete plan to try to touch something of Daniel's or Joshua's if I feel myself fade. But still, fear is settled deep in my bones and it stirs at the thought of Diane and Paul leaving us, at the silence of the house when Daniel is at work every day.

'We're all packed up,' she rattles on. 'I'm sure we'll be back again at some point. It goes without saying that if you want us to come again, then you just need to let us know.' She leans forward, to brush an airy kiss against my cheek. 'We're just trying to do the right thing,' she says.

'Of course,' I tell her, trying to make my voice stronger, more certain than it is. 'We'll get there, won't we, Daniel?'

We all stand around awkwardly, as though we are talking about the renovation of a room, or a pile of paperwork.

We will get *where?*

Paul appears with their case, his jacket zipped up so high that we can only just see his face. The case is huge and I realize they were planning on staying for much longer than they have. At least they tried. I still haven't told my dad what has happened to Joshua. If I did, would he be here with a too-big suitcase, plans bigger than he could manage? I think of the other Erica talking about him as though he was part of her and then shake my head. *No. Don't go there.*

'Ready to go, love?' Paul asks Diane. He nods at Daniel, at me. We help them into the car, the freezing wind snaking around us, whipping into our house.

***

'I'm late for work,' Daniel says when they've gone. 'Will you be ...?' he doesn't finish but I know what he means.

'I won't go,' I tell him.

'But you'll be on your own all day. Maybe you could

call the museum, talk to Carl about some hours or something?'

I push down the irritation that springs inside me. I don't want to be annoyed with Daniel. It is not part of my plan. But Carl is the last person I want to talk to. My maternity leave was meant to last until next spring and now, without a baby, this seems implausible. But what is more implausible is sharing this awful time with the loud, brash Carl who wouldn't understand my grief if it slapped him in the face.

'Okay,' Daniel says, seeing my expression. 'I know it's probably too soon to think about the museum again. You need a focus, or an escape that isn't your other life. Just think about it, okay? The book, if not the museum. Or call Zoe or your mum and get them to spend a bit more time with you. They keep asking me about you. You're shutting them out. You're shutting everything out. I know you're grieving, but we have to try and grieve and live at the same time. It will get easier. It has to.'

I nod as brightly as I can. 'Okay. I'll dig out my book stuff.'

He brushes my grazed cheek lightly. 'What happened?' he asks, concern in his face.

'It was when I came back. I landed too close to the wall. Terrible navigation skills,' I say. He smiles and I laugh, and there is a moment between us, a fleck of light in the darkness.

'Can you fight it?' he asks me.

I nod. 'I can try. I've been thinking about how. Remember that article that Nicholas gave me? About the girl in the eighties that it used to happen to?' I speak carefully, as though Daniel might suddenly recall the part where Helen became her other self. 'She said she just touched something belonging to her cat, because her cat was the thing she loved the most. It was always enough to keep her here. We decided around the time of my accident that if I touch something of yours, it might be enough. I haven't ever needed to try it since then because it stopped happening. And maybe yesterday I didn't really try to stay. I couldn't. But I will try to be quicker, and try to do something about it. I do want this life with you. It's just that sometimes ...'

Daniel nods. 'I know.' He takes his wallet and keys from the table. I kiss him again and this time he doesn't brush it away.

***

After Daniel has left the house, I wander around the rooms, collecting things for my book. It's so long since I worked on it that it takes a while to remember its intricacies, its directions and shape. I sit at the kitchen table for a while staring at my notes, reading about the people who told me their stories, smiles in their voices. If it weren't for Blackpool, the book was going to sing to its readers, these people and buildings wouldn't exist. The world would be different.

When Daniel suggested that I find something to distract me, I thought throwing myself into the project of the book might be a good solution. But all the book makes me see is the fine web that connects people, the everyday moments that changed their lives, paths appearing and disappearing with every second, every decision. All the what ifs make me think of the very thing I'm trying so hard to forget.

I rub my temples, trying to dull the fierce headache burning through my mind. I stumble up and grip the table, ignoring the dizziness that threatens to take hold of me any second. The sink is three steps away, and I only just make it before falling. I reach out, my eyesight fading, and feel around until I touch the cool metal of Daniel's spoon that he touched a few hours ago. I squeeze the handle and think of his fingers on it, and slowly, I can see the sink beneath me. The dizziness eases and I take a breath. I am here, I tell myself. I am staying here because I love Daniel and I can love this life again. I am taking it a second at a time.

The house is still and silent, the air cool as the central heating that I flick on clanks its way round the pipes.

I wander to the fridge, take the Blackpool tram magnet and turn it over in my hands before placing it back on the fridge door and treading lightly back through to the hall, up the creaking staircase, to the third room on the right.

If I am going to stay, to commit to working through our pain, then I should face this. It might help, I tell myself.

I push the door open. Everything is exactly the same as it was that night.

At first, we moved nothing because of the investigation. All a formality, people said, as Joshua's things and our hearts were handled roughly then put back in all the wrong places.

When all that was over, we shut the door.

***

I start to take things from his wardrobe next to the window: tiny, soft clothes and bibs, nappies, muslin squares. I place them in his cot. Grief tears at my insides, and I stop for a moment.

I am even more aware of the crippling pain now that I have experienced a few moments without it.

If I stay, if every time I feel this world fading, I always touch something of Daniel's to keep me here – a sock, fuzzy with wear; a cup of half-drunk coffee, the rim of a mug that has touched his lips; his still-damp toothbrush or whatever book his fingers have turned the pages of – then this pain will stay too.

I could clear this room, paint it smooth white or deep red. I could bolt shut the door and never enter it again. But the primal agony, the need to touch Joshua and kiss him and press him to me will never ever be stilled no matter what I do. It's this animal need that suffocates any choice, any control I might have.

I grab the things from the cot and stuff them back into

the wardrobe. There is no order to my attempts, and they tumble back out one after another from the shelves, tiny arms and legs flailing through the air.

I remember the day we moved this wardrobe into our house. It's a small, antique mahogany chest that's missing a door. We bought it from an antique fair in Manchester. I was pregnant, and Daniel wouldn't let me help him lift it. We laughed as he tipped it into the room and it almost toppled over. We said over and over again about getting another door for it, adding it to our eternal list of repairs, but it was never done. Nothing was ever done. The house and its needs suffocated us, an ocean of expensive, impossible jobs.

'He'll need a new door by the time he makes friends and they come round to sit in his bedroom,' I said.

'He'll need a new wardrobe by then,' Daniel said.

I squeeze shut my eyes but the image burns on.

Chapter 40

As soon as I hear the key turn in the lock later that night, I jump up and pour two glasses of Daniel's favourite red wine. I caught the tram to St Anne's and bought the bottle especially, along with some new wine glasses and two candles which now flicker gently on the coffee table. I hand Daniel's glass to him at the front door.

'A peace offering,' I tell him.

'You're here,' he says, a grin taking over his face. He sips the wine, closing his eyes. 'Perfect.'

'Of course I'm here.'

He glances at me, his grin disappearing as he sees my swollen eyes that I have tried to disguise with makeup. 'Are you okay? Did something happen?'

'I tried to clear some things from his room. I wondered if it might help me move forward somehow.'

'And did it?'

'Not really,' I admit. 'Maybe it was too soon. I just felt like this pain won't ever leave.'

Daniel sighs. 'It won't leave. But one day we will learn

how to live with it. Look, it's good that you could even go in there. It means you faced it. I don't think you could've done that a few weeks ago. So you are moving on, even if it doesn't feel like it. And I'd rather you were here, trying to get through things than ... well, you know. Speaking of which,' he takes my hand and leads me to the lounge. 'The best minds think alike. I have a peace offering too.' We sit down and he hands me a small red box. 'There's nothing new in there,' he tells me. 'So don't get too excited.'

I take off the lid. Inside is Daniel's watch.

'I was thinking about the article and using something of mine to keep you here. And if you want to keep it with you, then I'd love it. I want to be enough to make you want to stay, Erica. I know it's so hard. But I think we can get through it.'

I jump up and curl my body against him. He is in there. I can see glimmers of him. 'We just need to change our plan,' I say.

'Yeah. Although I must admit I've never had to change a plan quite this much before.'

We're silent for a few minutes, sipping our wine, pressed into one another in a way we haven't been for months.

'I did something today,' I tell Daniel, pulling my laptop towards us. 'I emailed my dad, and told him about ...' I clear my throat. I can't say the words yet. 'I told him what happened to us.'

'You did? That's good.' Daniel has tried to get me to

contact my dad before to tell him about Joshua but I never have done. 'And what did he say?'

I close my eyes for a second, trying to ignore the hope from so long ago that rears inside me. 'Nothing yet. But I wonder if it might be what he needs to come and see me.'

Daniel nods. 'Check your email,' he says, and I do. But there is nothing.

'Maybe he doesn't check them very often,' I say. 'Or he has my number, I think. Maybe he'll phone me.'

'Shall we put some music on?' Daniel asks after a few minutes.

I hesitate and he sees.

'Joshua won't mind. It doesn't mean you love him any less if you listen to some music.'

I roll my eyes. 'You sound just like the counsellor.'

Daniel laughs and it stirs something inside me I thought had gone. I disentangle my limbs from his so he can get up and put a record on. 'You might as well top up our wine,' I say. Since the day we lost Joshua, I have only had the one glass that Diane gave me, and tonight's gives me a pleasantly vague feeling that blurs the edges of reality.

'I was going to get the watch engraved,' Daniel says as he pours more wine. 'But I was too impatient. I wanted you to have it tonight and nowhere would do the engraving in just one day.'

'What were you going to have engraved on it?'

Daniel downs his wine. 'It's a bit cheesy. I was going to

get "*bid me discourse, I will enchant thine ear*". You know, from the ballroom in the Tower.'

I bite my lip. 'I would have loved that. Although it would have upset me too. It would have reminded me so much of our time before any of this happened. That day, at the Tower, when it was just us and we were so happy and hopeful. It breaks my heart.' The alcohol's effect of vagueness dissipates suddenly and violently, and I feel tears storming to my eyes.

But Daniel is shaking his head. 'I get that. Of course I do. But no, I wouldn't have wanted it to make you think of the past. I wanted it to say something to you about now.'

'Really? What?'

'Well, I'm no poet. You know that. You're better at this stuff than me. But I was thinking more along the lines of, give us more time, or a chance, and we will see happiness.'

I put my arms around him and kiss him. 'You're more poetic than you think.'

'So did it nearly happen? Today? Did you control it?'

I nod. 'Yes. And I just touched your cereal spoon and it stopped.'

'My cereal spoon. Wow. Romance is off the charts around here.'

'But that's the thing,' I say, on a roll with words and wine and something that isn't happiness – might never be happiness – but isn't the sharp agony of the last few months, 'it *is* romance. It's real romance because I wanted to stay, for you. I didn't want to think about the other version of me with Mike.' The last few words of my sentence droop and fizzle. I know my mistake as soon as I hear it fly from my lips.

Daniel is silent for an excruciating minute before speaking.

'The other Erica is with Mike? You've been watching yourself with him?'

I sit back and throw a cushion at him to try to lighten the mood, even though I know it's impossible. 'You make me sound perverted. I haven't watched anything like that.'

'But you're with Mike?' Daniel stares at me. 'Have you only just seen this? I thought you said you didn't go today?'

'I'm not with Mike,' I insist. 'The other me is with Mike. Not me.' Guilt twists inside me as I remember the feeling of Mike's lips on mine, the soft scratch of his gold stubble on my chin.

'But it's not new?'

I look down and shake my head. 'It's not me,' I mumble again.

'Why didn't you tell me?'

'Because it's not me. It's not a big deal. She's been with him for ages.'

'Oh,' Daniel says, 'great.'

'I know it must sound weird. But I bet in your other life, you're with someone else. It's just that you've not seen it.'

'Yeah. And if I'd disappeared and left you in this hell

alone for almost a whole day to see how I was getting on with this other woman, you'd be fine with it?'

'No. But my point was, I didn't go today.'

'You obviously wanted to on some level though, because you had to try so hard to stay! But you never mentioned Mike. And I know, because I would have remembered.'

'I am drawn to it because I am different there. I seem so fearless, so free! But I didn't go!' I shout. 'And you don't know how hard that is for me!'

'Hard for you? What about me?' Daniel says. He is standing up, the pressure of the last few months visible in his reddening face, his furious eyes. I have never seen him like this. He storms over to the record player, tearing the needle from the record so it squeals and stops. 'I have to be the one here without you! I'm the one who's always going to be wondering if you'll be here when I get home, or if you'll have found a world with your ex in it that's preferable to this one!'

I frown at him. 'You knew that this would always happen to me almost from the start. And you said it was fine. Now you're telling me it's not?'

'You told me you were leaving it behind.'

'What did I know?' I say quietly. 'How could I ever put something that runs alongside me, behind me?'

'You have to try. We shouldn't even be dealing with this right now, Erica. It's making things even worse.'

I scramble over the rockiness of our words, of Daniel's hurt, trying to get our steadiness and my confidence back.

'Please, let's not talk about it. I didn't want tonight to be about the other Erica. I wanted it to be about us. We're so different now,' I say, and a sob escapes. I wipe it away, and mascara, the first I've worn in months, melts onto my hand. 'I thought it was enough to come back and change things here, to get us back. I thought if I could always choose to stay then we would be able to get the old versions of us back. But we are so far from what we were. It's not going to be that easy, is it?'

Daniel dips his head and closes his eyes. 'No, Erica,' he says, calmer now, sad instead of angry. 'Nothing about this is going to be easy. Things won't be the same. We have to work out how to live this new life, not try to get our old one back or try to somehow replicate bits of the other Erica's.'

'But then why have I seen it? It makes things so complicated.'

'You've never known why. You probably never will.'

But I shake my head. 'There has to be a reason. Now more than ever.' I think for a minute, then turn to him. The wild feelings of last night rustle inside me, threatening to take hold again. 'What if I could change things?'

'How? You don't go to the past. You don't do anything. You just see things. You see *Mike*,' he says sourly.

'Not exactly. Not anymore.' I bite my lip. Does he want to hear this?

He looks at me, frowns. 'What?'

I take a breath. 'I became her. Only for a second or so.'

He stares and I continue. 'Just forget about Mike for a minute. What about if the other Erica could meet the other version of you?'

'Erica, this is ridiculous.'

'Is it? You've said yourself that you think we'd meet in my other life anyway. What if, somehow, I could make it happen? What if we could meet again in another life, and somehow turn all this into something else? I've never been able to make her do anything before, but it's all been leading to this.' The pull to the other world rises in me, the promise I made to forget it fading. 'I am trying to ignore it. But what if that's not the right thing to do? What if this is a chance to do things differently? Aren't you at all fascinated for me to see what we could be like in a different life?

He shakes his head and stands up. I am pushing him too far. 'Stop it. *This* is our life. It's hard, but we are living *this* one. End of.'

'Living? Really? You call this living? We are not living, Daniel! We are hurting, and it's not going to end.' More tears, gushing and ugly, flood from my eyes. My nose streams. *Romance*, I think caustically. Yeah, right.

'Have you ever even seen me in the other life?' Daniel asks, even though he knows the answer because he has asked me before, and I have always had to say no.

I take a sip of wine but it tastes different now, too rich and dry. 'Not yet. But that's good, if you think about it. We haven't even started yet. Surely that's better in a way. We have a blank canvas.'

'Erica. Enough.'

But it isn't enough. There is something burning inside me. Trying to pull at loose strands, emailing my dad and washing our old grey blanket, lighting candles and pouring wine, wasn't enough. Of course it wasn't. I need to do more than that.

'I want to be braver,' I say quietly. 'The other Erica is different because things didn't go so wrong with her family, and she is—'

'She is *not you*!' Daniel shouts. '*This* is you!' he takes hold of me. '*This*! This hurt and these memories and the pain! The happy times that you remember, and everything that's happened! Whether it's easy or enough or not, it's you, Erica. It's us. Can you really even contemplate a life without Joshua? Where we never had him? Is that honestly what you want?'

I look away from his blazing eyes, down at the carpet. I see the Champagne stain from our first day here and twist out of his grip. The happy times seem even further away than my other life, completely impossible to reach. They hurt me more than the sadness.

'You're right. I know you're right. But I still just wonder ...'

Daniel shakes his head. 'I give up,' he says, and my stomach lurches. I follow him out to the hall, to the smooth expanse of replaced tiles that mattered so much a million lifetimes ago. He stops just before the front door.

'If you don't want to do this with me, and you want to

opt out then that's fine.' Daniel takes the watch from where it sits in its box and stuffs it into his pocket. 'Don't have the watch to keep you here. Just go. See the other world you crave so much.'

'Daniel. Don't go. Don't do this.'

'I'm not doing this,' he says as he stalks out into the hallway and flings open the front door. The frost of the evening seeps into the house. 'You are.'

***

I stand frozen in the hallway for a minute before I take my coat from the hook by the front door and wander out across the road and onto the promenade, Pip curling around my feet and then leaping away, back to the house, as I venture further. I stare out in each vast direction until I see Daniel. He's a dot, moving further away until I can't see him anymore.

He's been taking long walks on the promenade since it happened. Sometimes, at the weekends, he leaves the house in the morning and doesn't return until the winter afternoons have turned black and crisp with cold. I've joined him on only one of his walks. His hands were rammed into his pockets, his face blank, his strides far too fast for me to keep up with. He always used to slow down for me, but now he does not.

I used to pull him back. Now I do not.

I turn, and head for home.

Chapter 41

I thought I'd be taken straight away, but once I am home, I don't become dizzy or nauseous and the world does not tilt and tip me from it. Daniel comes back around an hour later, bringing with him the bleak smell of cold, salted air.

I watch him sighing, making a cup of coffee that he doesn't even touch, tossing his watch on my bedside table as though he couldn't care less what I do with it, tearing off his black jumper and throwing it over the bedpost before crawling under the duvet. I wonder if the other version of me is as different as this version of Daniel. The thoughts tangle together in tight knots.

I reach my hand out and touch his face, which is still cool from his walk.

'I'm just trying to do the right thing,' I tell him.

'Then stay.'

I sigh, and my eyes travel to the copy of *The Shining* that holds our window together. It's been there for so long now that the pages are crisp: they will probably fall out if I try to ever read it again.

'I'm going to buy us a new copy of *The Shining*,' I say.

'Cheaper than new windows,' Daniel answers quietly, his voice grudging.

I shuffle towards him and he pulls me closer, our sighs lost in the groans of the house, the wind, the sea.

***

And so this is how the winter goes.

Daniel and I orbit one another, bumping gently sometimes when we have our better days. He spends long hours at the office to try and gain momentum with the business now that he is a partner. After both John and Daniel made huge investments, the work has slowed down in the past year or so and I can see anxiety as well as grief pull at him. I don't want to make things worse for him, so I always try to be at the house when he returns home. Most of the time, I manage to avoid thinking about the other Erica, about how light I felt when I became the same person as her, and instead remember how long I would be gone for if I did it again. I remember what Daniel has said about this life, and no other, being ours. I try to think what it would be like if I came home to an empty house because he was somewhere I could never, ever find him; if I woke up and his space next to me in bed was cool and empty. I force myself to try to feel how he would feel if he was doing something normal: stirring milk into coffee or turning off the shower and stepping out into a towel, or tying the laces on his shoes, and then he tried to find me and I had disappeared.

I try so hard to channel my thoughts to think only of this, of the negatives of disappearing and seeing a simpler life where we are not blurred by grief, where we might have only hope and the joy of meeting to come. But sometimes, when work on my book has slowed for the day, when Daniel isn't home yet and the black early evening wraps itself around me, dizziness and pain blind me so forcefully that there is sometimes an instant where I just can't fight it. I can't touch something of his or think about how he might feel, because I am already halfway there.

At those times, I follow the other Erica, unseen, out to the cool blue swimming pool behind the cottage; to the Italian markets where she buys bright, shining vegetables; to the old town where she clacks through the cobbled streets. Sometimes I watch her work whole shifts at a tiny crooked cafe that smells of brown sugar and strong Italian coffee. I see her take cash from the owner when the café is closed, and stuff it into her little white apron, watch him wink at her, see the way his eyes linger over her a little too long, and the way she blushes and chooses not to notice, just like I would.

She is me.

She is not me.

In the evenings, Erica and Mike sit outside the cottage with their friends, clinking glasses of wine, eating fat olives and fillets of white fish that they have grilled on the rusting barbeque. I see them kiss and drape their arms around each other as they laugh and share each other's drinks, taking greedy bites from one another's food. They are easy together, their relationship as smooth as the skin of a peach. The scent of charcoal and the smoky flesh of fish and foreign sun clings to me, even when I am back home in the dark dampness of our house.

I feel temptation rising up inside me each time I see her. Sometimes, I reach out, and pull my hand away just as it's about to reach her glowing, sunned skin.

She is me.

She is not me.

Chapter 42

It was my mum's idea to have the party on the day Joshua should have turned one.

'Not a party,' she said to me, her words clipped and cautious. 'A gathering. Something to celebrate him and remember him.'

'I don't know,' I said. 'I'll speak to Daniel.'

But Daniel doesn't know either. And now here we are somehow, the air smelling of sugar and false happiness. The March day is bright and warm, the kind of spring day that makes it feel as though winter never happened. We open the windows in the kitchen and the sounds of the gulls and the sea float through the house on the pleasantly salty air. It reminds me of the air I breathed the day I went into labour, and I take greedy gulps of it, as though it might somehow infuse me with the past, with Joshua again.

'Mummy made this,' Phoebe tells me when she arrives with my brother and Amelia, grinning as she places a huge cake in the shape of a rainbow on the table. 'I helped her choose what shape to do. I said we should have a rainbow because Joshua is in the sky now and so he'll like rainbows. I bet he's seen a lot of rainbows if he lives in the sky. I'd love to see a rainbow. I did think he might like a sunshine too, but I decided that a rainbow would have more colours in it. It's got green in it, and I think green was his favourite colour because he had a green bib, didn't he?'

His green bib with elephants around the edge. I'd bought it one Saturday when we were all in town, and I'd pulled the tags off and put it on him straight away. I wonder what's happened to it. Part of me wants to go upstairs right now and find it. But no. I can't do that because it will pull me under and Phoebe is here and talking to me and I have to stay, to let her pull me forward instead.

I put my arms around Phoebe and try to move her towards me. She is not a cuddly child, and she crooks her head awkwardly under my arm before pulling away. 'Are you still sad, Auntie Erica?' she asks.

I nod, tears burning my eyes. 'I am really sad. I miss Joshua very much.'

She thinks about this. 'Maybe you could look at some photographs of him? Or,' she says, another grin making her face round and sweet, 'maybe I will draw you a picture of him. Daddy brought my colouring things. Then would you be happy?' She looks at me, waiting for a simple yes or no answer.

'Yes,' I say. 'I would love that. It would help a lot.'

She races off towards the hall where her bright purple Disney backpack is. Then she stops and turns around. 'Wait. What colour were his eyes?'

'They were changing colour,' I say slowly. 'They were blue. But I think they were going to turn green, like Uncle Daniel's.'

'Wow,' Phoebe says breathlessly. 'I wish my eyes would change colour. Joshua was very clever to have colour changing eyes.' She thinks for a minute. 'So if I use a bit of blue crayon and a bit of green, will that be right?'

'Yes,' I tell her, fighting the urge to pull her to me again, to kiss her soft skin and smell her scent of soap powder and paint and school. 'Thank you.'

But she has already gone, busily pulling out her pencil case and paper from her bag, and Nicholas is next to me, putting down bowls of crisps and sandwiches on the table.

'Is she behaving?' he asks, looking at me carefully.

'Of course. She's drawing me a picture of Joshua.'

'Ah. I can tell her not to, if ...'

'It's the nicest thing she could have done. She's so special, you know. I still feel awful about that day in the park last year. I shouldn't have lost control with her there. Was she frightened?'

Nicholas thinks for a minute. 'Nah. I don't think so. She's probably forgotten. And she's your family. Even if it did scare her, that's okay. Families are scary. It's good she knows that.'

I laugh as my mum and Daniel join us in the kitchen. 'How are you?' Mum asks me.

'I'm okay,' I say, as Daniel's phone rings.

***

I wonder if I am imagining it at first, because I have rarely seen Daniel cry. He cried on the day Joshua died, but after the first few days his face became grey and frozen, as though someone had locked it. But I am not imagining it – there is a tear sliding slowly down his cheek. He makes no effort to wipe it away, just stares at me.

'It's happened,' he says.

I frown at him. We are alone in the kitchen; Mum and Nicholas have joined Amelia, Phoebe and Daniel's parents in the lounge.

'What has?' I ask, although my body is ahead of me and I already feel a deep ache of worry and sadness in the pit of my stomach.

'John's called in the administrators.'

'How bad is it?' I ask quietly.

He shakes his head. 'The house is safe. But all our money that I invested has gone.' He sits down again and takes my hand in his. 'I'm so sorry, Erica.'

'It's not your fault,' I say firmly. 'It was a risk and we took it together. We'll work it out. I'm speaking to Carl tomorrow to confirm my start date for me to go back to the museum. My year off is over, and my money will go up again soon.' But as I say the words, a wave of sickness rushes through me. The sounds of the sea I had thought were pleasant moments before suddenly feel too close, as though we might be swept away, house and cakes and all.

'We're never going to get anywhere,' he whispers so quietly that I can only just make out the shape of his words. 'With the house, and our money and this ... this pain.' He says pain softly but bangs his fist on the table and squeezes shut his eyes. I watch him, my heart sinking. All this time, I have found his optimism hard to believe. But now that it's gone, it doesn't seem like Daniel any more. The last of him has gone, floating away like a lost balloon so I can't even see it anymore.

'Daniel, you told me we would get through it. I believed you. I still do. You can't go back on it. You have to believe it.'

'Oh, what did I know?' he says, louder now. Phoebe appears at the door of the kitchen, grinning widely, drawing in hand.

'Uncle Daniel,' she says. 'I've done you both a picture. Want to see?'

He turns around and smiles at her, carefully putting a lid back on his emotion. 'Course. Bring it over.'

She hands it to us and we stare down at the drawing of a rounded Joshua with blue-green eyes, a broad red smile and a tuft of bright yellow hair.

'Thank you, Phoebe,' I say. I stand up and march over to the fridge. The stark contrast of what Daniel is going through and Phoebe's eager face and her simple intentions to make us happy, stirs a sense of energy inside me. I have to do something. I have to be the one who somehow thinks everything is going to be okay if he can't do it anymore. I have to be the one to take charge and change things for Daniel because he's at his lowest ebb and I don't feel like he will ever rise up again if I don't try to help him. 'I'm going to put it on here, under one of my favourite magnets.'

'I think that's a good idea. Because then every time you miss him, you can look at it. Auntie Erica, can we have the cake now? Mummy told me not to keep asking you but it just looks so yummy.'

I glance sideways at Daniel. 'We can have the cake,' I tell her. 'Go and get everyone from the lounge.'

I squeeze Daniel's arm as Amelia cuts through the rainbow-coloured cake. We are silent, and the omission of *Happy Birthday* is haunting and difficult. In the end, Daniel stalks over to the radio on the windowsill and turns it up loud. Pop music blares out, as incongruous as the silence.

We chew through the sweet icing, the buttery sponge, and I force myself to swallow it. Daniel doesn't touch his slice, and slides it towards Phoebe, who accepts it with round, excited eyes as though she can't believe her luck. The afternoon wears on. Daniel wanders outside into the garden, and his dad follows him. They sit on the bench under the gnarled apple tree and talk in lowered voices, and I see his dad pat Daniel on the shoulder, gesturing to him that things will work out. Eventually, Amelia packs away Phoebe's things and her cake stand and tin, and my mum covers uneaten sandwiches in cling film.

'We made it through,' I say to Daniel after they've all driven away. The sun is fading now and I shiver.

'Did we?' he asks. 'To what? What's next, Erica?' He is holding a plate, one that he picked up in an attempt to clear away, but then ended up just carrying around as he said goodbye to people. He looks down at it now, frowning as though he doesn't have any idea where it has come from. It's one that we found when we moved in, a delicately patterned china plate from another time, so thin that I can see the outline of his fingers beneath it. I hear our voices, hopeful and happy, the day I pulled it from the depths of one of the kitchen cupboards. We'll find out how old it is. We'll find some to match. We'll keep it forever.

He throws it, and it soars through the air, crashing down into a hundred pieces on the pavement. We'll have to clear that up, I think wearily, the blast of energy from earlier fizzling already. I will have to come out here with a dustpan and brush, and sweep it all away.

But I say nothing; I just put my arm around him, pull him back into the house and close the door gently behind us.

Chapter 43

On the night of Joshua's first birthday, I dream that I am twelve again and that we are in the car on the way to Blackpool. The smell of the toast and eggs that we had for breakfast is sticky, lingering on our hair and clothes. Nicholas is bony and teenaged, his skin smooth and for now unmarked by acne or stubble. He stares at me from his position in the front, craning his neck around awkwardly.

'What?' I say in the end.

'I just can't believe you time travelled.'

Nausea and fright shoots through me and I shake my head. 'I don't know what it was.'

Maybe it was a warning, I think, and maybe I should say more to Mum. Maybe I should make her turn around.

Mum clutches the steering wheel, leaning so far forward she's barely in the same car as us. I try to reach her, to reach the steering wheel and change the direction but it is too far away and no matter how much I stretch myself out, I don't get any nearer.

'Mum?' I say. She is crying. Her tears fall and fall. I hear them drip onto her legs, and then I see that she has Daniel's legs and is wearing Daniel's black jeans. Then she has Daniel's face, and he is crying too, and the passenger seat is empty.

I wake up and gasp for air, my hands still reaching out for the steering wheel that Mum gripped in my dream.

I sit up dizzily and pull the duvet around me. The superficial heat of spring faded at sunset and it's cold now. I stare down at Daniel, oblivious in sleep, the faint trace of a smile on his lips. It will disappear as soon as he wakes. When will be the next time he smiles?

He can't take any more. He has reached the end, the same end that I reached months ago.

***

I need to do more this time.

I should have done something, somehow, to save my parents from such sour disappointment, from walking down the wrong road, all those years ago.

I should have done something to save Joshua's life, to save Daniel and myself from what has happened to us.

But I did neither.

Being strong, putting Phoebe's pictures on the fridge, clearing up shards of broken china, is something. But it isn't enough.

I need to be fearless like the other Erica. Daniel is wrong about her because he hasn't seen her. I need to be more like the version of me I would have been if I hadn't seen my family fall apart, if I'd had my dad supporting everything I did, if I'd kept my friends and not disappeared all the time and not missed half my life when I was young.

I reach over and kiss him lightly on the cheek before stepping softly out of the room.

It happens easily. I am forever ready to escape these days. As soon as I leave the bedroom, I disappear to the other world.

Erica is sitting up in bed, a lopsided lamp giving her a warm glow. She is typing quickly and quietly on a wide silver laptop. The air is balmy and as I glide silently towards her, I smell lemons and a sharp, unpleasant tang of garlic.

Oh, Erica, buy some mints, I think, and then feel strangely guilty. I reach out my hand and it wavers. I see our skin together, hers glowing, mine pale.

I pull it away, doubt simmering inside me. Once I am there, Daniel will be alone. I might be gone for days. Do I really want to leave him for so long? I don't even really know what will happen to the world I've left behind when I become the other Erica. The last time was only a second, but what if this time is much longer? Can I really expect Daniel to just wait for me, for hours and days on end, when I know how much he hates me going?

And then I remember. He is not Daniel now. I could find another Daniel, one who isn't broken, one who smiles and laughs and can keep up with the pace of his own mind. I could make him a reality, and the other one a dream, an alternate reality that was never really lived out.

I have to try to help him. Otherwise, what has all this been for? I can do something. Even if he doesn't think I should, he won't be real soon, will he? I could get the old Daniel back. I *have* to do something this time.

I reach out, close my eyes, and feel the sting of becoming somebody else who is not quite myself.

***

Straight away, I feel the clear absence of grief that has been dragging around my neck and my bones, the pleasant lack of pain that has twisted around my soul too tightly.

The smell of garlic and lemons is gone, my senses immediately used to them.

I lean forward to read what is on the laptop in front of me.

The fearless traveller
by Erica

is spread across the top of the screen on a red banner, and underneath is a blog entry.

They say that sunlight makes you happier.

I've been in Italy for a few months now. Long enough to forget dark mornings when the heating hasn't come on yet and it hurts to stick even one toe out of the duvet. Long enough to forget leaving the house on those beautifully crisp Yorkshire mornings, when the fields have been painted silver-white with frost.

I sit back and stop reading for a minute as a memory comes to me. Our house in Yorkshire. Leaving for work at the travel agent's on winter mornings and scraping a thick layer of ice from the windscreen of an old Fiesta that's mine. My dad coming out and pouring a full kettle of hot water onto the glass, us both watching nervously, waiting to see if it would crack.

I push my hair from my face, the long strands that I'm not used to anymore wrapping themselves around my fingers.

So I have new memories.

The blog continues:

And I can vouch for it. I can definitely say that sunlight and warmth make you feel like more is possible. But that's not to say I'll stay here forever. The next place I go will be cold. Because although sunlight is good for you, a bit of darkness makes you appreciate it more.

You know nothing of darkness, I think fleetingly, but as I do, I feel a strange thud of something that isn't quite sadness, but a kind of longing, a vague unease. I try to pinpoint it, to recognise it. What does she want? It always seemed when I was watching her that she wasn't that homesick, that she was doing what she's always wanted to do. I expected to feel a sense of achievement, a pleasant bloom of satisfaction. Has she just been pretending?

As I stare at the screen, trying to look for answers that I know probably aren't there, a message lights up the phone next to me. I scoop it up, feeling somehow like I am being intrusive. It's your phone, I tell myself. *Yours. Mine.*

There is a passcode, and I enter it instinctively because it's the same as on my phone that I left behind: the year of my birth.

The message is from Mike.

Hey E. I'm heading back.

I'd forgotten that Mike called me E for a brief time when we first met. I can't think now why he stopped, or if maybe I told him not to.

Mike had been staying at the cottage last time I saw this version of my life, but now he doesn't seem to be. I wonder where he is now, and where he's going. I stare at his message for a minute, trying to beckon a memory of where he is and what he's doing. Nothing comes.

Heading back where?

I reply, hoping it's not too obvious that I don't know what he means. Faint guilt, edged with panic, ripples through me again as I think of Daniel in bed at home, waking up to find me gone. Perhaps there, I have already been gone for a few days.

But I'm doing this for both of us, I remind myself. I have to find the other Daniel. Get us together so we can start again.

And then what? What will happen to the other version of him? I squeeze my eyes shut then open them as I hear Mike's reply ping in. And as I read, I feel things fall quietly into place.

UK. Coming?

I reply without even thinking.

Count me in.

After I have replied, I scroll through the photos on the phone, trying to ignore the niggling feeling that I have stolen someone's property. There are a few of me and Nicholas. As I sit and look at the images, vague memories of when they were all taken begin to wash over me, fuzzy and remote as though they were from childhood even though the pictures look recent. Some are of colourful groups of travellers. Most of them are of places: turquoise seas, oriental buildings and vast green fields. The new memories that slot into my mind are bigger and brighter, more adventurous than any of my own, but even as I stare and stare at them, my emotions remain flat.

The final photo is of Mike. He is in a bright white shirt which makes his tan look even darker, his hair blonder. A new string of memories from when I took the photo flashes into my mind: sweet red wine in a tiny cafe, hot pizza in a box, long kisses as we stood on an elaborate bridge. This version of me likes Mike, I realise as something finally stirs inside me when I look at the photo. But there's no love. The feeling seems shallow and slightly unfulfilling, a clear rockpool without ripples or tides.

I think of my own ocean of feelings that I've left behind. I picture my phone, left on my bedside table at home. I have to try hard to recall the photos on there, to replace them in my mind with the ones I've just seen. I think they are mainly of Joshua but my mind won't let me recall specific ones. It will only let me think of the ones I'm looking at now. Anxiety flares inside me, the feelings of the old version of me taking over momentarily those of the new. I suddenly feel like I can't do this.

I take a deep breath, and put the laptop down on the stone floor. I think of Daniel, of my own bed with its warm, crumpled covers; the sound of the gulls screeching as they bounce on the wind outside the window; the scent of coffee and the rainbow cake from the party of my old yesterday; the memory of Phoebe's drawing of Joshua, of *home*. But it does nothing. I shut my eyes and open them again. I am still here. My panic ebbs in a way, somehow becomes detached, like the kind you feel for a character who is being chased in a film. How could I have been so sure that this was the right thing to do?

I look down at the phone again. Could I phone Daniel? Do mobile phones somehow reach alternative worlds? Maybe I could try. But would it be this Daniel, or the new one? Would he know who I am? I frown, staring at the numbers on the keypad, but they are meaningless. His number is lost in the confusion of my mind and I can't remember it.

As I stare at the phone, another text from Mike appears, brightening the screen.

Next week?
No,

I type quickly.

This week.

I jump up from the bed and open the chunky wardrobe door in front of me. A mass of colour greets me: red cardigans and pink dresses and blue skirts. I have never worn colour before; I've only ever worn black. I pull a short magenta dress with spaghetti straps from its hanger and pull it on, staring at the full-length mirror on the wardrobe door. I move closer to look into my own eyes that I know so well, that are exactly the same. Then I step away again and see the subtle differences. I stand taller, and my skin is darker. My hair is longer. My shape is different: curvier in some places from a summer of Italian cheese and wine, flatter in others from the lack of pregnancy. But there is a difference more elusive than any of that. I flatten the dress against my skin, and turn away from the mirror.

I find a suitcase under the bed and throw the tangle of clothes into it. As I do, the phone rings. I grab it and swipe to answer.

'What's the rush?' Mike says. His voice is lazy and slow.

'I just want to get back. There's only so much olive oil I can stomach,' I say, attempting to keep things light. It's the first time I have spoken as this version of myself and I am surprised at how it feels: louder, but without the confident ease I've come to expect.

I close my eyes and slump down on the bed, listening to Mike's voice as he talks about flights and prices and tickets and London. I can hear him tapping away at a keyboard as he speaks. I want to know why he's not living here at this cottage anymore, and where he is. The journey back to the UK with him won't work if it's clear I know nothing about him.

'So do you want to come to me?' he asks. 'Or are you going to meet me at the airport?'

'Airport,' I say, even though I'm not entirely sure which airport I'm near to. 'Will you do me a favour? Will you book my ticket for me? I'll, um, pay you back.' I feel worry pulse through me; I don't even know if I have any money. Surely I will be able to access her bank account, which is now my bank account?

'How come?' Mike wants to know.

'I just have a lot to, uh, do if we go in the next few days, It'd be doing me a huge favour.'

'You're the one who said this week. We could stay a bit longer if it's too much of a rush. I'm easy. And Joel doesn't care when we leave, as long as we're gone by October when the house is being used.'

'I know,' I say, even though I don't know anything. 'Look, don't worry,' I tell him. I pull the bag that's slouching at the end of the bed towards me and empty it onto the duvet next to me. In there is my passport, and a bank card. I exhale. 'I can book it.'

'Nah, don't worry. I might as well do two clicks instead of one. You sure you're okay though? You seem a bit on edge.'

As I flick through the passport, and pull out a tatty makeup bag that contains a lip balm and a cracked powder compact, my head pounds and sudden memories dance around like flames. Mike moving because of a job. Something to do with cars. He's nearer to Rome now. I open the compact, and more new memories wash over me gently. It was a temporary contract that's nearly up.

I snap shut the compact and turn it over. It's the same one I always use, just a shade darker. 'By the time I see you at the airport, I'll be fine.'

'Okay. If you say so. So are you going to stick around in London for a bit too?'

'I don't think so. I think I want to go home.' But as I say this, I remember that my home now is Yorkshire where I watched myself last year, and that Daniel will probably be in Blackpool. Won't he? 'Actually, I'd love to go to Blackpool.'

Mike snorts, 'Yeah right. You'd never survive there.'

'No,' I say slowly. 'Maybe I wouldn't.'

***

I don't speak to Mike much before I see him a few days later in the chaos of the airport. I spend my time wandering from place to place in the Italian cottage: from my bedroom to the terrace, where I watched myself laugh and drink with friends with whom I now live, who share bathrooms and cutlery with me and who I have short bursts of memories about. Joel, who owns the house and plays the guitar at inappropriate times of the night, always makes me have another beer when I probably shouldn't. Sophie is the one with the pink hair, and she always borrows my dresses without asking and then drapes them over my bed when she's finished with them, leaving them smelling of peaches and cigarettes. I wander through the sweet heat of the mornings to the cafe where I work; I remember I have left because Luca, the owner, tried to kiss me when we were alone in the storeroom together a few weeks ago, and keeps messaging me even though I have made it clear I'm not interested in him. I stand outside looking in, and the memories – frayed around the edges and incomplete – become stronger and more colourful. I'm surprised by the way the new recollections make me feel. I thought the colour of this life would be enough to fill my mind and my heart, but when I think about the people I'm surrounded by, I feel strangely empty, as though I am waiting for something more to happen.

***

It continues as we pull our huge cases through the throng of people, as we are herded through customs and we wander around the duty free. The surprise at how unexpectedly dissatisfied I feel softens and shifts its shape into a vague feeling of disbelief that I can't really place and don't understand. New memories rush at me from my childhood and teenage years, covering the old ones like thick grey smoke, fading them forever.

Chapter 44

'So, you've still not told me. What's the rush to get back home? Has something happened?' Mike asks.

I shake my head as we walk past an impressive pyramid of designer handbags. 'No. Nothing like that. I—'

I stop talking as the words that I was going to use desert me. We stop walking. Mike stares at me, waiting. Why am I going back to the UK? I feel like there was a reason, a huge reason that was compelling me to move back, and to visit Blackpool. But why Blackpool? Frustration claws at me, scratching at my senses.

'Did we have plans to go to Blackpool?' I ask Mike, who frowns, as confused as I am.

'You wanted to. But I didn't. We haven't mentioned it since. Have you been into Joel's weed stash? You were being weird like this the other day.'

I carry on walking and shrug, trying to ignore the feeling that I'm missing something huge. 'I don't know,' I admit. 'I think I've just had enough of being away.'

Mike nods, satisfied, which pulls at the end of a loose

thread somewhere else inside me. I feel like I'm wanting more from him, but I don't understand why. 'Fair enough,' he says, picking up a tester bottle of deep blue aftershave and spritzing it into the air before us.

And as I smell it – inky and earthy, a deep male sweetness – I remember it all.

Daniel's face. The feeling when I was with him, that I was with someone who knew me and valued me completely. The pain of losing the most precious thing we ever had. Our house, my job at the museum. The space where Joshua's highchair used to be. Daniel losing his job. Him turning into someone else whose sadness I couldn't bear to see any more because it hurt too much. The desperation to make things different. Why I am here now.

The memories spiral, suffocating me. I take a deep breath, the smell of Daniel infusing everything around me, and I glance at Mike, who is oblivious. I am suddenly hugely irritated by him. He's not the one for me. I need to find Daniel, not spend time with Mike. He is in the way. 'I do want to go to Blackpool,' I tell him, my snappy tone betraying my annoyance with him. 'It doesn't matter if you come with me or not.'

I wonder if he'll be hurt. But his face gives nothing away, if there is even anything to give. 'All right,' he says. 'Cool.'

***

But I can feel it fading again, my old life ebbing away as the new one washes over it. I say the names over and over again, trying to recall Daniel and Joshua's faces every few seconds. But every time I do, their faces are more blurred, their eye colour gone, their scents faded in my mind. When we sit down to have a burger for lunch, I hastily open the notes on my phone to type in the names I have silently recited for the last half an hour so they don't ever disappear completely.

Mike talks to me, about the price of the vodka he bought from Duty Free. 'It's not even that cheap,' he says. 'Probably been ripped off.'

As I look up at him, I remember what he did to me: left me at a party, crying, dumped.

I shake my head. Don't focus on Mike, I warn myself. He carries on, telling me a story about vodka and a morning after a night where he drank a full bottle and couldn't even remember where he lived.

'I had to sleep in the park. Are you listening?' he asks.

'Yeah. Just hang on a minute,' I say. I have to type these names before I forget them again. But before I have started typing, and as Mike resumes his story, they have gone from my memory yet again, as though they were written in sand.

Chapter 45

On the flight, I fall into a heavy sleep. When I wake up, my head is on Mike's shoulder. He is awake, flicking through the in-flight magazine.

'Beer?' he asks, offering me his cup.

I shake my head drowsily. I feel as though I've been drugged. I think through why I'm on a flight. I remember rushing to leave Joel's house in Italy, and I can feel a pull to home, to my parents' house in Yorkshire. But I can't see through the thick confusion to understand why. Italy was fine. There was no reason to take a risk, make a big change, was there? I didn't like working at the cafe, but I was going to try and get a job somewhere else. Money wasn't a massive issue because I have savings and I'd been living rent free at Joel's house for the last few months. He said we could stay until October, when some friends of his parents are going to come and stay at the cottage with their grandchildren. Mike got impatient a few months ago and moved somewhere new because he hates staying in one country for too long. But I'm not like that, am I? I feel a faint anxiety pulse through me. Why can't I remember anything?

'We'll be landing soon,' Mike says, interrupting my thoughts. 'You've slept the whole way.'

'Sorry,' I say, although I don't know why I'm apologising.

He shrugs. 'So what's the plan? Are you really going to do Blackpool? I don't think I want it to be the first place I go. But we can catch up there at some point, maybe. For like, a day.'

'I'm going to go home first,' I tell him. I remember before, when we were in the airport and I brought up his home town of Blackpool without really knowing why. I wonder if Mike thinks I want to go there because I want to meet his family, to make us more serious. I wonder if it *is* because of that. I can't think of any other reason. I visited my grandmother there a few times when I was young, and I know that my mum went to school there but I've never felt a pull to visit before.

If Mike is thinking any of this, he doesn't say it. 'So we can catch up in a few months? Do Blackpool then?' He turns to look at me, and I look into his eyes. They are a murky brown – not a particularly nice colour, I realise guiltily.

'Yes,' I agree. 'A few months.'

***

Mum seems changed, somehow, but I can't put my finger on why. The confusion I felt at the airport, about something I can't even define, follows me like a fog.

'Have you changed your hair or something?' I ask, trying to reach a feeling where I know what's missing, what's different. 'You seem different.' I reach forward and hug her and she hugs me back. She smells the same – of honey shampoo and washing powder.

'Nope. It's probably you. Maybe you're seeing things through new eyes after all your adventures,' she says, smiling as she puts on the kettle. We sit down at the table, and I stare down at it, at the place where I once scratched my initials as a child.

'So, tell me everything. What's the latest with Mike?'

I think of Mike, his natural charm and bold laugh. The casual way he kissed me briefly on the lips when we left for different trains after we landed in London. 'I don't really know. He's nice. We have a laugh, and get on well. But he's in London now. He has issues with the north,' I tell her, and she smiles. 'We'll see each other again soon though. I want to go to Blackpool for a few days at some point, and that's where his family's from so we might meet up.' My words are casual, but I feel underneath them the sting of my usual unease that I am taking the easy option with Mike. I know he encourages me to avoid commitment, falling into a comfortable love that trudges along the same track for so long that the road becomes rutted, impossible to deviate from. I never thought I wanted that, but spending time with Mike sometimes leaves me feeling a bit lacking, and it makes me wonder if the bits I'm trying to skip out of my life are somehow more important than I always gave them credit for.

'It's small world,' Mum says, interrupting my thoughts. 'You might have even seen Mike around when we went to visit Grandma in Blackpool when you were small.'

'Well, even if we did see each other years before we met, I don't think it means anything. I definitely don't think we're soulmates.'

Mum looks at me sharply. 'Since when have you ever wanted a soulmate?'

I frown at her. 'I don't. I just wonder sometimes if I should push for something a bit more,' I admit.

'I think you know the answer to that, Erica. You've spouted since you first were old enough to form an opinion that you don't ever want to end up boring and married like me and your dad.' Mum stands up and clanks about making the tea. 'You even said yourself before you went off travelling that we had made you realize everything you didn't want. That's obviously what you see in Mike. He's big on travelling about and having fun, isn't he? Things will never get serious and boring with him. You won't end up old miseries like us. Grab the biscuits, will you?'

I think about this as I go to the cupboard where the biscuits are. Maybe she's right. Maybe pushing for more will end in having less: a soulless house, a man I don't particularly like after all, messy children who take up all my time and money and a battered old table with secrets scrawls carved into the wood. I don't want that. I've never wanted that. Mike is enough, I tell myself firmly.

'Erica? The biscuits,' Mum says, breaking into my thoughts. 'They're not in there. You haven't been away for so long that you've forgotten the most important cupboard in the house, surely?'

I stare into the cupboard I've just opened. I could have sworn it would contain a tin of chocolate biscuits. But a bread bin and cereal are in there. I swing round.

'You moved things round.'

Mum shakes her head. 'Nope. Not since the nineties,' she laughs. She narrows her eyes at me. 'Are you sure you're okay? You seem a bit ... off.'

'I'm fine,' I say. 'Mike said the same. But it's probably just the flight.'

'I hope your room's as you remember it. I've used it as a bit of a dumping ground for my washing but I've cleared it all away since you said you were coming home. Not that you gave us much notice.'

'I know,' I say, taking a chocolate digestive from her. 'I think I'd just had enough of being away.'

I think. But I don't know for sure.

***

My bedroom is as I left it, which, after knowing I'm not behaving quite normally for some reason, is a relief. Photographs line the walls, their edges curling, and the ones near the window are yellowing after too much sunlight. Me and Nicholas, me at my graduation, with my backpack on our drive the first time I went travelling with Claire, my friend from school, who got married and then had a little boy a few years after we returned.

I sit on my bed, then take out my phone and type a message to Claire.

Back in the village. Meet up soon?

She replies straight away.

Definitely! Freddie can't wait to see his fave auntie.

I grin. I saw Claire just before I left for Italy and I speak to her about once a week. But it suddenly feels as though I haven't spoken to her in years.

An image from Claire flashes up on my phone then: her little boy, Freddie, in his highchair, his chubby face stained orange with spaghetti sauce.

And there is a flash, a tiny chink of light in the darkness of the strange confusion I've felt over the last few days. But it's gone before I can reach out to touch it and pull myself towards it.

Chapter 46

The days at home stretch on. I catch up with Claire and some other friends at the village pub that I know so well from spending so many of my evenings there when I was younger. I wander around the cobbled streets and over the fields that are soft with the approaching summer. I write my blog and look online for jobs. I speak to Mike every now and then. There's no pattern: sometimes we will talk for an hour, other times days will go by without us getting in touch at all.

'How's London?' I ask him one day when I sit at the kitchen table chatting to him on the phone.

'It's cool. Costs a fortune though. Wish Joel had a house here too that we could stay in rent-free,' he says and we laugh.

'Speaking of Joel, he's asked me to get in touch with you. He emailed you but it bounced back.'

I frown. 'My email should be working fine.'

'He said it didn't exist. It wasn't recognised.'

I try to shake off the uncomfortable feeling that descends

on me. Emails crash all the time. 'Must be a glitch,' I say. 'What did he want?'

'Well, some uncle has died and left him a fortune. He's even richer than he was. He's thinking of buying a hotel that's being built in Sydney, and he emailed us all the plans. Says we could all work there and have food and board for free. We'd earn a packet. It's right near the Opera House.'

'Wow. Sometimes I can't believe our luck that we met Joel,' I say. 'Are you going to do it?'

'Well, like you just said, it's pretty lucky. The chance of a lifetime, I suppose. Who could afford rent there? Plus we'd be earning too. So yeah, probably for a bit. Not forever, obviously.'

'What do you think you'll do until it's built?'

'I don't know. I'm checking out jobs here. There's one in a bank I might go for.'

'You in a bank? In a suit?'

'Yeah,' he says defensively. 'Just to earn some money. It's a decent wage. Worth going for it.'

'Wow. I never thought you'd get a serious job like that.'

'It won't be that serious. Not when I'm there to mix things up. What about you? Still got a random urge to go to Blackpool?'

I think. The longing I remember from a few weeks ago has faded, and I wonder again why I ever had it. 'I don't know. If you're heading there, then let me know. Maybe I'll tag along.'

'Yeah. I'll let you know. Depends what happens with this job.'

'Tag along where? What's next for you?' asks Dad when I hang up. He's making bacon sandwiches, buttering bread and slathering on brown sauce. 'Want one?'

I shake my head. 'No thanks. I'm heading out to see Claire soon. It was Blackpool I was talking about with Mike. His family live there and we said we might meet up. I don't know if it'll happen though.'

'Ah, Blackpool. You should go. It's very romantic there, you know.'

'Really?' I raise an eyebrow. 'I can't really remember it. But Mike says it's not somewhere I'd want to be blogging about. He doesn't like the idea of going back. He hasn't even told his mum he's back in the UK yet because he knows she'll want him home and he can't bear the thought.'

'He knows nothing. It's a special place. I was in Blackpool when I decided to try and win over your mum.'

'Really?' I smile. I always struggle to imagine what my parents were like when they first met. It's so hard to imagine a world other than the one you know.

'Yep. I was living in London then. But Grandma had had one of her falls, so I came back for a few days. There was a bonfire party I went to whilst I was up there – a load of old school mates. I only went because some woman was ill and I heard that your mum was taking her place. I had a bit of a thing for her,' he says, and I look for a twinge of nostalgia, but there's nothing. All his attention is on carving the sandwich into two halves, leaving a smear of sauce and grease on the worktop that he won't clear up, that Mum will roll her eyes at and mutter something about later. 'Anyway, after that party, the rest as they say, was history. I went back to London but it wasn't long before your mum joined me there and then before we knew it, we were married and moving here to settle down.' He settles himself down at the table and takes a huge bite of sandwich. 'I'm glad you're getting to travel about a bit, anyway,' he says between mouthfuls.

I narrow my eyes at him. 'Yeah, yeah. I know. But have you never thought you could have gone anyway? That maybe you could have had all the adventures you wanted with Mum?'

'Nah. Doesn't work like that once you have a house and a job and kids come along,' he says, just like I thought he would. 'You can't just give up all that safety. I know I say a lot that I wish I'd got to travel. But you should know that I wanted to be here with your mum, and I wanted to have you and Nicholas. I'm just glad you got to go off and have a bit of adventure, face your fears. That's all I'm saying. It's a long life doing the same old thing every day,' he says as he stands up, brushing pale crumbs from his chest.

'Oh, I sometimes wonder if I really am facing my fears.'

'Course you are,' my dad tells me without missing a beat. 'You're having a blast, seeing the world. Don't let anyone change that. And don't let anyone take your freedom.'

'No chance of that with Mike. He's freedom-obsessed,' I tell him, and we both laugh.

***

It's later that day that I find the book.

I am sitting on the pale pink carpet of my bedroom looking through some boxes of books for a travel guide for France that Dad mentioned he had but as soon as I find the book, the idea of travelling falls gently from my mind, like a dying leaf from a tree.

My fingers brush against the spine, and I immediately feel strangely tense, as though I have somewhere else to be. I've already met Claire for our rushed coffee that was cut even shorter when Freddie spilt his juice over himself and her and she had to leave to get them both changed. I have no other friends here, no plans to be late for. So why do I feel the anxiety that I am missing something, letting someone down?

I pull the book from the box and stare at it, trying to think why touching it has made me feel so strange. It's an old copy of *The Shining* that I bought when I was too young to read it. I remember hiding it from my mum and reading it under the covers of my bed with a torch. I haven't read it for years. It never scared me. Horror stories never do. I love them. So why is it making my heart race?

I turn the pages slowly. As I do the flutter of a trapped memory stirs and rises. This book, in a different house, a house that is my home. A broken window frame. Someone

I love flicking through the yellowing pages, grinning at me. Telling me I'm fearless. And then, in a flash, it all comes to me.

Daniel.

I gasp and the book falls from my hands as the floor disappears beneath me.

Chapter 47

It hits me immediately: the heaviness of the sorrow, the exhaustion of sadness pulling at me as soon as I am back.

I am sitting on the landing of our house. I stand up, my body tight with pain. I feel as though I'm going to be sick.

'Daniel?' I croak, my voice barely a whisper.

I hear a sound downstairs. He's here. I almost fall over myself, my legs clumsy and tangled as I make my way to him. 'How long have I been gone?' I ask, my voice still weak.

He spins around from his place at the kitchen table and rushes towards me, knocking over his chair in the process The colour of his skin shocks me. I am used to Mike, to my friends in Italy and back in Yorkshire, happiness and ease of life making their skin bright.

His hug is so tight I can barely breathe but it still isn't close enough. The scent of him makes sharp tears sting my eyes and I pull him even closer, my fingers sinking into the wool of his grey cardigan. I didn't know he had a cardigan; I'd forgotten that about him – his clothes and how he looked and smelt and sounded, and now here he is, the knit of the wool fine and smooth and warm against the skin of my fingers.

'I'm so sorry,' I say, my words squashed against him. I rest my cheek on his shoulder, feeling my torrent of tears soaking into his cardigan. 'How long?' I ask him again.

He pulls back reluctantly. 'So long, Erica. I didn't know if I would ever see you again.' His face is still bloodless, shock making his features stark and unfamiliar. He presses kisses on my forehead, on the tip of my nose and my collarbone. 'I can't believe you're back.'

'How long is ages?' I ask him. My stomach still swirls and my limbs ache. I want to collapse, to curl on the floor but I can't let go of him. He gestures to the tree outside. When I left, the pale pink buds were just beginning to sprout from the branches. Now, the blossoms are brown on the grass beneath, replaced by rich green leaves.

'Months, Erica. It's summer now.'

'It wasn't months where I was,' I say after a pause. 'And I didn't know how to get back to you.'

A storm passes over Daniel's features and he pulls back. 'Well then, you shouldn't have gone. You know, people have been suspicious about where you've been. I had to tell them something so they didn't report you as missing. I said you'd gone on holiday, a retreat. To recover.'

'It wasn't that far from the truth. They didn't believe you?'

'Your Mum and Nicholas helped to get people on board with the story. They obviously knew where you were. But I don't care about that, really,' he says, waving a thin arm. Has he lost weight? Or was he always this thin? He looks taller but he can't have grown. 'I care about the fact that you're back. It's over, isn't it? You disappearing? It has to be over now.'

I swallow and look away into the garden that's rich with green leaves. It suddenly seems so long ago since I saw it.

'Erica? You can't be serious. You can't be refusing to say you will avoid this at all costs from now on? You know how to stop it!' he says, the volume of his voice climbing.

'I was trying to make things better,' I say.

'By running from me? From Joshua?'

The name slices through my heart so quickly I don't notice it at first, but then the agony comes all at once, gushing through me in ugly bright rivets and I have to stumble over to the table and sit down next to Daniel's discarded chair that lies on the floor

'I wasn't running from you,' I tell him after a few minutes. 'I was running *to* you. To the you that you should be.'

'You can't just erase the pain, you know. If you erase the pain, you erase Joshua. Everything.'

I bite my lip, thinking of how my memories were washed away so easily. 'I know.'

'And say you do find the other me, which you probably won't, and we end up together in this parallel universe.

When does it end? When would you stop trying to find perfection? Who's to say nothing terrible will happen again, that this other Daniel won't end up on his own while you run from it all again?'

'I won't,' I say simply. Memories are slipping softly away, but I know this.

'How do you know that? You said you weren't there for that long.'

We stare at each other like cats fighting out territory. I sigh. 'Look, I know I'm not making any sense to you. I'm not making much sense to myself,' I admit. I stand up weakly and move towards him so I can put my arms around him again and breathe him in.

'Carl called, you know. Several times. And then he stopped. You'll have to get in touch with him.'

Carl? I think hard, my brain aching dully with the effort. Who is Carl? Daniel waits for me to answer, and I can't bring myself to tell him that I don't remember everything about this life yet, that I am balancing between two worlds, so intent on not falling that I can't focus on much else. If I tell him how precarious my grasp on this reality is he will be even more frustrated by my need to do this.

'Carl? From the cafe?' I venture, but I know it's the wrong answer because I can see the cafe in my mind now, dappled in shots of hot foreign sun. It's not here. It was there.

'Cafe?' Daniel frowns. 'No. The museum. Your job. He was expecting you to be in touch with a return date. It's all been waiting for you, Erica. But I have a horrible feeling that you'll be too late.'

***

I take my phone from Daniel and stare down at the messages that fly onto the screen. So many messages: from Zoe and Amelia, from Katie and Carl and the agent who asked me to send her a full draft of my Blackpool book. I ignore them, and open up the photos. A memory as blurred as a dream floats through my head, of looking at the photos on the other Erica's phone and not being able to recall these ones. Now, I can't remember hers.

'Ring him, Erica. Aside from the fact we're completely broke, you need to remember how much you loved it there.'

I flick through the numbers and my finger eventually hovers over Carl's. What does he look like? Did I like working with him? I glance at Daniel with an urge to ask him about everything I am missing from my mind. But his drawn face, the tension of weeks, months, of not knowing if I will ever come back pulls his features down and it makes me silent. I press call.

As soon as I hear Carl's voice it all comes back to me anyway. His slim-fit suits and loud ties, his brash voice and incongruity with the museum and what it used to be when Katie worked there. It could have been me, I remember. I could have had Carl's job if I hadn't disappeared on the day of the interview. The need to stay that I used to have washes over me. I don't have that now. And the other Erica has never experienced anything like that. I'm sure of it. She has no memories, as far as I can recall now I'm back, of going to other worlds. She never missed opportunities for change. Quite the opposite: she's the kind of person who has chances to try new things springing up like flowers in front of her as she moves through life.

She has a chance, I remember, at working for her friend in a hotel. Where? China, maybe? Or Australia? Somewhere I would never go in this life.

Chance of a lifetime, I remember someone saying.

'Erica?' Carl is saying, his voice reverberating in my ear. 'Are you there?'

Daniel prods me gently. 'Yes,' I say. 'I'm here.'

***

Carl, it turns out, is leaving the museum following an offer of a sales job for, he tells me cheerfully, double the salary.

'I'm glad you've had some time away,' he says awkwardly. 'I do understand how difficult it's been for you, and I don't blame you for needing the break. But I'm also glad you're back. We advertised your post eventually, when we heard nothing from you but there was nobody suitable so we didn't appoint. I leave next week and we really need someone who knows how things work to start as soon as possible. It's only part-time hours I'm afraid. The funding situation is a little precarious, and we still have reduced opening hours.'

'That's fine,' I tell him. The memory of my desk floats

into my mind, although I can't quite recall where the museum is in the town. Panic flares inside me. I have to take this job; I have to be able to do it. My paltry maternity pay came to an end months ago. And although Daniel's freelance work is slowly building up, his income is nowhere near what it was before his investment in Palms Architecture used up all our savings. But if I want to go back to the other world, to try to fill the urge to make things right so that we can live our best kind of life together, then what will happen to the museum? I glance at Daniel, who watches me tensely as I speak to Carl. If I take the job, and then disappear again for months on end, Daniel will never forgive me.

If I go again, I can't ever come back.

Chapter 48

7th September 2017

I am faced with a choice.

Every single day, I have to choose.

It is my birthday.

I stand at the kitchen window and stare out at the wilderness of our garden. The leathery leaves twist and thrash against one another. Some of them are already edged with the gold of autumn. The wind is cold even though it's only September. It screams through the gap between the glass and the battered wooden pane and I sigh and flick on the radio beside me.

The museum is shut today. I've enjoyed being back there for the last few months, although it's strange without Katie. Even William has gone. There is another volunteer now called Sheila, who eyes me constantly like a hungry cat. 'She's a pain in the neck,' Carl told me before he left. But I am thankful for her gaze. I need someone to pin me here. I am thankful too that the job is intact in my mind again.

I have even finally pulled out the notes from my book and emailed the agent who asked for a full draft last year, to see if she will still accept it.

Memories of the other life, of the tilts of Mike's voice and the smoky smell of his breath, the cool tiles beneath my bare feet in the cottage, the ripe warmth of the Italian spring, the strange familiarity of the house in Yorkshire, mostly fade into dark corners of my mind like forgotten dreams.

But the shimmer of hope, the promise of making things right, never leaves me.

Sometimes I go to the shop and buy flowers, and put them in a vase on the table. Other times, Daniel will cook us dinner and pour us glasses of dry, dark wine. We always toast to the future, to building something new. We have been back to the coffee shop, bracing ourselves against the smiling baristas and normalcy of other couples and the inevitable sting of highchairs. We have cleared Joshua's things from his room and put them in the loft. We have painted some walls, put up pictures to hide the cracked plaster beneath.

We manage to function, to breathe, to put one foot in front of the other.

But the house is falling down around our ears.

The flowers wilt.

The wine is left untouched.

And the arguments. They are never ending, looping around and around in tiresome knots.

The tension from today's is still here in the room, hanging above me like a shimmering heat.

'Maybe I will find you a Birmingham magnet,' Daniel said this morning, and to begin with there was such little tension between us that things could almost have been normal. He was eating a bowl of cereal, his spoon clanking merrily against the bowl. He smelt of his old aftershave that he'd not worn for a while, and had on a grey shirt I hadn't seen him in for years. He was going to Birmingham to meet a potential client, so we were up earlier than usual.

I looked across at him and smiled. 'I would love that.'

'Are you going to go to your mum's?'

I shook my head. 'No. I'm going to try and get on with the book.'

'But it's your birthday.'

'I know.'

I saw panic flash across his eyes. 'You're going to be alone all day?'

'Yes.'

He chewed and swallowed. 'Erica, I know temptation might get the better of you, but you'd never do it again, would you? Become her and live that life?'

I hesitated for a moment too long. His face fell.

'Are you kidding me? When you know you might never be able to get back? When you know I might be on my own for months on end, waiting?'

'If I found you, I think it would be the last time. I think it would change things,' I said, even though I wasn't completely sure *what* would happen if I found the other version of him. I just knew that I wanted to be honest with him about the urge I still had to try.

'Okay. Best case scenario. This wonderful other version of you that you think is so much better for me, finds the other version of me. What happens to all of this?' he motioned around the kitchen with his spoon, and all I could see was the gut-wrenching corner of the table where Joshua's yellow highchair used to be, the bowing window that never did get replaced, the soft black mould that climbed up the wall like ivy. But he obviously saw something different, something he would miss if it were gone.

'I think that the worlds would eventually merge somehow, and that you'd do what I did when I went. You'd slip into another version of yourself and feel strange and a bit confused for a day or so, and you'd put it down to tiredness because you wouldn't know what I know. And then after a day or two, you wouldn't know any different.'

'And you think that's okay?'

'Yes. I do.'

He banged his cereal bowl down on the table. 'I can't believe this, Erica! You said yourself that you forgot everything when you were in the other life. So how would you even know to find me? It's such a huge risk!'

'I'd write it all down.'

'You couldn't. You said nothing stayed with you. How would you take a piece of paper with you?'

'I'd do it as soon as I got there this time. Before I forgot everything.'

'But you might forget instantly next time. Don't be fooled into thinking you have it all worked out, Erica. This is a dangerous game. Way too dangerous for you to even think about.'

'I never said I had it all worked out,' I said, tension entering my words, clipping them into sharp sounds. 'I just can't help being tempted by a life where we might be happier, better versions of ourselves.' I've said it over and over and over again, but still he didn't hear me.

'But why would we be better? Because we wouldn't have lost Joshua?'

'Yes. Partly. Is that so hard to see? I have a chance to take away this pain for you, and it's so hard to just ignore it.' He was silent, so I carried on, desperate to persuade him. 'You would be given a fresh start! And then you'd meet a better version of me who wouldn't disappear and have weird issues with happiness and falling in love—'

'Of course you'd have issues! You've said yourself, you end up with Mike! Mike of all people! Mr Commitment-phobe who didn't understand the first thing about you! Can you even hear yourself?'

'I won't end up with Mike. I'm just with him now! But I'll change it. I'll deal with it.' Somewhere in all of this, I'd stopped saying *Erica* and I'd started saying *I*. We were blurring into one.

'You know what I think?' Daniel said as he shrugged

his coat on. 'I think this fearless version of yourself sounds like the most frightened version of you there could be. She's risking nothing. *That's* why she's so fearless. She has absolutely nothing to lose.'

I lowered my gaze as Daniel's words made the other version of me suddenly come to life in my mind: the feeling of something lacking, of wanting more than Mike gave me but knowing that to look for more would be to risk too much. 'You're right,' I admitted quietly. Daniel looked up and the frustration that had built up between us softened as our eyes met.

'The other me has this thing,' I said cautiously, 'about marriage. When I'm there, I want to avoid it. So I suppose I do have issues in that life too after all.'

Daniel raised his eyebrows, and I felt an echo of the past when I first told him about my disappearances and he was fascinated and interested. 'So she's not that different, then?'

'Maybe not.' Images flickered, dancing in my mind. 'I'd forgotten. But now you've made me remember that when I saw my parents, it was obvious that they weren't actually as happy as I thought they were.' I frowned as the truth about the other life shifted and changed its shape. 'I always thought they were happier, that their marriage would have changed me for the better, and that not having my disappearances would somehow wipe out all the things I'm afraid of. But really, it isn't that simple.'

Daniel stepped towards me and took my hands in his, hope brightening his face. 'So what are you saying?'

I shook my head, confused. 'You're right. I'm not that different after all. I have the same fears in that life that I've had in this one. And my parents were the ones who made the other version of me want to travel, to not get bogged down with marriage and commitment. But I don't think the life that people are pushing me to have when I'm there is one I'm particularly happy or excited about.'

Daniel cleared his throat. 'So all this time, you've thought the grass was always greener. But that's not really how things are. And it doesn't sound like you could have done much to change your parents' happiness either. You've felt guilty for so long about that. It must be kind of good to know that things weren't as they seemed.' Daniel stepped closer, let my hands go and cupped my face, kissing me gently on the lips. I closed my eyes and let the rare feeling of connecting with Daniel again wash over me.

If I'd left it there, we could have started to piece things back together. If I'd stopped talking at that moment, then his face would have stayed hopeful and calm. He wouldn't have stepped away from me. We'd have put back together a piece of our jumbled jigsaw.

But as soon as I began to rethink my plan, a need to solve the colossal problem of Daniel's pain sprang back up inside me. My happiness as the other Erica, my parents and how things never could have changed for them, was irrelevant. We'd been here time and time again, where hope was an illusion that vanished if we tried to reach out and hold onto it. The hope he had now was no different.

'Mike makes it too easy to coast along in the other life. He doesn't make me *want* to take risks,' I began slowly. Daniel nodded again and kissed me briefly on the lips. He thought we were finally on the same page, that I was going to let it go after all this time. I closed my eyes for a second before I spoke again, savouring the glossy bubble around us that I was about to burst into nothing.

'Maybe my parents were beyond saving. I can accept that about them. But I can't accept it about us, Daniel, about you. I can see now more than ever that if things ended with Mike, and I met you instead like I did in this life, but at a different time in a different circumstance, then it would become clear to me, just like it did in this life, that some things are worth risking. If I could meet you in that world, I'd change. We'd be together and we could start all over again. Things would be better for you. Your life would be so different.' The bubble popped, and Daniel stepped away from me, sighing.

I'd heard him sigh a million times this year: sharp, sad, exhausted sighs all day long. 'This is not what we're meant to be doing, Erica.'

He didn't elaborate and I didn't ask him to. Because there could be no elaboration that would make sense. What *were* we meant to be doing? What were you meant to do when the thing that was at the centre of your orbit had gone?

There were more words to come. So many that I had said a hundred times before.

Don't you wonder if I'd somehow done things differently with Joshua or been another version of myself, or not gone to the party where we met or agreed to go out with you, or maybe not even gone to get my hair cut that day when our hearts broke into a million pieces, you wouldn't be this person now who struggles with every breath? Don't you want me to try to change all the moments that led to this one, where we are lost and sad and broken? Don't you want me to try and fix it? Wouldn't you do it if you could?

But he had stopped listening to me so I didn't say any of them. They floated around the room with us like tiny ghosts. 'You have to choose,' he said. He took his glasses off for a moment, and rubbed his eyes. 'I'm not begging you to stay anymore, Erica. I've had enough. I love you way too much to spend my life wondering if you're going to disappear, or wondering if I'll be waiting for hours or months for you, or if you want to tackle this with me. What I do want is to take you out for your birthday tonight, to stick at this life. Together. Be at Luigi's at eight,' he sighed. 'Or don't come back at all.'

***

And so I can't go, can I? Because I'd like to think that what I told him was right, and that if I changed things for us, then Daniel's world would soften and ripen around him, the colours changing from the black and grey of winter to the pastels of spring, the vibrancy of summer. I'd like to think he would somehow be so much better off, that his grieving and anger would dissolve into nothing. But I can't be sure unless I go, and it happens. And then it will be too late.

***

And so I changed my plans so that I wouldn't be alone. I haven't worked on my book. I have surrounded myself with Daniel's belongings, with people in cafes and supermarkets. I have seen Zoe for lunch, and Mum has been round with cake and bunting and flowers in an attempt to bring some colour into this world. But now, it's 7pm. There's an hour to go until I am meant to meet Daniel and I am flagging.

I close my eyes, and feel the other life calling me, promising me answers and a way out. I picture Daniel in Luigi's later, waiting for me. We haven't been in a long time, but I know where he'll sit: at the third table on the right, next to the wall with the picture of Charlie Chaplin above him. He'll face the door. He will sit fiddling with the cutlery, his jaw set with tension. If I don't arrive, he will put his head in his hands, tufts of his hair escaping through his fingers. He will sigh, and stand, nodding a goodbye to the staff, explaining nothing.

And after that I don't know what he'll do or what will happen, because I cannot imagine a life without him, a life where he hasn't met me yet and hasn't turned grey with sadness. But maybe that's the whole problem. Maybe we are together too much and our shared pain has started to weather us both like the sea has weathered our house: splintering us, cracking the beautiful strength that we started out with.

***

My vision blurs and my head spins. I'm too dizzy to stand without leaning against something for support. It's gone beyond temptation and reasoning now; it's all instinct.

Fight or flight.

It has always been this day when it's too difficult to stay. There are so many reasons why. It's my birthday; the day I moved to Blackpool; the day I started to fall in love with Daniel; the day we got our house. It's clear to me that this is the one day where I'm not strong enough to stop it. I never have been.

It's a dangerous game. I know that. Of course I do.

But really, what can be so dangerous when the worst has already happened?

How can you fall if you are already in a heap on the ground?

How can you be dragged down by a wave if you are already at the bottom of the sea?

Chapter 49

I fall hard through time and space. My body jars, my head pounds.

And then I am watching myself. I sit on the bed in Yorkshire, reading a text message from Mike.

Going to Blackpool tomorrow. Coming?

I reach my fingers out. It's barely touching, the very edges of my fingertips to the very edges of her hair. But it's enough.

Chapter 50

'I'm not a massive fan of going back,' Mike says as he casually speeds onto the motorway. 'But my mum's been nagging me to go and see her; you said you wanted to go a couple of times, and I thought this party might be cool. Kev and Sophie always used to be pretty fun. The last time I saw them was at their engagement party, actually. Years ago, now. Same house. Can you believe they've lived in the same place all this time?' he snorts in faint disgust.

I shuffle in my seat and turn my eyes away from the window. I'm dizzy today, my head heavy. Maybe I had too much red wine with Mum and Dad last night. It's the day after my birthday, although Mike hasn't mentioned it. Maybe he's forgotten. He's not the type to remember dates.

'Anyway,' he carries on, 'So tonight's the party and I've said we'll crash there. Always used to. These parties were legendary when I used to live here. I never made it home. So tomorrow we'll find breakfast somewhere to help us recover then I suppose we'll call at Mum's. She's got a spare room so we'll stay there for a night then head back. We can do all the tourist stuff from hers. Then we're off. I'm not staying for more than a day or so.'

I nod, unable to say much because of the pain in my head. I felt strange last night too, and went to bed early, ignoring protests from my dad that he wanted to talk more about Thailand and where I might go if I return.

I've never had migraines before but this is what I imagine one to be like, all flashing lights and consuming pain.

***

I feel slightly better by the time we arrive at Mike's friends' house. The semi, with its square, bright rooms that are all open plan and its narrow staircase, is vaguely familiar to me. The party isn't like the one Mike was expecting and I can tell from his face that he's disappointed in how his friends have changed since he was last here. Neighbours and friends – all couples – of the people that Mike knows sit around and chat about mortgage rates and supermarkets and potty training. A baby crawls around the centre of the room, stopping every now and then to pull out the contents of someone's handbag or beam up at us all with a wet, gummy smile.

I feel Mike's eyes on me for most of it, see him do a terrible job of stifling his yawns. He tries to liven things up with his anecdotes from our travelling, to make people laugh with our stories of drunkenness and friends and other cultures we didn't understand. They laugh quietly, politely, exchange looks as though they're all thinking the same thing – that he hasn't changed a bit and really should have done by now.

'This,' he whispers when we both escape to bring our bags in from his car, 'is exactly where I never want to be. They used to be so much fun. And now look at them all!'

I nod as he feigns falling asleep and then smacks his forehead in frustration. 'I know. How boring,' I say, because that is what I've always thought, but somehow my words seem empty. Mike waits, because this is what we do: we are brought together by a delight in congratulating ourselves on skipping out all the things that make other people's lives so tedious. But the idea that all those things are life, rather than something to be avoided, jars in my mind and I don't want join in with him.

I look back up at the house. 'Come on,' I say, and I can sense that he's irritated by me because I haven't fully backed him up. 'Let's go back in.'

But when we get back, the conversation has remained firmly about interest rates and home improvements.

'Have you not found anywhere you want to settle yet, Mike?' someone asks him, and suddenly all eyes are on us, although not in the esteeming way he was hoping for.

He picks at the label on his beer bottle. 'Nope,' he says. I wait, as does everyone else, for him to elaborate, but he says nothing more.

These are your friends, I think. *Why can't you be nicer to them? Why am I here with you?*

'He just loves new places,' I say in an attempt to soften

Mike's brusqueness. They already know this but I can see they are grateful for me at least being friendly.

'And what about you, Erica? Do you think you'll put down roots somewhere soon?'

'Oh, I already have,' I tell them, the words flowing smoothly from my lips before I've even thought about them. 'I have a house in Blackpool.'

They stare at me and I stare back, wondering what I've said that's so wrong.

'Oh,' Sophie says, picking up her baby and plopping him onto her knee, where he becomes puce with anger and starts whimpering in protest. He makes me unsettled for some reason. I look away from him. 'Here in Blackpool? Mike said you hadn't been here since you were a child?'

'She hasn't,' Mike tells them, then looks at me, puzzled. 'Think she's had too much wine.'

I take a deep breath. I have no idea why I said I have a house in Blackpool when I haven't even been here for about twenty years, or why I'm filled with a sudden intense longing for something I can't identify. People stare at me, waiting for me to explain. Mike's eyes bore into me. *You're being weird,* I can almost hear him think. 'I didn't finish what I was saying,' I begin. 'I just meant, I have a house that I *like* in Blackpool. I saw it online. Of course I didn't buy one here, or anywhere else. I've been in Italy.' To me, my words sound transparent, as though I am saying revision notes out loud in an attempt to learn something.

But it seems to be enough. 'Oh,' Sophie says, 'I thought you were leading a double life for a moment there,' she grins, before gently putting her baby back on the floor.

***

After what seems like a lifetime, the party ends and we are released to a room upstairs.

'It's a bit of a mess in here,' Sophie says as she turns on the light. 'Our lodger, Em, moved out two years ago but we've still not got around to decorating.'

'That's okay,' I say as I stare around at the purple walls, the purple bed.

Mike gets in next to me, and tugs at my pyjamas. I turn around, my back to him.

'What's your problem?' he whispers, trying to plant kisses on the nape of my neck. 'Let's make at least something about tonight fun.'

I sit up, ignoring Mike's grumbles.

'Do you really think we should be together?' I ask him.

I see his silhouette shrug in the darkness. 'It's a bit late for this kind of chat, isn't it?'

My mind is so foggy that I stand up and press my knuckles to my forehead. 'No. I don't think it's too late.' I sit back down on the edge of the bed. How am I suddenly so certain about this? I was looking forward to spending time with Mike, wasn't I? I know I've had a few doubts lately, thinking I might be taking the easy road by staying with Mike for now, and I know I've had times where I've felt discontent and lonely. But I've never felt this strongly that I shouldn't be with him before. Am I mad with him because he was rude to his friends? If that's the reason, why is it not clear to me? The ache of disorientation is dull, almost painful. 'I think I should find a hotel tomorrow instead of meeting your parents.'

He doesn't answer, just pulls the covers over him. The bed, this room, the whole house, they all stir something inside me. It's like the first rustle of a storm, when the air is yellow and you feel the weight of the black sky, but you can't feel any rain or hear any thunder. There is a feeling of restlessness, an electric anticipation of something but I can't decipher what it is. *What?* I want to shout. *What is my problem?* I feel myself trembling, yet my words are steady and sure.

'Let's just be friends, Mike. I think there's someone else I need.'

'Someone else?' he snorts from beneath the mound of covers. 'Like who?'

'I don't know. I'm so sorry. You're okay though, aren't you? We were never going to make it, were we?'

Mike sighs loudly and turns over. His scent of cigarettes, of rushed kisses and beer, washes over me for what I suppose is the last time, and I wonder if he might be upset, ready to fight for me. *Let me go*, I will tell him. But there is only an irritated grunt. 'Whatever.'

***

The next morning when I wake up, Mike is still asleep. My head pounds. Maybe I did have too much wine. I stare at him for a minute. His skin is golden and smooth, his mouth slightly open as he breathes deeply, revealing the edges of sharp white teeth. He is good looking. He makes me laugh and he understands adventure, not being tied down, the things I thought meant so much to me. He's not always kind to everyone, but he's always been nice to me. I wonder what he would do if I woke him and asked him to forget everything I said.

But no. I won't do that because it's not what I want. I remember the certainty of last night, the feeling that being next to him in here was all wrong.

I will spend the day alone in Blackpool, see if he contacts me, and see how I feel tonight.

I slip quietly from the bed and pull on my jeans from yesterday. As I do, I hear the soft crackle of paper in my back pocket. I pull it out and flick my eyes over what seems to be a note in my own handwriting to myself, only I don't remember ever writing it.

You won't remember why you made this list,

I frown and look across at Mike to check he's still asleep.

But there are a few things you HAVE to do. The order doesn't matter, as long as you do them ALL.

1. End it with Mike. (Don't feel bad. He did the same to you.)

2. Go to Blackpool.

3. Find someone called Daniel Penn who was born on the 27th February 1985 and DON'T LET HIM GO.

4. If you're struggling, speak to Nicholas.

I don't know who Daniel Penn is. And Mike ended things with me once? I can't remember that either. The reason I wrote a note to myself is little more than an ember in a black grate, although the fact that I have already ended it with Mike, in Blackpool, tells me it's got to be somewhere in my subconscious.

I glance once more at Mike's sleeping profile, angelic as a child. Then I stand up and wander towards the narrow window. As I push back the heavy patterned curtains and stare out into the backyard of the house I'm in, beyond to row upon row of identical houses and bins and gates and children's slides and cars, the memories roar into colour like sudden flames, making my face burn with hot relief.

His loss.

I can see it all: Daniel, in this very room at the engagement party of Sophie and Kevin, the one Mike told me he went to years ago. Daniel's straight, wide smile, the glasses he used to wear with the thin black rims, his pleasant surprise at the taste of his wine and the way he stood in the room talking me through how he thought I should move on and make a new plan because Mike had ended things and apparently broken my heart.

I scramble from the window, gather my things and sneak from the room, from the house, as silently as a cat.

***

An hour later, I am sitting in a tiny cafe on the promenade. Everything around me seems distant and blurred. It's as though I am looking at the glass counter full of cans and chocolate bars, the red-faced staff, and my white mug, through cellophane. As I whirl milk through my tea with a plastic stirrer, I think over and over again of the memory of meeting Daniel for the first time. I picture everything about him, giddy with relief that I can remember him again, terrified that the memories might disappear at any moment: his green eyes and the sharp prickles of greying stubble on his chin; his drumming fingers as he thinks; his coffee and walks and habit of looking upwards, at buildings, instead of straight ahead. And with all the things I love about him, come all the things that I know hurt me so much. Joshua's face staring up at me from the Silver Cross pram that's now stuffed into a locked shed at the bottom of our wild garden; his elated smile whenever he saw me; the rolls of skin behind his knees and delicious softness of his head; the emptiness that ripped through me again and again when he'd gone.

I know now why I'm here. I know that I wanted to find

Daniel because I wanted to see a version of him who wasn't broken, whose relationship with me wasn't burned out. I wanted to be a version of me who wasn't struggling to stay afloat. It seemed like the right thing to do, after so long of not being brave enough to do anything. But suddenly, what seemed so simple to me before now appears ridiculous and impossible. I don't have the grief that the other version of me had, and so I don't have the desperation either. I have no idea where Daniel is, or who he is in this life. He could already be married to someone else – the thought threatens to make the tea resurface in my throat – or be living somewhere far away. He could have gone to Berlin and stayed there. Do I really, really want to see what Daniel would have done, and who he would have done it with, if he'd never met me?

My thumb lingers over the Facebook app icon on my phone, as it has done so many times in the past hour. One search and I will know everything: if he is the person I thought he would be, if he is single, if he even lives here, if there is a chance in a million that we could somehow be together again.

After everything, now it has come to it, I'm not sure I am brave enough to know. But I have no time to weigh up different options, or think clearly about any of it. The more the minutes tick on, the cloudier the memory of the other world I have left behind becomes and the clearer the café around me is, as though someone is wiping it clean. I try to play what I recalled before over and over again in my mind, but already there are gaps in Daniel's words, his expressions, his features.

And Joshua.

I am trying to keep hold of them both. But with every action in this life, a memory from the other is lost.

I sip my tea and the colour of Daniel's eyes is gone.

I set it down, glance outside at the faded bunting flapping sadly in the wind, and the noise of Joshua's delighted giggle disappears.

I take my purse from my bag, and the feeling of being at home with Daniel on a Sunday morning, the colours of our bedroom and the noises of our home, vanish from my mind.

I bang my hand down on the table in frustration that I am running out of time.

'Everything okay, love?' the waitress says.

I nod and put my hand up to my mouth, the tea sickly and sour in my mouth. The list I wrote to myself makes it all seem so certain, so calculated. But how could I be so sure that I wanted to be here, and do this? To lose all the memories that now seem so precious to me?

If you're struggling, speak to Nicholas.

I swipe through my phone, my fingers shaking, until I get to Nicholas's number. He answers on the third ring.

'Nicholas!' I say, relief at his familiarity flooding through me. 'I didn't know if you'd be teaching.'

'Nope. Free period. How was your birthday?' he asks. 'Did you get the gift card?'

'Yes. Thanks,' I say hastily. 'Look, I need to see you. Is it at all possible?'

'Course,' he says. 'Pop round later if you want.'

'I— Pop round? To Oxford?'

There's a silence, the faint buzz of a phone line, the clatter of cutlery behind me in the cafe. Infuriation fills me as I know I've said something wrong, but my mind is a flurry of jigsaw pieces from two different puzzles.

Nicholas is the one to break the silence, his voice amused. 'Oxford? Are you feeling okay? When have I ever lived in Oxford?'

'Never mind. Look, I'm not okay. This is why I need to see you,' I tell him. 'I'm running out of time. I don't even know if you'll be able to help me. But I know you'll try.'

'Erica?' Nicholas says. 'You're worrying me. Can't you tell me now?'

I catch a sob in my throat, aching with the memories being pulled from my mind, with the old life being painted over with the new. There isn't even time to speak to Nicholas. A longing for Daniel, for the memories I am losing, engulfs me. I want to touch him, to see him and tell him I was wrong. I'm wasting time, I realise, because this Nicholas, for whom thousands of different moments leading up to now have changed where he lives and who he is, knows nothing of disappearances to other worlds, of my need of someone to understand and protect me. He knows nothing of who I really am, and the chasm I suddenly feel between us is suffocating. I need to work out how to get back home and he can't help me because he doesn't know enough. 'I am from somewhere else,' I begin, the words tripping over each other in their eagerness to be heard and believed as quickly as possible. But there isn't *time*.

'Hold on,' Nicholas says, and I hear him speak to a colleague.

As I wait, the name of our baby disappears. I empty my bag on the table, ignore the alarmed looks from the waitress and the other people in the café. I rifle through the lip balms and pocket tissues, the bottled water and underwear and facewash. But there is no more paper anywhere. I haven't written it down. I take a huge breath and try to recall it. Joey? No. It began with a J. I am drowning, panicking and flailing under deep, deep water. In a minute, I won't even remember how he looked and I won't remember why I am talking to Nicholas. The items on the list I wrote will mean nothing.

'Right,' Nicholas says. 'Sorry. All yours. What were you saying?'

Something flies into my mind then, lighting it up like a firefly. It's something I have to ask Nicholas, above all else, before it disappears. 'How's Phoebe?'

***

I run blindly, the salty wind stinging my eyes. I can hear shouts, and I know it's the people from the café, that I haven't paid for my drink, but I can't turn back. I *have* to get home.

Nicholas's words ring in my ears over and over again and the pain I thought I'd left behind roars through me. 'Phoebe? Who's Phoebe?'

And now, Phoebe is fading into darkness with everything else I remember, her bright voice and face becoming murkier with every second. I stumble along the promenade, not even knowing why I am running, or where I am running to, until I see it.

Chapter 51

The house is as lost as I am, its shutters banging softly in the September breeze. I run to the door and hammer on it, tears streaming down my face, sobs bursting from me.

There is no movement from inside, no sign of anyone having lived there. The front window shows an abandoned room. A kaleidoscope of memories flashes into my mind: spilt Champagne on carpet, a hundred tealights and a ring twinkling in the centre of them; a bowl in the sink; a piano and a record player in the lounge; a book holding closed the window in the bedroom. A cot and a pram and a yellow highchair.

I am trembling so much that it takes me minutes to grip the paper from my pocket in one hand and my phone in the other. As I try to type, my fingers slip and flail and my phone falls to the ground. I pick it up, crouching as I finally press the search key. I can't put it off any more. It's the only way I'll be able to find him.

There are over twenty people who meet my search, but

when I see his profile picture I know it's him. My heart leaps. He's grinning, his wide, beautiful grin that starts from his eyes, the one I haven't seen for so long. Maybe this is the right thing.

I click.

And then I scream, and the world stops spinning.

***

There is no sound: no gulls sobbing above my head, no gentle rush of the tide, no rustle of the overgrown grass around me. Just the beating of my heart and the gasps of my breath.

Then the sounds all rush back at once. I see a man in a yellow coat running towards me from the promenade.

'Is everything all right?' he asks, panting slightly from the unexpected sprint towards me. I can see a few other people staring from across the roads, dog walkers and cyclists with gaping mouths.

'Is there somebody you want me to phone for you?' the man in the yellow coat asks when I don't reply. His eyes crinkle in concern and I see a sheen of sweat twinkling on his forehead. I feel like I have seen him somewhere before but my mind won't move from one thought to another. Nothing makes any sense because a black dread, a fear so big it has eclipsed everything else, is all I can feel.

'Can I get you home?' the man asks next. 'Where do you live?'

I sob, holding my hands to my face. 'Here,' I tell him, as he looks around at the neglected house in confusion.

'I live here!' I shout again. I stumble to my feet, and hammer on the soft, rotted wood of the back gate until it finally gives way. The man follows me as I stagger over to the shed at the back of the garden.

'My pram,' my voice is clotted with tears. 'It's in here. It's my house.'

But the man only looks sadly at me.

'Look in there! Get my pram! I want my pram!' I scream at him, and he takes a step back. I'm scaring him, I realise. I am scaring myself. I am a madwoman. I have a madwoman's shaking hands. I hold them out, and they seem so bare.

'Something is missing,' I mumble, and then the kaleidoscope is back, glittering memories shifting in and out of focus in my mind. 'It's my wedding ring,' I tell him. 'I'm not wearing my ring because I never got married.' I choke with sobs, and the man steps towards me again, placing a firm and heavy hand awkwardly on my heaving back. 'I don't want these hands!' I wail. 'They have never even held him! They have never touched him! I held him and gave him his milk and cuddled him to sleep. I loved him so much.' I look up at the man, my eyes streaming. 'They aren't my hands!'

He nods, patting my back. 'I think I'll go and get more help,' he says, cocking his head on one side. He hauls me back to the front of the house and perches me on the crumbling front wall. 'Stay here.'

But the dog walkers and cyclists have moved on now, and as soon as the man disappears from view, there is nobody else to see me. The house slides and blurs and the wall dissolves beneath me. Time loops and twists around me and back on itself, coiling and spinning so fast I can see nothing at all but a blur of blue flashing lights.

***

I am calm now, my blazing feelings burned to still, cool ashes.

I am with Daniel in his car. His edges are smudged, but I can tell he is younger. His hair is blacker at the sides, his skin slightly tighter, his movements sharper. I can't move, or speak, or reach out to touch him and I know he can't see me. I should be out of my mind with relief, with confusion, but I have no real mind. I know, somehow, that I don't exist to anyone in this moment. I am in a strange state of flux where all my memories of both worlds are within my grasp. I could steadily reel off Daniel's habits, and Mike's; I can visualize my teachers from school in Yorkshire and Blackpool; the precise leaf-green of the lamp-shade in my bedroom in Blackpool and the beige of the stone floor of the cottage in Italy. I can coolly recall every detail of my life with Daniel and Joshua; every detail of my life without them. But there is a vague question fighting to be seen through the robotic certainty: what is this?

As though he's trying to help, Daniel turns up the radio and the newsreader reels off the date.

September 7th, 2013. My twenty-eighth birthday. The day I went to the Lake District with Daniel.

I have seen the moments of this day more than once in my original life: the ice cream on Daniel's lip as we sat by the glittering lake, the way I felt light and happy because I had been with him all day, as though Mike ending things a few days before might not have been so terrible after all. The memory I recall of living the alternate version of that day in the other life is vague and unimportant. It seems I was working at the travel agent's in the village and saving for one of many trips abroad. I think I went for drinks at the local pub with Claire.

But which version of life is the one I can see right now? I try to look up, at the road, to see where we are, but I can't move. This isn't like the disappearances I've become used to, where I can silently follow who I'm watching. I am stuck, my eyes fixed on Daniel.

He is glancing at the bag beside him on the passenger seat. And as he does, my strange state of being nobody caves in, giving way to an avalanche of emotion. I am me. I am the Erica who knows everything about Daniel, and who knows what is about to happen.

But I still can't move.

I try to scream, but as in all the worst kind of nightmares, I am mute with paralysis, my voice ripped from me.

I try and try, but I am still and silent as a corpse. *Keep your eyes on the road!*

He is always doing more than one thing at a time. The

posts on his Facebook page that I have just seen at the house are blood red in my mind, flashing and darting. But my limbs are dead.

We'll miss you.

Gone too soon, mate.

So tragic.

I watch him fiddle with the navy rucksack, which isn't zipped shut and is stuffed with what looks like a change of clothes. My heart is torn by the sight of his clothes, pushed in his bag in a hurry because he'll probably have been late, busy in that Daniel way of his that means he always crams too much into minutes that are always shorter than he thinks they'll be.

I try to move, to *be*, but I am powerless. All I can do is observe.

The horrified squeal of brakes.

The smashing of glass.

The smell of blood.

The chilling, heart-stopping silence.

Chapter 52

I watch it all from above, like a spirit.

Daniel pulled from the car, his pale head lolling on one side, blood already blackening around his nose and mouth, sticking in his hair like jam.

The police officers speaking into their radios.

The mangled cars being pushed back from the road.

I try time and time again to scream his name, try to will myself back to him, to a world where he is grey and tired and hurting, but is at least mine and here.

Memories of a thousand moments I never before thought were important drift through my mind like clouds over the sun: smiles and frowns and invitations and refusals. I think of my first ever version of this day, ripping through all the other images to get to the one that matters.

***

'I was meant to play football over in Manchester later but I'm awful at it. And between you and me, I don't actually

really like it that much. So if you want to do something, we can. Totally up to you.'

I stare down at the wreckage of Daniel's car and see through the crushed metal and smashed glass to the carrier bag that has been thrown from the seat, the carrier bag that contained his football boots.

'Are you sure?'

'Yeah. Really sure. I've never even scored a goal.'

'I meant about doing something.'

'I'm sure.'

***

I try again to reach out, to somehow reach Daniel and touch him, but instead I seem to be moving further away from him. I float along, like an autumn leaf on a cool breeze.

Then, without warning, I am thrown so hard that I feel as though my bones will shatter.

I am on the ground, gravel scraping the skin of my cheek like glass. The cars and police and radios buzz around me. I stumble to my feet, towards the accident.

'Daniel,' I say, my voice no more than a croak. *Daniel, Daniel, Daniel.*

I am on the verge of forgetting again, but this time I can't. I can't make the wrong choice or let myself be carried to somewhere I am not meant to be. I can't forget the grief, or the loss, or all of the moments that might have stopped this one.

I flit past the police, past the paramedics. I am invisible to them as I float between two worlds.

I brush my fingers against Daniel's cool skin, his jet-black hair, his soft stubble and the hot blood that covers him. I press myself against him, my sobs shaking both of our bodies, until he fades away completely, and becomes nothing.

Chapter 53

When he is gone, I am gone too. I am in a different place, and I know immediately, instinctively where that is and who I am without even opening my eyes.

The ball of grief that has always felt so suffocating when I return is so welcome that I want to extract it from my body, to cup it in my hands, to kiss it and all the memories it contains.

I am home.

***

When I arrive at Luigi's, it's after nine. The waiters shake their heads sadly. *Gone*, they mouth, hands upturned like small children.

I run from the restaurant and gaze out across the glittering promenade. And there, moving along the horizon, his steps furious, hurt, marked by grief and memories and life, is Daniel.

I race towards him, across the blinding lights of the

roads and trams and people, through the blazing colours and shouts, over the damp, hard sand.

I shout his name over and over again, the cold air ripping through my chest, the joy that I am never, ever going to forget it again propelling me so far forward that I almost fall.

'Daniel,' I say as I reach him. I can't stop saying his name and I am crying huge gulping sobs and laughing too. I grip him and pull him towards me, his warm skin and soft stubble and smell of ink and earth and home overwhelming me.

'You left,' he says simply. 'I waited over an hour. I told you I can't do this anymore, Erica.'

I put my hand on his face, which is cool with the wind but warm with the blood that surges beneath. 'I was so desperate,' I say.

'And?' he says, because he can't quite give up on me like he said he would.

'I never, ever want to go back. I promise. I swear on everything we have ever touched.'

He looks at me for a while. 'What happened?'

I shake my head, the image of Daniel's head lolling and sticky with black blood still bright and terrifying. I don't tell Daniel that if I hadn't met him at the party, and he hadn't taken me out to the Lake District on that day instead of getting in his car to drive to Manchester to play a game of football, then he would have lost everything. I'll never tell him that. Because then he would think I had saved him. When really, all this time, he saved me.

'I didn't have you,' I say simply, because really, that's all there is to it. Nothing changed my life as much as the moments leading up to me meeting Daniel and all the moments that went after. 'Nothing is worth not having you,' I tell him. 'Nothing. I know it's taken me way too long. But I'm here now.'

'Timing has never been our strong point,' he mutters as he takes my hand in his.

'Oh, I'm not so sure about that,' I say.

'I got you another birthday present,' he tells me, and digs in his pocket. He hands me a small box. Inside is a bracelet. The letter J dangles from it and twinkles in the moonlight.

'I've been thinking a lot lately about what you've been saying, about how we might have had a better life. And I've tried to see it like you do, Erica. Honestly, I have. But I just can't get there. When we bought the house and we had each other, and Joshua, and everything was ahead of us, I was so happy.' He glances at me as we stride over the rippled sand and I smile at him, nodding for him to continue. 'Some people never know that kind of happiness. So my conclusion is always the same. It was shorter than we expected and hoped. And losing it has almost broken us beyond repair. But we still had it. Part of that happiness was having each other, and we still have that. And we *had* Joshua, and he was perfect and we can remember how it felt to have him, how it felt to be that happy, for the rest of our lives.' A memory scorches my mind and squeezes my chest: my wedding finger bare, hands that weren't mine.

'I know that now,' I tell him. 'I really, really know that.' I slide the bracelet onto my wrist, the silver cool against my skin. 'I love it. I'm so lucky,' I say, relief that I am with Daniel in this life almost choking me.

'I kind of got it for both of us. I think we were both trying not to think about him. I was as guilty of it as you. But it doesn't work. Not thinking about him doesn't make the pain go away and it makes me feel guilty too. He deserves us to think about him, doesn't he?'

I nod vehemently, wiping a tear that skims my cheek.

'But if it doesn't work for you, and it's too soon or it's too much pain,' Daniel continues, his endless stream of words a part of him I want to pull and hug to my chest, 'then that's okay. We can put it in a drawer, or we can swap the charm for another. But we have to do it together.'

'I would never do that. I'll never swap it.'

Daniel puts his arm around me. 'Shall we head back? It's late.'

I shake my head. 'Let's walk. We have the time.'

'All the time in the world.' We walk for a while, the glittering tide nearing us with each wave. Daniel picks up the pace, walking too quickly, and I reach out and pull him back.

Epilogue

7th September 2018

I am in the back garden.

Nothing is remarkable, except the fact I am here.

The September sun is tempered by stretched fluffs of cloud and a cool breeze that ruffles the napkins that I have just put onto our outdoor table, making them soar for a moment before falling down to the uneven grass beneath.

'Do you think we should eat inside?' I ask Daniel.

He smiles. 'Nah. We're going to get the most out of summer, even if it kills us. The garden's the nicest bit of the house now. We have to make people enjoy it with us.

He's right. We've spent hours in the garden this summer and it finally feels like our hard work and dedication is paying off. The shed has been pulled down, there is a decked area at the back, and everything apart from the tree that stands above us has been pruned, trimmed and chopped away.

'Zoe and Ben will be used to Australia temperatures though,' I remind him. 'They might be freezing.'

'They will drink their way through it. They might have spent six months there, but they're still British,' Daniel says.

'Did I hear my name?' Zoe asks as she totters through the back gate, early as always.

***

I help Zoe unload her carrier bag of wine and beer into the fridge, eying her subtly as I do. 'Did you not bring non-alcohol beers today?'

'No!' she gasps, her eyes wide.

'Yes,' I tell her.

'When?' she bursts out. 'When is ...?'

'February. I was going to tell you earlier, but I wanted to wait until we were face to face.'

She looks at my stomach. 'Wow. I didn't notice, but now you've told me it's pretty obvious.' She looks up and I see her eyes are glassy with tears. Zoe never cries. She prides herself on it. 'So. Boy? Girl?'

'Girl,' I say, as tears fill my eyes too.

'Girl,' Daniel says, coming into the kitchen with Ben. I look at him, giving him a secret smile that says I can tell he's close to tears too, but that Zoe and Ben probably haven't noticed.

'Boy,' Zoe says.

We all wait for Ben, who grins and claps Daniel on the back and says, 'Boy or girl.'

And so it goes.

***

The others arrive shortly after in a flurry of hugs and gifts and tissue paper. After I've opened the presents – a beautiful cashmere blanket, a basket of bath bombs, and a new horror book – Nicholas and Daniel go outside to light the barbeque. Mum and Diane take over the slicing of buns, and the chopping of lettuce and tomatoes. They work shoulder to shoulder, taking conspiratorial turns to glance back at me as I sit at the table.

'I'm fine,' I smile at them. 'And I can help, you know.'

But they wave away my offers.

'You can colour with me,' says Phoebe, plonking down a fluffy turquoise pencil case on the table and pushing a picture of a unicorn towards me. 'I'm doing the Rapunzel one. But you can do that one if you like.'

I pick up a pencil and start to shade the unicorn purple. Phoebe looks across to assess my work. 'Oh,' she says approvingly. 'You're good.'

I gaze at her for too long so she smiles hesitantly, lowers her eyes again and busily scribbles Rapunzel's hair bright yellow. Then she looks up at me. 'Daddy told me you're writing a book. Can I see it?'

'It doesn't look like a book yet. But it will do soon.'

'So will you make it into a book?'

'I've written all the words and chosen the pictures. But someone else will make it into a real book. Really soon, actually. And when it's done, we are all going to have a party and you will see it.'

Phoebe's face lights up. 'I'm coming to the book party?'

'Of course you are,' I tell her. The launch is organized for October at the museum. Excitement darts through me at the thought of my book, which I've worked on solidly for the last year and finally has a publisher and release date. The exhibition that sparked the idea so long ago has been reinstated at the museum and the guest list for the launch is longer than I'd ever hoped. Katie is planning to come back for it. We went to stay with her in Brighton in the spring. Even my dad, who eventually replied to my email last year and has visited me a few times since, has tentatively suggested he might come. The relationship is strange, new and old at the same time.

Planning for the launch night and putting the exhibition back up, photograph by photograph, has reminded me so much of that other time, when I was so frightened I might disappear and miss a chunk of my life. I never disappear now. I'm more firmly anchored to my life than I have ever been. Sometimes I have fleeting moments where I remember something from the other Erica's life: the scent of the Italian summer, the feel of the fabric of a top she used to wear, the peculiar feeling of looking in the mirror at a reflection that didn't fully feel like my own. But the moments are gone in an instant, lost in a million other more important ones.

***

After we've eaten, and the garden is strewn with plates and cups, the clouds clear and the sun glows down, warming us and making us forget the chill of the shady breeze from a few hours ago. I sit with Amelia and Zoe, and we watch Phoebe fling herself over the grass in a string of leggy cartwheels, and see Daniel laugh as he talks to Ben. He still isn't the version of himself he used to be. But he is here, and he is laughing again and he is Daniel.

'Hey,' Zoe says as she sees me place a hand on my rounded belly. 'Do you remember the time we had a barbeque here, and you were pregnant with Joshua ...?' Her sentence dies out. 'Sorry. I didn't think what I was saying. I shouldn't have brought him up.'

'That's okay. I remember,' I tell her. I close my eyes and feel the hazy glare of sunshine on my face, the ripple of tiny limbs inside me, the distant pulse of pain that is as much a part of me as my heartbeat and is matched by a throb of hope. I hear the scratch of the record as it stumbles from one track to another in the house, the wail of the seagulls and the crashing of the waves. 'I remember it all.'

***

'There's another present for you here,' Daniel says when everyone has gone and we sit amongst the discarded tissue paper in the lounge. 'I was going to give it to you when you had the baby. But it feels like something I should give you today instead.' It's a box: a duplicate of an empty one that sits on my dressing table. Inside is a bracelet charm to match the *J* charm I already have.

'Obviously, I didn't know which letter to choose

because we don't know who we'll get, or what will happen,' he says, his words edged with caution. 'So I chose this one instead.'

It's a tiny silver heart. I smile and clasp it next to the J on the bracelet I've worn every day for a year: days when I have cried endless tears and not been able to get out of bed; and days when I have laughed and kissed and been somewhere close to a strange new kind of happiness. 'I love it. And I love you, so much.'

'We made it through another year,' Daniel says. 'Happy birthday.'

'And happy first-date anniversary.' I lean forward and kiss him as the last golden beams of sunlight stream into the room.

Acknowledgements

Thank you to Charlotte Ledger and Emily Ruston for being so brilliant at their jobs, and for being the most supportive editors I could ever ask for.

Thank you to Lucy Bennett for designing a wonderful cover.

Thank you to everyone at One More Chapter for all their amazing work and excellent party planning.

Thank you to the Creative Writing staff and students at Manchester Metropolitan University for helping me to move my writing forward.

Thank you to my friends for their genuine excitement and enthusiasm about my books.

Finally, thank you to my family for so much, every day.